Livi Starling

Loves

The *Livi Starling* series

Livi Starling

Loves

Karen Rosario Ingerslev

PURE&FIRE

Livi Starling Loves
First published in the UK by Pure & Fire in 2016
Pure & Fire, England
www.pureandfire.com

ISBN: 978-0-9934327-4-3
eBook ISBN: 978-0-9934327-5-0

'Create in me a pure heart, O God,
And renew a steadfast spirit within me...'
— Psalm 51:10

~ 1 ~

I'm just getting started

Somewhere in the world there is a rich old lady called Cleo Honeywell. She was once a piano teacher living in a big old house at the top of our village. Rumour had it she kept wild swans. For years it had been my greatest ambition to get inside her house and I spent many fruitless hours begging my sister to let me learn piano. My chance finally came one summer when the house was put up for auction. Of course, Jill and I could never have afforded the place, even if we sold all our body parts, but we joined the rest of Little Milking in feigning interest at the open viewing. There weren't any swans but there were a couple of mounted deer heads in the sitting room and a stuffed stoat in the downstairs lavatory. I drew out our visit by pretending I had a stomach bug, which meant I got to taste some of Cleo's posh peppermint tea. Then I sat on the toilet for quite some time, imagining I was a princess and the stoat was my pet. As I left the lavatory I stole some pot pourri as a souvenir of my visit. Then I gave Cleo a hug and told her I would miss her.

The visit was always marked in my mind as one of the most exciting moments of my life. For many years I wondered where Cleo Honeywell was living now. I thought she was the richest person I would ever meet.

But that was until today when I went round Joseph Cashbottom's house.

I should have known it would be fancy. It didn't even have a number. It was just called 'Morenum House.' It was in a part of Leeds I'd not visited before, where the air smells fresher and the local park isn't covered in dog poo and lewd graffiti.

Joey had given me a hand-drawn map, complete with landmarks such as the local grocery store (indicated by a smiling tomato) and their next door neighbour's dog (a great salivating beast which was depicted as standing in my way with a sword).

I approached his street with caution, expecting to be attacked at any moment, but, as it happened, I didn't see the dog. I was too busy gawping at Joey's front lawn. It looked like something out of a film, with dazzling cherry blossoms and lines of tulips and even a little stone birdbath. I let out a long breath. He wasn't exaggerating when he'd said they had *'a few big trees.'* They had more trees than I had books.

As I made my way down the winding driveway,[1] my heart beat with a combination of horror and awe as I realised, *He's rich!* The moment I reached the door, however, this thought was displaced by a far more pressing matter: *I'm wearing second hand shoes.*

I ducked behind a bush as I debated running home and asking Ruby if she had a smart pair that I could borrow, perhaps her new school shoes with the line of little diamonds,[2] then I kicked myself as I realised that would still constitute *second hand.*

"And what if Joey recognises them!" I said out loud. "Then I'd look like I was too poor to own *any* shoes."

"Livi?" Joey's sudden call caught me by surprise and I lunged headfirst into the bush.

"Ow!"

"Livi?!"

I clambered out of the bush, rubbing my pierced face. "Oh! Hello Joey!"

"Are you alright?"

"I got a twig in my eye."

"Why were you in the bush?"

I tried to think of something sensible. "I was just smelling it."

"Oh." Joey gave me a curious look. "I've never done that before." He came beside me and sniffed. "I see what you mean..."

I forced a smile and waved his map. "I found your house," I squeaked.

"Yeah!" Joey grinned and headed for the door. "Come on then. Lunch is almost ready."

I gulped and trotted after him.

---

[1] Which, may I add, was long enough for me to figure out that *'Morenum House'* was an anagram of *'Run Home, Mouse.'*

[2] Fake ones, obviously, but still far more appropriate than my faded pink charity shop shoes with holes in both soles.

Joey's mother, Janine, met us in the doorway. I glanced casually at her footwear. She was barefoot.

She took one look at me and gasped. "Livi, your eye is bleeding!"

I rubbed my eyebrow and blushed.

"She was smelling the bush," Joey explained.

"Oh!" Janine looked a little confused but composed herself before saying, "Joey, take Livi to the bathroom so she can wash her eye."

I followed Joey into their house and down a smartly decorated hallway. I resisted the urge to squeal at the number of rooms leading off in different directions.

We turned a corner and Joey pushed open a door for me. "Here you go."

I went into the bathroom and locked the door firmly behind me. "Wow!" I whispered as I perched on the windowsill. Even their downstairs bathroom was as big as my *bedroom*. I poked the toilet roll, marvelling at how soft and springy it was. Beside me sat a crystal bowl full of pot pourri. I ran my fingers through it and wondered whether they would miss a small piece. *No!* I scolded myself. *I can't steal from Joey!* I thought for a moment before pulling off a sheet of the soft toilet paper. I folded it neatly and tucked it into my pocket. *That's surely allowed,* I reasoned.

Next, I peered at my reflection in the mirror and scowled. I had a cut right across my eyelid. I also had leaves in my hair. I picked them out and carefully washed my face. Then I turned from side to side and groaned. Fresh blood was already seeping out of the cut.

Joey knocked on the door. "Are you alright, Livi?"

"Yeah!" I patted my eye one last time and unlocked the bathroom door.

He gave me a friendly smile.

I nodded politely and chewed my lip. I wanted to say, '*I didn't know you were rich,*' but somehow this didn't seem appropriate. Instead I said, "Your house name is an anagram of '*Run Home, Mouse.*'"

Joey raised his eyebrows. "Did you figure that out yourself?"

"Yeah."

"Cool..." He paused. "What's *my* name an anagram of?"

I shrugged. "I'm not *that* good at them." I didn't want to dwell too long on his surname.

9

"Oh. Okay. Let's go into the living room." Joey led me back down the hallway and into a beautifully furnished room at the front of the house.

I pulled off my ugly second hand shoes and tucked them out of sight. "Do you know Kitty Warrington?" I asked casually.

"Does she go to our church?"

"No. She's at my school."

"Then how would I know her?"

I gave a coy shrug. I didn't want to admit that I'd assumed their families might be in some kind of rich club together. "Dunno."

"Well, what about her?"

"Oh, nothing." I pointed to a photo of a blotchy-looking schoolboy with crusty eyes. "Is that you?"

"Yeah!" Joey picked it up and held it towards me.

"Why is your skin all scabby?"

"I had chicken pox."

"How old were you?"

"About eight."

"That's amazing! I had chicken pox when I was eight."

"Seriously?" He looked at me incredulously. "How cool is that?"

"Yeah!" I pointed at another photo featuring an even younger Joey and two older children. "Who are they?"

"Jacob and Julie— my brother and sister."

"Julie?" I raised my eyebrows. "That almost sounds like *Jill.*"

"Oh yeah! Weird. We've got so much in common."

"I know! I don't have a brother though."

"That's a shame."

I nodded at the picture. "Are they here?" I wondered what kind of shoes Julie would wear.

"Jacob's back from university. But Julie left home years ago. She lives with her husband."

"You're the youngest?"

"Yup."

"Me too!"

"Amazing!"

We stared at one another and grinned. I tried to think of something else that we might have in common but I soon grew distracted by the open fireplace, sheepskin rug and crystal chandelier which all seemed to be screaming, *Who are you kidding? You're nothing like him!*

Soon we heard Janine calling from some room far away.

"Time for lunch!" said Joey.

I tried to sound nonchalant as I said, "Groovy." I followed him down the hallway and into a large dining room where we were met by a table of expectant faces. I gulped and raised a self-conscious hand to shield my bleeding eye.

"This is my dad," Joey said, pointing as a man stood up and came towards me.

"You must be Livi!" his father exclaimed. "How nice to meet you."

"You too, Mr... Cashbottom."

"Call me Ronnie," he boomed.

I nodded. "Nice to meet you, Ronnie."

"That's my brother," Joey continued.

A lean young man with glasses got up and shook my hand. "Jacob," he said smoothly.

"Livi," I squeaked.

"And that's Uncle Terry."

An older man at the end of the table raised his hand. "Excuse me for not getting up," he said gruffly. "I have plantar fasciitis."

"What?"

"A bad foot," Joey whispered.

"Oh," I muttered. "I'm sorry."

"Don't be sorry!" Uncle Terry roared. "It's not your fault!"

I blushed. "Okay."

"Take a seat, Livi!" Janine trilled, ushering me and Joey into seats in the middle of the table before heading out of the room.

We sat down and I copied Joey in laying my napkin carefully over my lap. Then I looked up to see everybody grinning at me. They shot the odd glance at the cut on my face but, to my relief, nobody mentioned it.

"Would you like some elderflower cordial, Livi?" Jacob asked, holding up a fancy jug of strange-looking yellow liquid.

I looked at Joey. "Are you having any?"

"Of course," he said, holding out his glass for his brother.

"Then yes please," I said.

I watched as Jacob slowly filled our glasses. I had never heard of elderflower. I hoped it wasn't an actual *flower*. I didn't like the idea of drinking daisies or tulips or bits of tree. I tried to pretend it was apple juice.

"Is that enough?" Jacob asked, filling my glass right to the top.

"Yes thank you," I whispered.

"Try it!" Joey raised his own glass cheerily.

I took a sip. It was rather sharp. "It's quite nice," I muttered.

"That's the correct answer!" Joey grinned. "My mum made it."

I looked at him in horror. "I mean it's *really* nice. It's the best drink ever." I swallowed hard and silently commanded myself, *Be cool*. But then I counted six pieces of cutlery in front of me and almost wet myself.

"So, Livi," Ronnie began. "Tell us about yourself."

Fortunately, I was spared the ordeal of answering his question by Janine who reappeared at that moment with a tray of glass bowls filled with pink gloop. "I thought we'd start with prawn cocktail," she said.

I eyed the food cautiously as Janine put a bowl in front of me. I had no idea prawn cocktail was an actual dish. I thought it was just a crisp flavour.

Once she had served everybody Janine took her seat and said, "Ronnie, would you like to say grace?"

He nodded before beginning heartily, "Thank you heavenly Father for this meal and for the privilege of having Livi here to share it with us..."

I squirmed and wondered whether I ought to have brought something— a bottle of champagne, perhaps.

Ronnie finished his prayer and Janine said, "Bon appétit!"

I forced a smile and scooped a bit of prawn cocktail onto my spoon. I gave it a little lick and winced. It was disgusting. I tried again and then quickly gulped down some drink. My eyes started to sting as I alternated between little nibbles of gloop and mouthfuls of bitter cordial. I debated whether I could sneak the prawn cocktail into my pocket without anybody noticing.

Joey's brother must have caught me looking disturbed because he leant across the table and whispered, "Just leave it if you don't like it. Or do what Joey does and hide it under your cushion."

I gulped. "I'm not going to hide it under my cushion," I assured Janine.

She chuckled. "I'm sorry you don't like it, Livi. We have roast duck for mains and a lemon tart for dessert. Will those be okay?"

I nodded helplessly, feeling like I was going to fall off my chair. I had expected lunch to mean a sandwich or, at best, some popcorn chicken. I'd had no idea Joey was inviting me for a three course meal. I fidgeted with the fancy napkin on my lap and wondered if this was officially a date.

Once everybody had finished their starter Janine gathered up the bowls and stacked them with mine, barely touched, right at the top. "I'll get the duck," she said.

Jacob got up from his seat. "Do you want some help, Mum?"

"Thanks, dear. That would be lovely. Oh and Joey will you come and carry the potatoes?"

Joey gave a cheeky groan but followed them out nonetheless.

I sucked in my cheeks. *Was I meant to be helping too?* I half stood up and then sat back down.

Ronnie turned to me and smiled. "Joey tells me you're rather good at animal impressions?"

I blushed.

"Can we hear some?"

"Er..."

Joey reappeared and plonked a bowl of roast potatoes onto the middle of the table. He was followed by Janine who held a platter of multicoloured vegetables and Jacob who was carrying the duck.

As Ronnie got up to carve the meat he exclaimed to his family, "Livi was just about to perform some of her animal impressions."

"She's currently being a *Rabbit in Headlights!*" Uncle Terry added with a chortle.

Ronnie looked at me and chuckled. "I'm sorry, Livi. I don't mean to embarrass you."

"It's okay," I insisted. "I'm not embarrassed. Actually, I can do a *Dying Duck* impression." I pointed to the duck.

They all looked at me curiously.

"Go on then," said Joey.

I squeezed my eyes shut and started to quack in a choked up manner, twisting my head from side to side as my voice became more strangled. I had practised this impression with Ruby and was aware that its impact lay in the tension of not quite knowing when the duck was finally dead. So I writhed around for a little longer before letting out one last rasp and slumping down dramatically. I looked up to see everybody looking rather bemused.

"Well done, Livi," Janine said. "That was a wonderful impression." She started to pass round plates of food, adding delicately, "There's plenty of meat if anyone wants some more..."

In the silence that followed, Joey let out a snigger and said, "Is anybody else thinking about how *this* duck died?"

His family gave a friendly laugh and Janine repeated, "It was a wonderful impression."

I blushed and poked my food with my fork.

To my relief, the main course was delicious. So was the lemon tart. I could hardly believe that there were people in existence who dined so extravagantly. However, despite how tasty the meal was, each bite was accompanied by an increasingly overwhelming sense of not belonging. I was petrified that Joey's parents would ask about my home life or quiz me on the names of the obscure vegetables that were accompanying the meal. At one point, I realised that Joey would probably expect to be invited round my house in return. I gave a silent moan. There was *no way* that could happen! I didn't speak again after my duck impression and was hugely relieved when lunch was over.

"Thank you, darling," Ronnie congratulated his wife as he chomped his final mouthful of lemon tart. "That was delicious."

"Yeah, thanks," I muttered, following Joey as he got down from the table.

"What was your favourite bit?" Joey asked me as we left the room.

It pained me that we were still within earshot. I frowned but he didn't notice. "I liked the roast potatoes," I said feebly, hoping that was the right answer.

"They're from the garden!" he replied.

I breathed a sigh of relief and followed him into a small sitting room, or *'den,'* as he called it.

Joey flung himself onto a beanbag and grinned. "What do you want to do?"

"I don't know."

We stared at one another for a moment before Joey exclaimed, "Oh! I know!" He ran to a shelf and took down a large box. "Check these out!"

I plodded over and sat on the floor beside him. "What are they?" I asked, watching as he lifted the lid on what looked like a pile of dirty old stones.

"My rock collection," he said proudly.

"Oh!" I pretended to be interested as he passed me a handful.

"I had loads more but my mum made me chuck most of them away. She said they took up too much space. These are the best ones."

I turned one over in my hand. "This one's shiny," I said politely.

"It's amazing, isn't it? I like how it curves on one side."

I forced a smile. "Yeah."

As Joey took each rock out one by one and set them in a line, I glanced at the clock and wondered how much longer I should stay. When Joey had invited me, he'd said, *"Come for lunch."* Since lunch was well and truly over, perhaps he was just boring me with his rocks as a way of getting me to leave.

"Well, I'd better go..." I said.

Joey looked up in surprise. "Oh... Alright."

Immediately I worried that I had spoken too soon. But it would have been odd to change my mind so I stood up and wandered into the hallway. "Where are my shoes?"

He shrugged. "Where did you leave them?"

I looked at the front door. "I don't know..."

We paced up and down the hallway, peering into rooms and checking behind various ornamental animals and umbrella stands but my shoes were nowhere to be found.

"Mum!" Joey yelled. "Did you move Livi's shoes?"

Janine came out of the kitchen. "No. Have you lost them?"

I gave a bashful shrug. "Sort of..."

Ronnie emerged from the study and asked, "Is everything alright?"

"Livi's lost her shoes," said Janine. She called up the stairs, "Jacob, have you got a moment? Livi's lost her shoes."

Jacob appeared at the top of the stairs. "Do you need some help?"

"Not really..." I said hoarsely.

But, before I could protest any further, the whole family launched into a search for my shoes. Even Uncle Terry was on his hands and knees in the conservatory, muttering faintly about his plantar fasciitis.

At one point, the phone rang and I overheard Janine saying, "Hello Julie! Joey's got a friend round and she's lost her shoes..."

"It doesn't matter!" I said. "I can go home like this..."

"What do they look like?" Jacob enquired. "Maybe I've seen them and just didn't realise."

Before I could reply, Joey's father came out of the living room holding my tatty old trainers. "Found them!" he sang. "They were under the sofa."

I took them, mumbling a hasty, "Thanks."

"I'll call you back, Julie," Janine said into the phone. "Ronnie's found the shoes." She hung up and watched as I pulled them on. "Oh, they're nice," she said kindly. "I like the laces. Very fancy."

I blushed. "It's ribbon. The actual laces broke."

"Well, it's very inventive," she insisted.

"Thanks." I forced a smile before adding, "Thank you for having me."

"It was our pleasure," Janine replied.

"Any time," added Ronnie.

"Great to meet you," said Jacob.

"Wonderful duck impression," added Uncle Terry.

I nodded dumbly before following Joey down the hallway to the front door. "Bye then," I said.

He grinned. "Shut your eyes and put your hand out."

"Alright..." I closed my eyes and held out my hand.

He placed something small and cold on my palm. "Open your eyes!"

I looked down. It was one of his rocks.

"That one's my favourite," he said. "I want you to have it."

I felt my cheeks burn as I stammered, "But... I... Are you sure?"

"I'm sure."

"Okay." I rolled it round in my hand. From a certain angle it did look sort of interesting. "It's like a fish with jaggered teeth," I attempted.

"Exactly!" Joey exclaimed. "I knew you'd get it."

I gulped. "Well... It was nice to see you."

"You too."

I gave a coy wave and walked away, my heart pounding wildly. It took me eleven whole seconds to make my way down the driveway. I rather hoped Joey would be watching me the whole time but I didn't dare turn round to check.

As soon as I got home, I logged onto FriendWeb to update my status. *'Just got back from a fun lunch.'*

A few seconds later, Joey commented on my post, *'Hey! It was great to see you. Come again some time!'*

I sat back and grinned, turning his rock over in my hand. I set it down on my souvenir piece of toilet paper and typed, *'Thanks. I will.'*

'Good. You should,' he replied.

As I sat there, wondering what to say next, my sister came in and sat on the sofa.

"Hi," I said casually, logging off FriendWeb before she could see that I was on it.

She glanced at me. "What happened to your eye?"

"Oh nothing. I just got a bit of a bush in it at Joey's."

Jill turned in surprise. "I'm not sure I want you playing with boys in bushes," she said briskly.

"We weren't playing in a bush! I was just smelling it."

She raised an eyebrow. "I know what it's like. I don't mind you having a boyfriend—"

"He's not my boyfriend!" I spluttered.

Jill smiled to herself as if she knew some secret joke.

I sniffed and turned away.

"What's that?" she continued nosily, indicating the rock from Joey.

I coughed. "That's my rock collection."

"Your what?"

"*Rock collection.* Or it will be. I'm just getting started."

J is for Jill

Being more than fifty miles from the nearest coast, Leeds doesn't provide much opportunity to grow a rock collection. Joey had said he'd got most of his from a beach called Filey so I asked Jill if she wanted to go there for her birthday.

She grunted and said, "I don't do birthdays."

Ever since the year Jill turned thirty her birthday has been something of a sore point. On that fateful year, urged on by Aunt Claudia to do something 'special,' Jill had opted to spend the big day in Ipswich.[3] We met some of Jill's friends for lunch where the celebration of Jill's birthday was usurped by the announcement that her best friend, Lorna, was getting married.

The group started screeching and I saw Jill turn pink as she exclaimed, "That's great!"

Lorna beamed and said, "I don't have any unmarried friends left. Will you be my maid of honour?"

Jill frowned. "Is that because I'm your first choice or because you haven't got anyone else to ask?"

Lorna slapped her on the arm and giggled. "I'm joking! Of course you're my first choice."

After a long silence Aunt Claudia piped up, "You know what they say: some people were born to be bridesmaids."

Jill thumped the table with a maniacal laugh and said, "Who wants another drink?"

After lunch, Lorna surprised Jill with a visit to *Scrummy Feet*, a pedicure treatment which involved a tank of fish chewing the dead skin off our toes. I found it exciting and imagined that each foot was a pig suckling twelve piglets at once. But Jill was paranoid

---

[3] Not the most spectacular town for a celebration, but rather more lively than Little Milking.

that the fish were transferring verrucas and kept squirming and shooing them away and Aunt Claudia branded it *'horrendous'* before standing up and killing half a dozen fish.[4]

After that, Lorna asked whether Jill wanted to watch *'Everybody's Getting Married,'* a new comedy at the cinema, but Jill said she was feeling nauseous from the fish experience and would rather just go home.

Later that evening I found her sobbing over a bucket of ice cream, unable to get Aunt Claudia's bridesmaid comment out of her mind. Her giant flashing *'Look Who's 30!'* badge[5] lay mutilated in the sink.

Her 31st wasn't much better. Jill opted for a small gathering at our house in which we were instructed to *'act normal'* and *'refrain from mentioning anybody's age.'* Since Jill had stated explicitly that she didn't want any presents everybody turned up with a cake instead.

I giggled and said, "Now you have to pick your favourite friend, Jill!" which, with hindsight, wasn't very helpful.

In order to spare their feelings Jill cheerfully declared that she would have a slice of them all, at which Aunt Claudia leant over and said in a loud whisper, "Aren't you watching your weight, love?"

In the silence that followed, Lorna announced that she was pregnant.

So it was with a little trepidation that I went downstairs to greet Jill on this year's birthday morning.

It was the last day of the Easter holidays, which meant I had a massive pile of neglected homework to do. I had got up early with the good intention of doing a bit of Maths before breakfast but had got distracted with making a card for Jill. Wanting to depict something light-hearted and fun, I had drawn a picture of her riding an elephant and waving. However, as I grabbed my crayons to shade in the elephant's grey face, I worried that the inclusion of an elephant might somehow imply that Jill's impending old age would never be forgotten. I thought for a moment before turning to the inside.

'Dear Jill,' I wrote. *'I hope you have a happy birthday. Remember: you're not old until you have grey hair and wrinkly*

---

[4] She found one squashed between her toes when we got home.
[5] A gift from me.

ankles, which you don't yet. Love from Livi.' I made the elephant extra grey and wrinkly so that she would appreciate the comparison.

It had taken a long time to find her a suitable present. Since Jill had insisted that she didn't want a fuss, it seemed a waste to buy her anything too fancy. Then again, I didn't want to be thoughtless and not get anything at all. So, after much deliberation and a lot of counsel from Ruby, I had bought her a singing egg timer. Jill has recently decided to put more effort into learning how to cook so I figured this would be a valuable addition to the kitchen. At least she couldn't accuse me of giving her something that I wanted for myself—[6] I have hated eggs ever since I blamed them for my chicken pox when I was eight.

When I'd finished colouring in her card, I retrieved the egg timer from the back of my wardrobe and wrapped it in some tissue paper. Then I padded out of my bedroom, pausing on the stairs as I listened for signs of Jill having a breakdown. I couldn't hear any crying so I sucked in my cheeks and made my way downstairs and into the kitchen. My sister was sat at the table, surrounded by piles of empty CTC boxes.[7] She was working away, dressed in scruffy old jeans and an oversized hoodie, looking as though she had completely forgotten it was her birthday. I wondered whether it would be rude to remind her.

I gave a cough. "Happy birthday."

She looked up and gave a thin smile. "Thanks."

I sat opposite her and handed her my card and gift.

She blinked at the card. "Is that me on an elephant?"

"You have to read the message," I explained.

She nodded and opened it. Then she pursed her lips and stared at my words for a long time. I wondered if she was having trouble reading my writing. "Thanks," she said finally.

"You're welcome! Now open your present."

She unwrapped my gift with a sigh and said, "Oh!" I grinned as she turned it over in her hands. "What is it?"

"A singing egg timer! It sings, *'Achy Breaky Heart'* when your egg is done."

Jill let out a chuckle. "That's great. Thanks, Livi."

"We could try it now," I suggested. "Have we got any eggs?"

---

[6] Unlike the time I got her some rollerskates.

[7] CTC stands for *'Colin's Tasty Chicken'*— Jill's employer and the third most popular fast food chicken outlet in the north of England.

"I'm afraid not."

"Oh. Well... What do you want to do then?"

"I want to finish this report."

I screwed up my nose. I understood she didn't want a big fuss, but it didn't feel right not to do *anything*. "I'll be back soon," I said before jumping up and running to my room. I closed the door behind me and grabbed my phone. Then I tapped in Ruby's number and wandered over to my window while I waited for her to answer.

She picked up after the second ring. "Hi, Livi!"

"Go to the window," I instructed.

A few seconds later Ruby's ginger head appeared in her bedroom window. She waved. "What's up?"

"Jill isn't doing *anything* for her birthday. I was thinking of throwing her a party."

Across the street, Ruby cocked her head to one side. "I thought Jill said she didn't want a fuss?"

"I know, I know..." I flapped a hand about. "But she probably just didn't want the hassle of having to arrange something herself."

"Mmm..."

"Jill doesn't really have any friends in Leeds. I was thinking you and your family could come over."

"Are you sure Jill would like that?"

"Of course!"

"What's she doing at the moment?"

"Nothing. It's really boring." I grabbed my teddy, Sausage-Legs, and had him crash spectacularly into my window.

Ruby giggled. "Alright. I'll ask my mum to bake a cake."

"Good thinking."

"See you soon."

"Don't take too long. Oh, and bring lots of eggs."

A short while later I saw Ruby and her family emerge from their house and cross the street. I waited for them to knock before grinning to myself and heading down the stairs. Jill had got up from the kitchen and was standing at the front door.

"It's the Ricos," she said as she peered though the frosted glass. "What are they doing here?"

Right on cue, Belinda warbled through the letterbox, "We're here for your party, Jill!"

I feigned astonishment. "What a nice surprise!"

Jill gave me a suspicious look and carefully opened the door.

Without a moment's pause, Oscar— wearing a blue jumpsuit with matching cape— leapt through her legs and into the hallway. "I've got my birthday suit on!" he yelled.

Belinda tittered. "He's been saying that all morning! He's so excited, bless him." She gave a stunned Jill a great soppy kiss on the cheek before wandering into our house, followed by Ruby, Violet and Stanley who were carrying four trays of eggs between them.

Jill gaped at them but, before she could say anything, Ruby piped up, "Livi said to bring eggs."

Jill glared at me. I gave a sheepish shrug and tried to think of something witty to say.

Thankfully, I was saved by Belinda taking Jill by the hand and leading her into the living room. "We're honoured to be sharing your birthday with you," she cooed.

I turned round, giggling to myself, and almost bumped into Violet.

"Hello Livi," she said solemnly.

I looked her up and down and suppressed a smirk. Recently, Violet has taken to dressing all in one colour. Today, she wore a purple dress, a purple tie-dyed cardigan, purple socks and a pair of purple ballet slippers. She had topped off the whole outfit with a lilac beret.

"What colour is it today then?" I asked.

She sniffed. "Where do you want the eggs?"

"Leave them with me." I took them from her and ushered her into the living room.

I carried the tray into the kitchen and carefully laid it on the table, humming to myself as I counted the eggs. There were thirty in each tray and four trays in total. That was a lot of *'Achy Breaky Heart.'*

Suddenly, Jill appeared in the doorway looking livid. "How dare you invite them over!" she hissed. "I said I didn't want a fuss."

I peered into the living room. Belinda was directing Stanley to an itch halfway up her back and Violet had taken her beret off and was muttering to herself in the corner.

"It's not exactly a *fuss*," I said. "Plus, I didn't tell them your real age."

Right on cue, Belinda called, "You look very young for 30, Jill!"

"See!"

Jill scowled and put a hand to her head.

"It will be fun," I assured her.

"Of course it won't be fun," she snapped. "Belinda's just started talking about ironing boards."

I sniggered but Jill smacked me on the arm. "I'm being serious, Livi. I have so much work to do before tomorrow."

"You've been off work all week and not done anything!" I said incredulously. "Why would you save it all for your birthday?"

She just growled and muttered, "I can't believe you invited them."

"Well, they're here now. We can't exactly ask them to leave."

Jill exhaled slowly. "Even though I'm not shouting right now, make no mistake about it, I am very angry with you."

"I understand."

"Very, *very*, angry."

"Okay..."

"Very, very, very, very—"

"I get it. And I'll never do it again."

"Right." Jill gave a steely nod. "Let's get this over with."

We went into the living room just in time to hear Belinda conclude, "I think the real problem lies in the size of the iron rest."

Jill pursed her lips and sat down beside Violet. "It's nice to see you all," she said stiffly.

"We wouldn't have missed it for the world!" Belinda exclaimed. She glanced around the room and added, "What a wonderful party."

"All of my favourite people, all in one place!" Oscar sang. He gave a toothy grin. "That's what you say all the time, isn't it, Mummy?"

"It is," Belinda said with a titter.

"Are Auntie Jill and Livi some of your favourite people?" Oscar continued.

"They are!" Belinda insisted. She turned to my sister and said earnestly, "You truly are."

Oscar twirled a lock of orange hair round his finger before asking my sister, "Are *we* some of *your* favourite people too?"

Jill rather overdid it as she nodded and forced a dazzling smile. "Absolutely."

Oscar beamed. "That's good. Because we see you all the time."

"You do," Jill agreed, grinning even more inanely. "This is the third time you've popped over this week."

"Why don't we play a game?" I said quickly. "Anybody got a good game?" I looked round at them all.

"We could play *Charades,*" said Stanley.

"Yeah!" Oscar squealed.

"Good idea," I said. "Let's play *Charades.*"

"Would you like that, Jill?" asked Belinda.

Everyone turned to look at my sister who went pink. "Yeah, alright," she muttered.

"How about *Special Charades?*" said Ruby. "We could have a theme, like *Easter* or *Animals...*"

"It should be Jill themed," Violet interjected. "Since it's her birthday."

"Auntie Jill themed Charades!" Oscar exclaimed. "I'll go first."

Jill looked a little alarmed as Oscar ran to the middle of the floor and stared at her. He thought for a moment before giggling and miming pushing something over. Then he clutched his hand and pouted.

"I know what that is," Jill said tersely. "That's me spilling my drink the other day."

"Yeah!" Oscar ran to give Jill an unwanted hug.

"I'll go next," I offered, jumping to my feet. "I've got a good one!" I started to flap my arms up and down.

"Flying?" Violet yelled. "Did Jill ever fly a plane?"

"Leaving the nest?" suggested Stanley. "You and Jill moving to Leeds?"

I shook my head and started again. I stood up straight and indicated a moustache with my finger.

"Facial hair?" Ruby guessed wildly.

"Auntie Jill eating a caterpillar!" cried Oscar.

"A man?" Stanley ventured.

I nodded and pointed to Stanley.

"A man?" he repeated.

I nodded again.

Jill looked confused.

"A man Jill knows?" asked Belinda.

I cocked my head to one side, as if to say, *'Sort of.'* Then I alternated between depicting the man and flapping my arms up and down.

"Oh, I know!" Ruby shrieked. "Fester!"

I gave her a withering look. "No!"

As I waved my arms ever frantically, I saw Jill looking more and more furious.

"Come on! It's really easy." I repeated my mime, exaggerating the features of the man all the more.

"We give up," Belinda said, shaking her head.

"Tell us!" Oscar demanded.

I pouted. "I was being Colin from *Colin's Tasty Chicken.*"

Everybody except Jill fell about laughing.

"Oh! That was a tough one," Belinda exclaimed.

I avoided Jill's gaze as I went to sit back down. "Who's next?"

"Me!" Violet called. She got up and started to mime what looked like Jill losing her last job.

Before anybody could guess, there was a knock at the door. Jill got up and went to answer it. I peered out of the window. It was the postman with a parcel from Aunt Claudia.

"What is it?" Oscar ran to my sister and poked the parcel with a podgy finger.

"I'll open it later," Jill said, tossing it onto the side table.

"But I want to see what it is," Oscar whined. "Please open it now!"

Jill forced a smile. "You can open it for me if you want."

Oscar's eyes grew wide as he yanked the parcel off the table and brought it into the centre of the living room. He ripped off the paper and gave a squeal as a book fell to the floor. *"A... journey of dis...covery on the road to... middle-age,"* he read clumsily. "Ooh. Can I have it?"

Jill snorted. "Yes."

"Oh I've read that one," Belinda piped up, peering over Oscar's shoulder. "There's a wonderful chapter on early menopause."

To spare Jill's embarrassment, I quickly said, "That's silly. Jill isn't middle-aged."

"Of course not!" Belinda agreed. She gave Jill a little pat on the head. "You've got a good run ahead of you yet."

"Years and years and *years,*" I exclaimed.

Jill glared at me.

"Anyway," Violet said. "We were in the middle of my turn."

"I think that's enough *Charades,*" I interrupted, ignoring Violet's wounded stare. "Who wants to boil some eggs?"

Nobody said anything so I nudged Ruby and said, *"Ruby?"*

"Oh!" She looked at me in surprise. "Alright."

I grabbed her by the arm and hurried her out of the living room and into the kitchen. "I don't think Jill's enjoying her party," I confided.

"That's a shame," Ruby whispered. "What do you think the problem is?"

I bit my lip and said nothing. Then I grabbed the singing egg timer and a pan from the cupboard. "Ready for something cool?"

Ruby nodded and passed me an egg from the table.

We covered the egg and the timer with water and set the pan on the stove. Then we watched in silence as we waited for the water to boil.

"Nothing's happening," Ruby muttered after several minutes.

"Keep waiting," I insisted.

After what felt like an eternity, a squeak erupted from the timer followed by some warbled singing.

Ruby and I looked at one another and gasped.

"That's amazing!" Ruby spluttered.

"I know!" I ran to fetch another egg. "Let's do another one."

"Okay!"

I sifted out the boiled egg and laid it on the work surface before filling the pan with fresh water. We popped the next egg in and waited.

We had wasted nine eggs before Oscar the gifted child came in and pointed out that the timer would have sung whether there was an egg in the water or not.

Ruby looked at her brother and giggled. "You're so clever!"

"I kind of knew that," I said. "But it's more fun when you do it properly."

Oscar shrugged. "It's time for cake."

I turned the hob off and followed Oscar and Ruby back into the living room. Everybody was gathered round a bright pink cake laden with candles. There were so many candles that there wasn't much space for any writing, although Belinda had managed to squeeze on a small J in blue icing.

"What a nice cake," my sister said politely as Stanley lit the candles.

"It's a new recipe," Belinda replied. "I'll teach you how to make it one day."

Jill nodded but said nothing.

Stanley finished lighting the candles and blew his match out. "Right then..." He looked round at the rest of us.

We were about to start singing when Oscar said, "I want to sing the *other* birthday song. You know... The good one."

His mother gave him a bemused look.

"Can I sing it?" Oscar begged.

"I don't know," said Stanley. "Jill might not like a different song."

Oscar stared at my sister. "Why can't I sing it?"

Jill forced a smile. "You can sing whatever you want."

Oscar grinned and got to his feet. He stared intently at Jill as he bellowed, *"You are another year older, and all the angels sing: Don't forget your Maker, don't forget your King..."* He waved his arms at his family, as if commanding them to join in, which they did after a little hesitation. *"...He made the earth, he made the sun, he made the stars and everyone. So don't forget your Lord Jesus— the greatest gift of all. Don't forget your Maker, now you're...[8] fifty years old!"* Oscar finished the song with a roar and took a bow.

Jill gave a curt nod. "Well done." She turned to her cake and blew her candles out. It took five puffs to get them all.

In the silence that followed, Belinda explained, "It's an old family song. You're more than welcome to use it whenever you want."

"Great." Jill pulled the candles off her cake and started to cut it rather haphazardly.

"Can I have the piece with the J?" Oscar asked, giving the coveted slice a poke.

"Jill should have that piece," said Violet. "It's a J for Jill."

Oscar cocked his head to one side. "I thought J was for Jesus."

"It is," Stanley said briskly. "But, today, J is also for Jill."

Oscar shot my sister a bewildered glance. "But she's not holy."

The colour drained from Jill's face as she stopped cutting her cake and handed me the knife.

Belinda forced a laugh. "Oh Oscar. What a cheeky pumpkin you are!"

Nobody spoke after that. Once or twice Belinda tried to throw a cheery smile in Jill's direction but my sister avoided her gaze. I hastily distributed several slices of cake which were nibbled with the enthusiasm of guests at a wake.

Finally, Stanley said, "Well, this has been a lovely party. I think it's time for us to go now."

Giving her first genuine smile of the day, Jill leapt to her feet and said, "Thank you so much for coming. Please take some cake with you..."

"Oh, don't give us any more cake!" Belinda exclaimed. "That's yours."

---

[8] Here, Oscar paused and looked at Jill in confusion. But, rather than stopping his song to ask how old Jill actually was, he continued with great gusto...

"Don't be daft," my sister insisted. "You always take cake home when you leave a party." She grabbed some napkins and wrapped up half the cake.

"And a party bag," I added, running into the kitchen to fetch Belinda a carrier bag of hard boiled eggs.

Jill didn't talk to me for the rest of the day. I did my best to make things up to her by tidying the living room and offering to cook her an omelette but she just glared at me and threw the rest of the eggs in the bin.

As I picked at the icing on the ruins of her birthday cake the piece with the J seemed to call out to me from the middle of the plate. *J is for Jesus... J is for Jill.* I gave a sigh and uttered a quick prayer. *God, I really want Jill to believe in you... She would be so much happier if she did.* I sucked in my cheeks as I made a decision: *One way or another, I will save Jill by the summer.*

~ 3 ~

The new girl

Despite our customary complaining all the way to school, I was more than a little relieved when the Easter break came to an end on Tuesday morning. Jill still hadn't forgiven me for her surprise birthday party and my preliminary attempts to tell her about Jesus had not gone down well.[9] I had also grown rather bored with all the free time that I had and, although I was reluctant to admit it, was missing some of our lessons.

"Ugh, I can't believe we're back at school already," I moaned as Ruby and I neared the school gates.

"I know!" Ruby exclaimed. "It would have been cool if school had burnt down or something."

"Yeah!" I sighed and pretended to be disappointed.

As we crossed the playground we saw Ms Sorenson emerging from the car park.

"There's Ms Sorenson!" Ruby said cheerfully.

I nodded and gazed intently at our favourite teacher, hoping she would look up and wave, but she didn't see us. I sucked in my cheeks as I wondered what our timetable would be like this term. I hoped vainly that Maths might have been scrapped in favour of more Personal and Social Development classes.

"In some ways, I suppose it's nice to be back," Ruby conceded as we wandered into the building.

"Back to normal!" I agreed, pushing open the door to our form room.

But it turned out that day would be anything but normal.

---

[9] I had begun by leaving a couple of Belinda's Bible bookmarks in Jill's shoes but she had mistaken them for Belinda's doing and started cursing 'that judgemental cow' as she ripped them into pieces. Later, I had perched my Bible carefully on the oven, open to a passage about the Kingdom of Heaven, but Jill had threatened to cook it if I didn't remove it immediately.

We had barely entered the room when Ruby gave me a nudge and pointed. There was a girl sitting at Miss Fairway's desk.

"Who's that?" I asked in surprise.

The girl looked up and caught my eye.

I attempted a smile but she just frowned and looked away.

I blushed and followed Ruby to our desk, shooting only quick glances at the girl so that I wouldn't be caught staring.

"She must be a new teacher," said Ruby. "She looks at least twenty."

"She's wearing a school uniform! She's our age."

"Oh!"

"Unless she's really stupid," I suggested. "And is re-taking several years."

Ruby cocked her head to one side. "She doesn't look stupid. She looks quite bright. And *really* pretty."

I sniffed as I gave the girl another sideways glance. I supposed she was pretty in a strange kind of way; with beady eyes, a very narrow chin and whiter than white blonde hair. The boys, it was plain from their gawping, had already cleared a space for her at the top of their imaginary *Hot Girls League,* and many of the girls were looking at her with a combination of curiosity and envy.

Kitty Warrington and her gang wore looks that clearly said, *'This is our school and we're in charge.'*

A few of the other girls were looking hopeful, as if wondering whether she might like to be their friend. Even Ruby seemed intrigued and kept grinning at me.

I pursed my lips and stole another peek at the new girl. She looked a little hostile. And she had a slight monobrow.

"She's not *that* pretty," I insisted.

Once we had all taken our seats, Miss Fairway arose and said, "Good morning everyone. I'd like to introduce you to Caroline MacBrodie. She'll be joining you from today."

The class gazed at the new girl. A few people exchanged optimistic glances.

"She's from a place called..." Miss Fairway paused and looked at Caroline. "Pebbles?"

"Peebles," the girl corrected shrilly.

Across the room, Wayne Purdy guffawed and yelled, "Where?"

"It's in Scotland," Caroline snapped. "Which is above England. I suggest you get a map and ask someone to help you read it."

A few people giggled as Wayne scowled and muttered, "I know where *Scotland* is."

"Yes, Peebles." Miss Fairway cleared her throat. "Caroline was just telling me that her dad has a new job in... What was it again?"

Caroline gave Miss Fairway an unimpressed stare before standing up and speaking for herself. "I'm Caroline. My dad moved to Leeds for business. I could tell you what he does but it's exceedingly boring and, unless you know what asset management is, you wouldn't understand." She paused before adding, "You'll have noticed I'm quite tall for my age. Before you go thinking I'm some kind of freak, I ought to tell you that I'm a model; so chew on that before you mock me."

My jaw dropped. When I'd arrived at the start of September, I'd wanted to hide under the table as Miss Fairway introduced me to my bemused classmates.

"This is Livi Starling," our teacher had said. "She's from a place called Little Milkman."

"Little Milking," I had squeaked.

Wayne had snorted and yelled, "Where?"

I'd whispered, "It's not on the map." Then I'd stared at the floor as Miss Fairway asked who wanted to look after me.

After a very long silence, Ruby had put her hand up.

I marvelled at Caroline's audacity as she concluded her speech, "I've seen the league tables for this school and it's not the best. But I can take Dance as an option next year so that's what swung it for me."

I glanced at my classmates. They were looking as stunned as me.

Even Miss Fairway seemed taken aback as she said, "Thank you, Caroline. We're all very pleased to welcome you to Hare Valley High and we'll do everything we can to help you feel at home."

Caroline sniffed. "In that case, I'd like to sit near the window. It's probably my Scottish blood but I find this school a little stuffy."

The class gawped as Caroline sauntered over to an empty desk at the side of the room, pausing to open the window before sitting down. She tucked her bag under her seat and swept her whiter than white blonde hair away from her face, seemingly oblivious to the wonder that had filled the room.

A few people nudged one another. Kitty Warrington and Molly Masterson were locked in desperate whispers.

"Her accent is so... exotic," I heard Rupert Crisp say dreamily behind me.

I turned and tutted. Just before the Easter holidays Rupert had expressed something of a minor crush on *me* and, as unwanted as his affections were, it seemed a little fickle of him to have gone off me so quickly.

Ruby had turned pink. "She's cool," she gasped.

"Yeah." I shifted uncomfortably. Not only was Caroline MacBrodie the *new* new girl, but she was a much better new girl than me.

Miss Fairway was blinking at Caroline in astonishment. She didn't need to ask who wanted to look after Caroline. It was perfectly clear that Caroline could look after herself.

Our first lesson was French. Ruby and I watched as Caroline wandered into the classroom and picked a seat at the back of the room. After opening the window, she yawned and drummed lightly on the table.

The rest of the class avoided her gaze as they scrambled for seats as far away from her as possible and proceeded to stare at her from behind their French textbooks. Nobody spoke to her. They all looked too frightened.

"Do you think she's alright?" Ruby whispered.

I shrugged. "She looks fine."

"Maybe she's trying to act brave. She might be terrified deep down. Shall we see if she wants to sit with us?"

I bit my lip as I stole a glance at Caroline. I wasn't sure if I wanted her to sit with us.

"What would Jesus do?" Ruby continued.

I screwed up my nose and ignored her imploring stare. I didn't want to do whatever Jesus might do. I wanted to do what was safe and I *hoped* that Jesus would understand. I tried to think of a reasonable excuse for leaving Caroline alone but I couldn't think over the noise of Ruby jabbering beside me.

"Think about how you would feel... Scotland's a whole different country... What if she cries herself to sleep tonight?"

"Oh alright!"

Ruby grinned. "Go on then."

"Ruby!" I rolled my eyes. "Why do *I* have to do it?"

She blushed. "I'm too scared. Plus, you know how it feels to be new. You can relate to her better."

I got to my feet. "Fine. I'll be Jesus."

I forced a smile as I headed for Caroline's desk. She didn't look up until I had positioned myself immediately beside her and, even then, she gave me only half a glance before shuffling her chair slightly away.

"So..." I squeaked. "You're a model? That's pretty cool."

She gave me a sharp look. "Don't patronise me."

I jumped back. "What?"

"Don't you know that a high proportion of models suffer a mental breakdown before the age of twenty?"

I raised my eyebrows. "Why do you do it then?"

"Because with this face I'd be stupid not to."

I nodded slowly. "I suppose so... Hey, I'm Livi, by the way. Do you want to come and sit with me and Ruby?"

Caroline looked me up and down. Then she glanced across at Ruby who was waving nervously. "I already have a friend called Libby. It's such a common name."

"Oh, no! I'm *Livi*, not Libby."

"You're what now?" Her lip curled into a sneer. "Is that some kind of car?"

I shifted uncomfortably. "Actually, it was a biscuit."

She stared at me. "I'd rather sit alone."

"Okay." I headed back to my seat, my head reeling.

"What did she say?" Ruby asked eagerly.

"She said she'd rather sit alone."

Ruby's face fell. "Perhaps she's nervous. It must be really scary for her."

I wrinkled up my nose. "I don't think so. I think she's just rude."

We watched as Caroline pulled some make-up out of her pencil case and reapplied her lip liner.[10] Not too far away, Kitty Warrington was staring at her intently.

Madame Maurel came in and greeted us with a cheery smile. "Bonjour classe. Comment allez-vous aujourd'hui?"

As the rest of us responded with our usual half-hearted grunt, Caroline sang gaily behind us, "Très bien merci. Et vous?"

Madame Maurel looked up in surprise. "Oh! Who are you?"

Without a moment's hesitation, Caroline stood up and recited in perfect French, "Je m'appelle Caroline MacBrodie. Je suis de Peebles en Écosse. Je peux parler français, allemand, italien et mandarin chinois."

Ruby dug me in the ribs. "What did she just say?"

"How should I know?"

---

[10] We later learnt that she didn't actually have any pens in her pencil case. It was full of make-up and she did her work with an eyebrow pencil.

Whatever it was, it had clearly impressed Madame Maurel. The whole class turned and watched as our teacher put a hand to her chest and muttered inaudibly before coming towards Caroline and applauding.

"I cannot tell you how 'appy I am," Madame Maurel exclaimed. "Come and sit with me at ze front."

Caroline gave a thin smile and picked up her bag. Then she followed Madame Maurel to the front of the room and sat in our teacher's chair.

I looked round at my classmates, certain that *somebody* would take the opportunity to call Caroline a geek. But they were all staring at her in awe. I sucked in my cheeks and frowned.

"Right zen," Madame Maurel said. "You may have 'ad two weeks off school, but zat is no excuse for sloppiness. Especially when some people are more zan able to perform wizout a fuss." She shot Caroline a sweet smile and began to write our morning's assignment on the white board.

Caroline gave the rest of us a snide glance as we pulled out our exercise books and made a reluctant start.

I tried not to focus on Caroline as I attempted the grammar exercise but it was hard not to get distracted by her since she was sitting in the way of the board. She finished the assignment in less than five minutes and Madame Maurel began praising her in French while Caroline beamed and said, "C'était facile..."

A short while later, Madame Maurel sent Caroline round to mark our work. I pretended not to care as she gave me a massive red cross with her lip liner.

"That was a great speech you made earlier," I said politely.

She nodded. "Could you understand it?"

"No..."

"Then you're just patronising me again, aren't you?"

I blushed.

Ruby looked like she was about to wet herself. "I can't feel my legs," she whispered as Caroline walked away.

I shot her an exasperated look and watched as Caroline stopped at the next table and picked up Darcy Bell's exercise book. Both Darcy Bell and Georgina Harris, who was beside her, were gazing at Caroline in wonder.

"What did you say earlier?" Georgina simpered.

"I said I could speak French, German, Italian and Chinese Mandarin," Caroline replied smoothly.

The class gawped at her.

"Oh, you should talk to Aaron!" Annie Button exclaimed, pointing to Aaron Tang. "He's Chinese!"

Caroline looked across at Aaron and shook her head. "No he's not. He's Malaysian."

Aaron's eyes grew wide. "Thank you," he whispered.

The class watched in stunned silence as Caroline made her way down the desks. Nobody seemed to mind that she was scrawling all over our work with ugly great crosses. If anything, most people took back their books with great glee as though they had just received an autograph from a celebrity.

Finally, she reached Kitty Warrington's table. I nudged Ruby and we exchanged bemused smiles. This would be interesting.

We watched as Kitty sneered and said, "Hey, Caroline. It must be tough being new?"

"Not particularly." Caroline picked up Kitty's exercise book and started to skim-read Kitty's work.

Before she could mark it, Kitty yanked her book back and said, "Anyway, I thought I should introduce myself." She gave a smug grin and held her hand out.

Caroline stared at her.

Kitty dropped her hand before saying pompously, "I'm Kitty."

Caroline smirked. "Like a cat?"

The class gasped.

Kitty's jaw dropped open.

Beside her, Molly Masterson turned scarlet.

Caroline snatched Kitty's book back and put a massive red cross through it all. "Try harder next time," she said. Then she slammed Kitty's book down and sauntered off.

Kitty stared after her, her face etched with a fearful combination of fury and dread.

The class gaped at Kitty and awaited her response. Then, as Caroline continued walking through the classroom, every eye left Kitty and followed Caroline instead. Nobody said anything. Nobody needed to. But, in the silence that followed, it was clear that a powerful exchange had taken place.

Sheena Ali broke the silence by saying loudly, "I like your shoes, Caroline."

Caroline turned and smiled. "Thanks. They wouldn't suit your skin tone."

After that, there was complete chaos as everybody clamoured for Caroline's attention.

"I love your accent, Caroline." That was Rupert Crisp.

"Can you say '*haggis*' in French?" That was Rupert again.

I rolled my eyes and turned to Ruby but, to my dismay, even she was looking a little mesmerised. "Do you think she's seen the Loch Ness Monster?" she whispered.

"I don't care!" I hissed back. "And *no*, I'm not going to ask her."

Ruby gave me a wounded look and pouted.

For the rest of the lesson, I watched in frustration as my class grew more and more enamoured with Caroline MacBrodie. Nobody did any work and Madame Maurel barely minded. In fact, at one point, Madame Maurel even took Caroline's seat under the window while Caroline swivelled in the teacher's chair and led a silent lesson in her own brilliance. She sat in front of the white board, holding our attention with her fierce glare, while glances that had once been reserved for Kitty Warrington were thrown frivolously in her direction.

I even heard Connie Harper utter the words, "I would eat my own face just to be her friend."

When the lesson came to an end Caroline had more than a dozen volunteers to help carry her bag.[11] Across the room, Kitty Warrington was looking rather pale. Molly, Melody and Annie were watching her uneasily, as if unsure of what to do.

I rubbed my head in disbelief as I gathered up my books. In less than two hours Caroline MacBrodie had single-handedly toppled Kitty Warrington from the post of coolest girl in school. And she had done it by being a complete cow.

---

[11] In the end, she bestowed the honour upon Ritchie Jones who was more than happy for Caroline to remark, "I don't expect there's much substance once one gets beyond your looks so we'll just keep this surface level."

~ 4 ~

Ms Sorenson always knows what she's doing

Despite the fact that our class had appointed Caroline MacBrodie as their new queen, it transpired that Kitty Warrington was not going to give up her crown without a fight. For the rest of the morning[12] she could be seen brooding darkly as she conferred with Molly Masterson. Every now and then, she looked across at Caroline and scowled. Beside them, Melody and Annie watched anxiously as they waited for their orders.

Fester, to my disgust, had almost swooned when Caroline entered his classroom. He had responded to her request to sit by the window by nodding so enthusiastically that he pulled a muscle in his neck. The upside of this was that it rendered him immobile and he was forced to conduct the whole lesson from the recovery position at the foot of his desk.

"We're going to be looking at coordinates," he said, wincing as he fumbled for his lesson plan.

The class ignored him and carried on talking.

"Silence!" Fester roared from the floor. "I won't stand for any nonsense."

"No, but you'll lay down for it," Caroline muttered.

The class erupted in laughter and a few people started throwing paper balls.

"I mean it! You'll all be in detention at this rate." Fester held up his mobile phone. "One more word and I'll ring Mr Riley."

The class quietened down immediately. An incapacitated teacher on the floor was far preferable to a visit from the head teacher.

"There are worksheets on top of the register," Fester continued. He kept his head perfectly still as his beady eyes roamed round the room. He caught my gaze. "Livi, hand them out, please."

---

[12] A tedious Maths lesson with Fester.

I winced and slid off my chair, ignoring the contemptuous looks of my classmates as I grabbed the worksheets and passed them round.

"What a geek," several of the boys muttered.

"Teacher's pet," added Molly.

I returned to my seat with a scowl.

Ruby shot me a sympathetic glance and pulled out her pencil.

A few people sniggered as Fester said, "Thank you, Livi. That was very kind."

I straightened out my worksheet and tried to make myself look busy. It was incredibly boring, and I was fairly sure that we had done the exact same worksheet before, but I didn't want to encourage any further communication with Fester by asking.

Halfway though the lesson, Ruby cocked her head towards Fester and whispered, "Do you think he's okay?"

I followed her gaze. Fester was trying to pull himself off the floor with the use of a nearby table leg. I felt a pang of pity for him as he writhed around like a worm.

"We can't help him," I reasoned. "Everyone would hate us."

We looked round the room. Nobody was working, unless you count Connie Harper and Sheena Ali who were helping Caroline sharpen her eyebrow pencils. Caroline was giving a lengthy discourse on how pathetic Leeds city centre was and, nearby, Georgina Harris and Darcy Bell were hanging on her every word. On the other side of the room Kitty was watching her like a hawk and making the odd snide comment to Molly.

Ruby turned back to her worksheet. "I suppose." She paused before adding, "Isn't it funny that, when Caroline knew how to speak French, everybody thought she was amazing. Yet all you did was hand out worksheets and everybody called you a geek?"

I whacked the desk with my pencil case. "Hilarious!"

Fester made it off the floor just as the bell rang for lunch. Most of our class cheered and sprang to their feet. Georgina Harris and Darcy Bell almost clashed heads as they lunged towards Caroline.

"Shall I show you where the canteen is, Caroline?"

"Do you want me to carry your lunch, Caroline?"

Caroline sniffed and thrust her bag at Ritchie Jones.

The other boys watched in envy as Ritchie took it with a bow and said, "What have you got for lunch, Caroline? I have some dried fruit if you fancy a *date*."

Caroline glared at him.

Ritchie cleared his throat and tried again. "If you were a bogey, I'd pick you..."

He turned to give some of the other boys a grin but, before he could get too cocky, Caroline said, "Seriously, I said surface level. That means no talking."

Ritchie blushed and mimed zipping up his mouth.

As Caroline sauntered out of the room with her procession of fans, Kitty Warrington got up and slowly followed her out. She kept her distance, stalking through the shadows as she stared with loathing at the back of Caroline's head. The hate in her eyes was so intense that I was surprised Caroline didn't catch on fire. Molly strode behind her, wearing an ugly sneer and, behind *her,* Melody and Annie scurried like agitated field mice.

I nudged Ruby and she nodded, linking arms with me as we followed them across the playground and into the canteen.

Caroline had chosen a table in the far corner and was sitting pretty while several of our classmates fought for the seats around her. Ritchie Jones, still carrying Caroline's bag, dutifully hunted around for her lunch and passed it to her as though he was handling a newborn baby.

Georgina Harris butted Darcy Bell out of the way to secure the seat beside Caroline, although she soon regretted it when Caroline turned to her and snapped, "You remind me of my puppy. She yaps just like that."

Ruby and I found a quiet table several feet away and watched the scene from behind our lunchboxes. Kitty was glowering at the side of the room as she summoned up the courage for her confrontation. Eventually, she strode over to Caroline and poked her on the shoulder.

Caroline turned and grinned. "Oh hello. Cat, was it?"

Kitty pursed her lips.

I waited for some fireworks; perhaps a slap or some hysterical hair-pulling.

But, after a slight pause, Kitty looked down at Caroline's lunch bag and said, "Is that from *Tizzi Berry?*"

Caroline held it up with a sneer. "Limited edition: *Tizzi Tokyo* range."

Kitty smirked before pulling out the exact same bag. "Snap."

Caroline looked at her in surprise. "My dad had to order it from Japan."

Kitty gave a laugh. "My dad *went* to Japan for mine."

Caroline raised an eyebrow. "Wow. You must really love him."

"What?"

"I don't love my parents," Caroline said scornfully.

"Oh, I don't love mine either," Kitty insisted. "But I know how to get them to do what I want."

Caroline nodded. "I once stole fifty pounds from my dad's wallet."

Kitty sniffed. "I lost my mum's necklace and blamed it on the cleaner."

Caroline faked a yawn. "I pushed my brother in a lake and tried to drown him."

Kitty opened her mouth and closed it again. Finally, she muttered, "I faked my own death."

Caroline stared at her for a moment. Then she grinned and patted the seat beside her.

Kitty gave a pompous smirk and sat down.

Next, Caroline turned to Molly and snapped, "Are you sitting with us, or what?"

"Yeah, obviously," Molly stammered, shoving an affronted Georgina out of the way as she plonked herself on the other side of Caroline.

After a moment's pause, Melody and Annie ran to join them.

Ruby blinked at me. "So, who won?"

"I have no idea," I mumbled. As far as I was concerned, they were all complete losers.

As I studied our timetable for the new term, I was pleased to note that we had Ms Sorenson's class that very afternoon. However, my stomach churned as I wondered what Ms Sorenson would make of Caroline. All morning, people had been falling at her feet.[13] I wasn't sure what I would do if Ms Sorenson fell in love with her too.

Wanting to secure seats as close as possible to Ms Sorenson's desk, Ruby and I left the canteen before lunch was over so that we could get to class early. We lingered in the corridor, wondering when it would be appropriate to go in, but our enthusiasm turned out to be unnecessary because, even after the bell had rung, most of our classmates still hadn't arrived.

"Where is everybody?" Ruby wondered aloud.

---

[13] Literally: first Fester and then a whole line of sixth form boys who tripped over one another as she passed them in the corridor. We even saw Rupert Crisp clinging to her ankles in the canteen after she told him and several of the other boys to, *"Go and play in the traffic. I've got enough dogs at home."*

"Take a guess," I muttered as we followed Rupert, Wayne and the rest of Caroline's rejects into the classroom.

Ms Sorenson was sitting at her desk, making a list in her filofax. Before we could sit down, she arose and said, "Come and stand by the window."

I felt a pang of dread as I wondered whether Caroline had already run ahead and charmed Ms Sorenson into considering the benefits of sitting under an open window.

It soon became clear, however, that Ms Sorenson had not yet been acquainted with Caroline.

"Where are the rest of your classmates?" she asked, frowning as she glanced at her watch.

At that moment, Caroline came sauntering into the room with Kitty on her arm. The rest of the class trailed behind them.

Ms Sorenson scoured her register and said, "You must be Miss MacBrodie."

Caroline scanned at her timetable and retorted, "You must be Ms Sorenson."

Our teacher raised an eyebrow. "Do you have bright green teeth?"

"What? No!" Caroline looked at her in confusion.

"Then you're chewing gum," Ms Sorenson said coldly. "Get rid of it and line up at the side."

I breathed a huge sigh of relief. *Thank you, Lord!*

Caroline scowled and went to spit her gum out.

Once everyone had assembled by the window, Ms Sorenson said, "Good afternoon, 9.1. Now then, what is a biography?"

I half raised my hand and then lowered it again. The rest of my class had stayed silent. I bit my lip. I was torn between wanting to please Ms Sorenson and not wanting to be called a geek again.

Ms Sorenson kept staring at us. She's not the sort of teacher who gives her students an easy way out.

Eventually, Kitty drawled, "It's the story of your life, Miss." She glanced smugly at Caroline who shook her head and sneered. Kitty blushed and whispered, "What?"

"The story of your life?" Ms Sorenson repeated. "Is that it?"

The class looked at Kitty before nodding ardently.

"No," I said loudly.

Everyone turned to stare.

I avoided their gaze as I squeaked, "It's the story of *somebody else's* life, isn't it?"

Ms Sorenson beamed. "Thank you, Livi. That's right."

My heart leapt. All around me, my classmates were muttering snidely but it was worth it. I stole a glance at Kitty and Caroline. They were both glaring at me. Caroline nudged Kitty and whispered something. Then they looked at one another and tittered. I stuck my nose up at them and turned back to our teacher.

"In a moment, I'm going to put you into pairs," Ms Sorenson said. "You will sit together this term and, over the next few weeks, you'll write your partner's biography."

Ruby clutched my arm as Ms Sorenson grabbed the list from her filofax.

"Don't worry," I whispered. "She'll put us together. Ms Sorenson always knows what she's doing."

Ms Sorenson cleared her throat and began to read out her list. "Molly Masterson and Wayne Purdy go and sit over there..."

Molly and Wayne frowned at one another. I tried not to show it but, privately, I agreed that it was a rather odd pairing.

Ms Sorenson pointed to a desk before continuing, "Rupert Crisp and Kitty Warrington."

That was even stranger.

Kitty opened her mouth to protest but Ms Sorenson put a hand up and said, "Go and sit down." As she continued reading out names, I started to feel a little anxious. None of the people who were being paired up were friends with one another.

Ruby was shaking as she clung onto my arm. "Please, please, please," she said under her breath.

"...Livi Starling and Annie Button."

My heart sunk. I looked at Ruby in disappointment as I picked up my bag and followed Annie to the desk Ms Sorenson was pointing to.

Ruby's jaw hung open. She raised her eyebrows as if to ask, 'What's going on?'

I shrugged desperately. 'No idea.'

"Hey Livi!" Annie whispered as we sat down. "We've never sat together before. Isn't this weird? You're gonna have to tell me all about your life because I forgot: is your dad an actor or not?"

I grimaced and looked at the floor. I couldn't possibly work with Annie Button. The last thing I wanted was to share my secrets with one of Kitty's minions. I wondered whether to express my reservations to Ms Sorenson but she was already in the middle of telling Kitty off for complaining.

"No, Miss Warrington. This is non-negotiable. Sit back down."

"But Ms Sorenson, I hate Rupert!"

"I'd like to add that I'm not too keen on Kitty either," Rupert said, shaking as he raised his hand.

Ms Sorenson forced a laugh. "I know." She looked round at the whole class before saying firmly, "Any more complaints and you can have an instant detention."

I buried my head in my hands as I sunk down in my seat.

Ms Sorenson continued calling out names until there was only one pair left.

"Ruby Rico and Caroline MacBrodie."

I looked up in shock.

Ruby had gone bright pink and was beaming from ear to ear as though she and Caroline had just been announced the prom king and queen. The rest of our class were looking incredibly jealous.

Caroline screwed up her nose and looked Ruby up and down. "Seriously? Can we at least sit by the window?"

Ms Sorenson gave her a stern look before pointing to a desk on the other side of the room.

Caroline tutted and snatched up her bag. "I hate this lesson," she muttered.

Ruby caught my eye and gave a nervous grin as she followed Caroline to their desk.

I narrowed my eyes and frowned.

Ms Sorenson took her position at the front of the class and looked round at us all. "We'll start off slowly," she said with a smile. "This lesson, you can do whatever you like—" We leapt up in excitement but she continued loudly, "—as long as you stay in your chairs."

The class groaned and sat back down, regarding our partners with differing degrees of disdain.

I glanced across at Ruby. She was still grinning happily as she gazed at Caroline. Caroline took no notice as she fiddled with her phone and yawned.

"What's your middle name?" Annie asked me suddenly.

I ignored her.

"Livi? What's your middle name?" She tapped me on the arm.

I pulled my arm away. "I don't know."

"What do you mean you don't know?"

"I don't want to tell you. Just be quiet. I'm trying to think." I turned my head away from Annie and craned my ears towards Ruby and Caroline. It looked like they had begun a conversation and my heart beat wildly as I feared for what would happen if they made friends. For the rest of the lesson I kept my eyes fixed on them as I fielded Annie's annoying questions.

"How can you not know your own middle name? Do you mean you don't have one? Or did your birth certificate get water on it and make it hard to read, because I know someone who lost theirs at the swimming pool—"

I gave a growl. "It's Teeson, okay?"

Annie raised her eyebrows. "Teeson? Is that a name?"

I nodded and looked away.

"How do you spell it?" Annie pulled out a pen.

I sighed and wrote it down for her.

Barely thirty seconds later, Annie piped up, "Are you sure it's a name?"

"Yes. It's my dad's surname."

"Your dad's surname? You mean Starling isn't your dad's surname? Whose surname is it then? Did you get named after your mum, because I know someone who never knew their dad and—"

"Yes, Starling is my mum's surname," I snapped. "What about you? What's your middle name?"

Annie beamed. "May. It's spelt M.A.Y."

"Fine." I carelessly wrote it down before turning back to Ruby and Caroline.

They were definitely talking about something. I couldn't hear much over the noise of our classmates although, at one point, I thought I heard Ruby ask, "Have you ever seen the Loch Ness Monster?" I didn't catch Caroline's reply but it made Ruby turn bright red.

For the first time in one of Ms Sorenson's classes, I was overjoyed when the lesson came to an end.

As soon as our teacher dismissed us, Caroline stormed out of the classroom, pausing briefly to grab Kitty's arm. "I missed you so much," she drawled.

"I missed you too!" Kitty exclaimed.

"Me three!" Molly added as she came up behind them. She linked arms with Melody and the four of them sauntered out.

"Bye," Annie said quickly. She grabbed her belongings and ran to join them.

I went over to Ruby who was slowly packing up her things.

"Well, what did you think?" I asked cautiously.

"I think..." Ruby sniffed. "Caroline MacBrodie is mean. And Ms Sorenson does *not* always know what she's doing."

~ 5 ~

Rock. Flamingo. Joey

It didn't take long for Caroline to grow tired of the undying affection of the rest of our class. On Friday lunchtime, she held a special meeting in our form room in which she defined her select posse of friends. Ruby and I peered through the window[14] and watched as Caroline arose and delivered a speech. Her words were met by gasps and a lot of shaking. After that, our classmates were sent out one by one until only Kitty, Molly, Melody, Annie and a mute Ritchie Jones were left.

I don't know exactly what was said but, not long after, we saw Georgina Harris and Darcy Bell comforting one another in the toilets.

"She's not worth it," Georgina whispered, glancing round as though afraid Caroline might hear.

"Yeah." Darcy nodded, although she didn't look completely convinced.

They were soon joined by Connie Harper and Sheena Ali who were sobbing helplessly.

"I thought she liked us," Sheena whimpered.

"I want to die," added Connie.

Without thinking, I let out a little splutter.

The four of them turned and glared at me.[15]

"I'm sorry," I said. "I just don't get why you care so much."

Connie sniffed. "You're just jealous. At least we were friends with her once."

"For three days," I retorted.

"That's three days longer than you!" Georgina snapped.

---

[14] Having been barred from entering by Ritchie Jones who held up a sign stating, 'Invite only.'

[15] It was at this moment that I noticed they were all wearing Caroline-esque monobrows drawn with eyebrow pencil.

I sucked in my breath. "I was trying to be nice," I muttered as I yanked the door open and walked out.

Ruby followed at a trot as I stormed down the corridor. "What's wrong?" she asked, eyeing the frown on my face.

"Our class is stupid," I said irritably. "I don't understand why horrible people are always so popular."

"Do you secretly wish Caroline wanted to be your friend?"

"No!" I yelled. I paused before admitting, "Well, yeah. A bit. Actually, I wish *everybody* wanted to be my friend. I don't understand why I'm not more popular. I'm a nice person, aren't I?"

Ruby nodded fervently. "You're really nice, Livi. That's the problem. Nice people get killed. Think of Jesus!" She paused before adding, "The only way to be more popular than Caroline MacBrodie is to be *meaner* than Caroline MacBrodie."

I gave a long, miserable sigh. For the faintest moment I wondered what would happen if I started insulting all my classmates.

Before I could consider it too deeply, Caroline came sauntering round the corner with her chosen elite gang. She took one look at us and drawled, "Oh. I almost stepped in something ugly."

Kitty, Molly, Melody and Ritchie roared with laughter. Annie paused for a moment before giving a nervous giggle.

"You're so funny, Caro," Kitty simpered as she clung like a spider onto Caroline's arm.

"Thank you, Puss-Cat," Caroline replied.

Ruby and I glanced at one another.

"Puss-Cat?" I exclaimed.

Kitty turned and narrowed her eyes at me. "It's my nickname. Got a problem with that?"

I didn't even try to hide my amusement as I spluttered, "Nope. No problem!"

Kitty glared at me and tightened her grip on Caroline's arm. "Come on, Caro. We might catch something if we linger too long."

Caroline gave us a cold look before slithering away. The last thing we heard as they turned the corner was her ordering 'Molly-Doll' to ask 'Young Boy' to give her her phone.

Ruby and I looked at one another and burst out laughing.

"Puss-Cat and Molly-Doll?" she whispered.

"Young Boy?" I hissed back. I could only assume that alluded to the fact that Ritchie was to be seen and never heard.

"I'd rather be unpopular," said Ruby.

I grinned. "Me too."

~*~

After a disappointing start to the new term, I couldn't wait to get to youth group that evening.

I'd been looking forward to it all week, especially after Joey sent me a message on FriendWeb which read, *'Oi, Starling! Don't forget youth group on Friday!'*

I had considered responding with, *'Oi, Cashbottom! I'll see you there!'* but, in the end, I decided to play it cool and wrote instead, *'Thanks for reminding me. I almost forgot.'*

Stanley dropped us off a little early and I took my time getting out of the car as I looked to see if anybody[16] else had arrived yet. The light was on in Eddie and Summer's living room but I couldn't see anyone through the window.

Violet, dressed all in green, marched up the drive and knocked on the door.

Summer answered. "You're the first ones here!"

Violet gave her a hug and went into the house. Ruby started to follow her.

"One moment," I called politely.

Summer nodded and left the door open for us.

I feigned a yawn before crouching down to do up my laces.

"You're about to take your shoes off," Ruby said. "Just leave them undone."

"I've got to tie them," I insisted. "I don't want to trip over."

"Their door is right here." Ruby took four giant strides towards Eddie and Summer's front door and turned back triumphantly.

"I know. I just always have to have my laces tied."[17]

"Alright." She looked confused as she left the doorstep and rejoined me on the pavement.

At that moment I saw Joey arriving in his mother's car and promptly got to my feet, leaving my laces untied. My heart leapt as he spotted us and waved.

Ruby dug me in the ribs and said in a sing-song voice, "Oh *that's* what you were waiting for."

---

[16] Or rather, *somebody...*

[17] In truth, they had been undone ever since I pulled them on. I'd been so keen to get to youth group that I had sprinted out of my house as soon as I saw Ruby and Violet emerging from theirs. I didn't even bring a coat.

I shrugged. At a recent sleepover I had been forced to tell Ruby all about my rendezvous at Joey's house and she hadn't stopped teasing me since.

Janine had barely stopped the car before Joey threw open the passenger door. He leapt out a little quickly and tripped on the curb, causing Janine to lean over and exclaim, "Joseph Teddy! Are you alright?"

"Fine!" he yelled. He slammed the car door shut and hobbled across the street.

Janine blew him a kiss and said, "Have fun." She waved at Ruby and me before driving away.

Joey came towards us, grinning from ear to ear, his blond hair slightly ruffled from his fall. "Hey Livi!" He nodded at Ruby. "Hey Ruby."

Ruby smiled politely.

"Joseph Teddy?" I asked in surprise.

"Yeah," he said sheepishly. "My middle name."

I tried to think of something witty to say but my mouth detached itself from my brain as I blurted out, "I could call you Teddy Bear."

Joey blushed. "Please don't."

"I wouldn't!" I stuttered. "I was just joking."

"Oh." Joey forced a smile. "Hey, I've got something for you." He held out a small blue rock. "It's from Filey."

I took it and turned it over in my hand. "Thanks. It's nice."

"Have you got any more since I last saw you?"

"Uh..." I pretended to sneeze as I stalled for time. As much as I had tried, I hadn't found anything worth adding to my rock collection. "I found a stone in my shoe yesterday," I said weakly.

He nodded. "You should come to Filey with us some time."

My voice squeaked as I said, "Okay!" I cleared my throat and held up the new blue rock. "It looks a bit like a turtle, don't you think?"

Joey laughed. "A bit!"

"Hey, we could stick googly eyes on them and make them into little rock animals!" I attempted a *Jolly Rock* impression as I danced the rock through the air.

Joey screwed up his nose. "I don't know. They're just cool as rocks, you know?"

I gulped. "Oh."

Ruby looked like she was trying not to laugh. "Shall we go inside?" She repeated her four giant strides up Eddie and Summer's drive.

We wandered into their house and into the living room where we joined Violet on the sofa and proceeded to sit in complete silence. I racked my brain for something interesting to say, fearing Joey would think I was incredibly dull.

The silence was broken by Violet who said, "Livi, you're sitting on my Bible."

"Oh!" I passed it to her. "Sorry."

She gave me a terse smile and got up to greet Grace Moore, who had just arrived.

Ruby looked from me to Joey and said, "Well, this is fun."

Joey looked like he was psyching himself up for something. Finally he asked, "Wanna hear a joke?"

We nodded.

"What did one rock say to the other rock?"

"I don't know."

"You rock my world!"

I forced a laugh.

Ruby looked confused.

"Do you get it?" he asked. "I just made it up."

"Yeah, I get it!" I said.

"I don't," Ruby said blankly.

"It's really funny," I insisted. "Because they're *rocks* and they *rock* each other's world."

"I got *that,*" Ruby said slowly. "But I thought there was a deeper meaning or something."

I looked at Joey and he grinned. I hoped his grin meant there *was* a deeper meaning, one meant only for me. I felt myself blushing and quickly diverted any attention by jumping up and shouting, "Nicole's here! Hey Nicole!"

Nicole, who was just taking her coat off in the hallway, waved before coming to join us.

"Oh there's Mark!" Joey added. He got up and ran towards him.

After that, we had a few minutes of deliberately ignoring one another as the rest of the group arrived.

Eventually, Eddie and Summer came in and we all quietened down.

"We'll start with a game," said Summer. "Find a partner."

I looked at Ruby before glancing quickly at Joey. He opened his mouth but, before he could say anything, Mark grabbed his arm and yelled, "Howdy partner!"

I turned back to Ruby. "Wanna be partners?"

She looked a little hurt. "Yeah. If you want to."

"Obviously!"

"Word association!" Summer continued cheerily. "One of you starts with a word and you continue to say the first thing that comes into your mind associated with the previous word. If you pause or repeat a word then your partner gets a point."

I looked at Ruby. "You start."

She grinned and said, "Banana,"

"Yellow," I said rapidly.

"Beach," she responded at lightning speed.

I paused. "Rock."

"You paused!" Ruby sang. "One point to me."

I gave a thin smile and started again. "Flamingo."[18]

"Pink."

"Heart."

"Love."

I felt myself shaking as my brain cautioned me, *Do not say Joey, do not say Joey...*

"You're taking too long!" Ruby exclaimed. "Another point to me."

"Fine." I tried harder to get my mind off Joey. "Caroline."

"Horrible."

"Sprouts."

"Round."

"Rock."

"You've said that before!" Ruby cried.

I blushed. "Whoops."

By the time Summer called the game to an end, Ruby had won by about fifteen points. She looked mighty pleased with herself as Eddie told everyone to come and sit in a circle.

Once we had settled down, Eddie opened his Bible and read, *"You are the light of the world. A city on a hill cannot be hidden. Neither do people light a lamp and put it under a bowl. Instead they put it on its stand, and it gives light to everyone in*

---

[18] That week, I had added *Snobby Flamingo* to my list of animal impersonations. I perfected it after watching Caroline show off during a netball game in P.E.

the house. *In the same way, let your light shine before men, that they may see your good deeds and praise your Father in Heaven.*" He stopped and looked round at us all. "What do we make of that?"

Violet put her hand up. "We need to tell people about Jesus."

Eddie nodded. "Anything else?"

"We're created to make a difference," said Grace Moore. "So we shouldn't hide."

I sat up straight and nodded along. "Don't be ashamed of yourself," I offered, shooting a glance in Joey's direction to see if he agreed.

He nodded and added, "Also, don't be ashamed of Jesus."

Eddie pointed to us both and said, "Great teamwork. Don't be ashamed of yourself and don't be ashamed of Jesus."

I caught Joey's eye and grinned. I liked being on his team.

"What's it like being a Christian at school?" Summer asked. "Is it hard to let your light shine?"

We all nodded.

"People think you're weird if you're a Christian," Bill piped up.

"They expect you to be all judgemental," said Violet.

I gave a thoughtful, "Hmmm." I didn't want to break it to her that in her case it was true.

A discussion began about appropriate ways of sharing our faith. Grace Fletcher suggested making friends with people first so that they would know there's more to you than their stereotypes of Christians whilst Nicole felt it was best to get it out of the way and tell people as quickly as possible.

"That way you don't have the awkward thing of not knowing whether they know or not," she explained.

Joey put his hand up and said proudly, "We have a club." He looked at Mark who nodded.

"A club?" Eddie echoed.

"Yeah," said Mark. "For all the Christians at our school and for anyone who wants to know more. We meet on Wednesday lunchtimes."

Joey grinned. "It's called ALIEN."

I raised an eyebrow. "ALIEN?"

"It stands for *Abundant Life In Emmanuel's Name*. And also, you know, because Jesus said his followers are not of this world."

I had no idea what *'Emmanuel'* meant but I nodded as I said, "Sounds great!"

"Yeah. You should start one up."

"Okay!" I squeaked. I nudged Ruby. "Wanna start up a lunchtime club?"

She looked at me a little warily. "If you want."

I barely concentrated for the rest of the evening. I kept glancing sideways at Joey, turning away before he saw me, then turning back to see if he was looking at me.

Eddie and Summer called the evening to an end with the challenge to look out for ways to let our light shine.

"It's not about being anything *more*," Eddie explained. "Just simply being true to who you *are*."

As everybody got up to leave, I caught Joey's eye and grinned.

"Are you going to church on Sunday?" he asked.

"Are you?"

"Yeah, of course."

"Yeah, me too! I'll see you there."

He nodded and opened the front door. Janine's car was waiting in the street and she waved as Joey trotted towards her.

I turned to Ruby. "What should we call our club?"

"Oh, you really want to do that? I thought you were just trying to impress Joey."

"I don't say things just to impress people!" I exclaimed. "I really want to start a club."

She cocked her head to one side. "Okay..."

We pulled our shoes on in silence as we tried to think of a name. Then we followed Violet out of Eddie and Summer's house, still deep in thought.

As we approached Stanley's car, I said, "I suppose ALIEN sounds quite good."

Ruby gave me a funny look.

"What do you think? Got any better ideas?"

She shook her head.

"ALIEN it is then! And we should probably have it on Wednesday lunchtimes."

"Because that's when Joey's is?"

"*No.* Because that's the middle of the week so it's the perfect way to... keep Jesus in the centre of everything."

Ruby gave a funny laugh and said, "Alright." She looked down and pointed. "Your shoelaces are undone."

I followed her gaze. "Well, it doesn't really matter. We're going home now."

~ 6 ~

Not of this world

It was Monday evening and I was round Ruby's house. We were meant to be doing some History homework but had ended up getting sidetracked with making posters for our club. We'd been discussing it all weekend and, spurred on by Joey and Mark's proclamation that the club at *their* school had grown to twenty members last term, we had high hopes for a spree of conversions amongst our classmates if we did things correctly.

"We could baptise people in the changing room showers," I suggested, stretching out in the middle of Ruby and Violet's bedroom floor as Ruby rooted around in Violet's art drawer, pulling out brightly coloured card and sparkly pens.

Ruby nodded. "Imagine how cool it would be if our whole school got saved?"

I grinned as I grabbed some yellow card and a silver marker. "We'd be totally *amazing* Christians." I wrote *'ALIEN'* in big letters before pausing and asking, "What does it stand for again?"

"Abundant Life In Emmanuel's Name."

"Oh yeah…" I wrote it down and stared at it. "What does *'Emmanuel'* mean?"

"It's another name for Jesus. It means *'God with us.'*"

I nodded. "Okay."

I couldn't remember what else Joey had said about it so I just drew a few aliens and wrote beneath them, *'Come and join a club that's out of this world! Are you a Christian? Would you like to be a Christian? Would you like to find out whether you'd like to be a Christian? Do you think you're not interested but really you might be?'*

"That covers pretty much everyone," I said triumphantly. "Hey, do you think we need a bigger room?"

We had booked out Miss Dalton's Religious Studies classroom, feeling it to be appropriate, but I was suddenly aware that it could fill up pretty quickly.

Ruby cocked her head to one side. "Maybe. We could ask Miss Waddle if we can use the Drama studio?"

I looked down at my poster and sucked in my cheeks. I wasn't sure Miss Waddle would be particularly accommodating, especially since I had given one of the aliens her silver shoes. "Let's just see who comes this week," I said. "Maybe, if it's really popular, we can hold it in the gym."

"Yeah!" Ruby sat back against her bed. After a moment, she let out a long sigh.

"What's wrong?" I asked.

She screwed up her nose. "I was just thinking about Ms Sorenson's class. I can't believe I have to sit next to Caroline all term."

"And I have to sit next to Annie," I added glumly.

"Annie's not too bad," Ruby insisted. "At least she doesn't pretend to throw up in her mouth every time you speak."

"I suppose. But she's still one of them. There's no way I want her writing my biography."

Ruby puffed out her cheeks. "I wish Ms Sorenson had put us together."

"Me too. Maybe she'll realise she's made a mistake."

Ruby nodded.

"If not," I continued, "I hope she doesn't expect us to go into lots of detail about our lives."

As it happened, Ms Sorenson *didn't* realise that she had made a mistake and she *did* expect us to go into lots of detail about our lives. The very next day she invited us to ask one another questions about who we lived with and where we had grown up.

Annie willingly told me that she lived with her mother and father and her aging great uncle who had just got out of bed after hibernating for the winter. Her grandma lived round the corner and Annie's family had lived in the same Leeds house her whole life.

"What about you?" she asked.

I looked away, determined not to tell her anything.

She poked me. "Well?"

"I grew up in Suffolk," I said with a growl. "I live with my sister. My mum died when I was a baby."

She continued staring, wide-eyed. "And your dad?"

"None of your business."

Annie looked a little lost. "I can't write your biography if you don't tell me all the details."

"Then don't write it," I snapped.

She gave an irritated tut and sunk down in her chair.

I glanced across the room. Ruby looked as miserable as I felt.

Beside her, Caroline began to moan loudly, "This lesson is such a waste of time. Anyone who needs to take a class to learn personal and social development clearly belongs in a laboratory."

I gave Ms Sorenson a quick look, desperate for her to notice and tell Caroline off. I wondered how bad things had to be before she reconsidered her previous arrangements and let me and Ruby work together instead.

"This school is full of little people," Caroline continued. "And I don't mean short."

I stared harder at Ms Sorenson, willing her to do something.

But, although our teacher did cast the odd glance in Caroline's direction, she just sat behind her desk and said nothing.

~*~

As soon as the lunch bell rang on Wednesday, Ruby and I leapt out of our seats like party poppers at a surprise celebration.

"ALIEN!" we roared.

Mrs Tilly, who had been in the middle of setting us some English homework, jumped in alarm. "Girls! I haven't dismissed you yet. Sit back down!"

The rest of our class giggled as we returned to our seats.

I fixed a cool expression on my face and pretended to copy down our homework assignment, although really I was scribbling a note to Ruby: *'Did you remember the name badges?'*

She nodded and patted her bag.

"...I want at least two sides and that does not mean extra large writing," Mrs Tilly finished. She looked at me and Ruby before saying, *"Now* you can go."

We grinned and ran to the door, leaping expertly over Caroline's outstretched leg.

"This is going to be amazing!" I yelled at Ruby as we sprinted down the corridor.

She just panted in excitement.

We arrived at Miss Dalton's empty classroom and pushed the door open.

"Maximise the space," I instructed as I dragged the nearest table to the side of the room.

Ruby joined me in rearranging the furniture. Once we had finished we attached our name badges to our jumpers, making sure they were perfectly straight. Then we crammed ourselves into Miss Dalton's chair and waited.

In my head, I rehearsed what I would say when everybody came. *'Hello and welcome to ALIEN! I'm Livi and this is Ruby. We're the joint presidents of ALIEN. Put your hand up if you don't know Jesus yet...'*

Outside, it started to rain. We turned to watch as it streamed down the window. I glanced at the clock and noted that we had been waiting for five minutes.

A short time later, Ruby made as if to say something and then fell silent again.

I chewed the inside of my cheek and wondered where everybody was. After another ten minutes, I was starting to get uncomfortable wedged in with Ruby on a chair designed for one so I got up and began to pace the room.

Finally, Ruby voiced what I had been fearing. "I don't think anybody's coming."

"A bit longer," I muttered.

We waited for most of the lunch hour but nobody came except for Violet who popped her head in right at the end and remarked, "You stole my art supplies to make your posters, didn't you?"

"Yeah," said Ruby. "Hey, are you coming in?"

Violet stuck up her nose. "No thanks. You spelled *'Emmanuel'* wrong."

"I can't believe nobody came," I said as Violet closed the door behind her.

Ruby sighed. "I suppose it does clash with the Chess Club..."

We looked at one another for a moment before pulling off our name badges and quietly putting the room back together.

As we emerged from Miss Dalton's classroom, our heads hung low, we heard a voice cackle nearby, "Oh look! It's the aliens!"

We turned to see Caroline and her gang jeering at us.

"We're not the aliens," I said hotly.

"Yes we are," Ruby whispered.

I looked at her. "What?"

Caroline's gang guffawed as Ruby explained, "Jesus said his followers are not of this world."

I opened my mouth in alarm and shook my head as I turned back to Caroline. "We're *not* aliens," I insisted, ignoring their laughter. "The *club* is called ALIEN. It stands for *Abundant Life In...*" I blushed as I fumbled for the rest of it.

"*Emmanuel's Name,*" Ruby finished for me.

"Who?" Caroline sneered.

"It's another name for Jesus," I said.

She looked at her friends and burst out laughing.

"Well we finally know why you look so weird," Kitty piped up. "You're aliens!"

"You should go back to your own planet," Molly added.

Melody tittered and pointed to the poster on the door. "Are you the one with the silver shoes, Livi?"

I quickly pulled the poster down. "Shut up."

"Let's go," Caroline said coldly. "I'd hate to see what happens when an alien gets angry."

As the gang sauntered off, singing *'Emmanuel'* in creepy alien voices, Annie turned and gave me an embarrassed smile.

I scowled and looked down at our poster. Somebody, probably Violet, had corrected my spelling of *'Emmanuel.'* Somebody else, probably Caroline, had written, *'Freaks!'*

"Can't we just call it *Abundant Life In Jesus' Name?*" I asked Ruby after they had gone.

"Then it wouldn't spell ALIEN."

"Oh yeah." I bit my lip. "Does it *have* to spell ALIEN?"

Ruby rolled her eyes. "You're the one who wanted it to."

"I think I've changed my mind. We need to make it sound more exciting. It has to sound like a cool club."

"Oh!" Ruby grabbed me. "We should call it The COOL Club!"

I raised an eyebrow.

"It could stand for... *Children Of Our Lord!*"

I chewed the inside of my cheek as I considered it. "Yeah. That definitely sounds cool."

For the rest of the afternoon we racked our brains for ways to make The COOL Club sound enticing.

"The problem is nobody thinks *God* is cool," I whispered to Ruby during Science. "We need to get people interested."

"I know," she said gloomily. "But how?"

The answer came to me on our way home from school. We were crossing a street when a nearby billboard caught my eye.

"Ruby, look!" I tapped her on the arm and pointed.

She followed my gaze. "What? The chicken poster?"

"Yeah!" I nodded and kept pointing.

The poster was part of a *Colin's Tasty Chicken* teaser campaign of which Jill had had some mild involvement. All around the city posters had sprung up featuring witty one-liners such as, *'Chicken round my house. — Colin,'* and, *'Let's talk about chicken. — Colin.'* This one read, *'I eat chicken, therefore I am. — Colin.'*

Ruby stared at it for ages. "What about it?"

"It's perfect!" I exclaimed. "According to Jill, Yorkshire chicken takeaway sales have doubled since the campaign began.[19] We need to do the same kind of thing to get everybody interested in God."

Ruby's eyes widened. "That's a great idea, Livi!"

We grinned at one another before running all the way to her house where we ransacked Violet's art supplies and began making new posters.

"Think of things God might say," I said. "Things like... *'I don't question **your** existence.'*"

"That's good!" Ruby grabbed some blue card and wrote it down.

"Do you know where you're going?" I continued. *"I'm watching you..."*

Ruby nodded and reached for more card. She paused before suggesting, "How about something nice like, *'I love you...'?*"

"Oh yeah. That's good too."

The door opened and Dennis the dog padded in and started sniffing our work. I gave him a courtesy stroke but he smelt particularly awful.

"Don't touch our posters," I warned him. "God will see you."

He cocked his head to one side and whimpered.

We spent the next couple of hours coming up with slogans and creating several copies of each one. The plan was to put them up anonymously around school so that people would see them everywhere and wonder what they were all about. In the bottom corner of each one, we wrote, *'Join The COOL Club. Wednesday lunchtimes in Room 43.'*

---

[19] Unfortunately, CTC's biggest rival, *Captain Barry's Chicken* (CBC) had enjoyed the majority of those sales due to their very popular counter-campaign: *'I've got a bigger house than Colin. — The Captain.'*

Eventually, Violet came upstairs and said, "Mum wants to know if Livi's staying for dinner." She took one look at her pile of art supplies and added huffily, "And, since you like to use other people's things, you'll probably want to eat all our food too."

I exchanged a bemused smile with Ruby. "I'd better go," I said, tipping Dennis off my lap. "Jill's probably made dinner."

She nodded and walked me down the stairs.

Belinda met us in the hallway. "Hello Livi! Are you staying for dinner?"

"No, it's alright. Jill will have made something... She's started learning how to cook."

"How wonderful!" Belinda trilled. "Tell her we're all very proud."

I said goodbye. Then I crossed the street and let myself into my house. I found Jill in the kitchen heating up potatoes in the microwave.

"Where have you been?" she complained. "Dinner's been ready for ages." She dumped a rock-hard potato onto a plate and put it down in front of me.

"Just at Ruby's... Do you like our posters?" I held one up and gave a proud beam.[20]

Jill screwed up her nose as she read it. "Have you just copied the Colin campaign?"

"It's for our new club. The COOL Club."

Jill gave a snide laugh but I ignored her and laid out a few more of the posters. "It's a club for Christians or people who want to find out more. And the posters are to get people talking about God because—"

Jill put a hand up. "I don't care."

I pursed my lips and put the posters away. Then I wolfed down my dinner as quickly as possible before storming to my room where I scoured my Bible for a suitable verse to counter Jill's contempt. I wrote it on a post-it note and stuck it on the bathroom mirror. *'You have said harsh things against me, says the Lord. Yet you ask, 'What have we said against you?'*[21]

I thought it would give her some food for thought. But she confronted me in the morning with a livid scowl and a not-altogether repeatable reply.

---

[20] *'I've got the biggest house of all. — God.'*
[21] I gave the reference (Malachi 3:13) in case she felt the urge to go and look it up for herself.

~ 7 ~

Welcome to The COOL Club

Ruby and I snuck into school early the next morning to plaster our posters up and down the corridors. Ruby had turned up wearing a balaclava, asserting that this was the best way to do it without anybody knowing it was us. I pointed out that her balaclava was embroidered with her initials and that the scarf she had provided for me was see-through. So we just settled for doing it as quickly as possible and then running back out of the school gates and hiding behind a nearby wall while the rest of the school arrived.

Miss Fairway frowned at us when we finally turned up to morning registration. "You're late!" she barked.

"Oh, I know," I said, feigning remorse. "We got lost."

"We forgot the way," mumbled Ruby.

"And then we got sidetracked by some interesting posters in the corridor," I continued smoothly. "Did anybody else see them?"

A few people murmured in agreement and I gave Ruby a sneaky thumbs-up as we ran to sit down.

Throughout the day, we heard the odd comment as people pointed out the posters and wondered where they had come from. Most people seemed to think they were weird although, to my excitement, a fair few found them entertaining.

In Geography, we even heard Georgina Harris say, "The one about having a big house is funny because, you know, it's like the chicken poster."

"I wonder who did it?" Darcy Bell added. She looked at Caroline, as though expecting her to be the only one capable of such an act of genius.

"Don't look at me," Caroline snapped. "I don't believe in God. And, if I did, it wouldn't be that one."

Darcy blushed and turned to our baffled classmates. "Who did it then?"

Ruby and I exchanged thrilled glances and pretended to be just as confused.

The speculations continued into the next week and, the following Tuesday, we returned with even bigger posters. This time, we wanted to get as many as we could into actual classrooms since many of the ones in the corridors had fallen prey to vandalism.[22] I especially wanted to put one up in Ms Sorenson's classroom, mainly because I hoped it would cause Ms Sorenson to want to join our club. I spent her lesson in anxious excitement as I considered the posters in my bag and wondered how to ask her. We were meant to be sharing stories with our partners about our early years and, as usual, I was trying (and failing) to ignore Annie.

"Hey Livi, what's your earliest memory?"

I yawned. "Don't know."

"Okay... Do you want to know mine?"

"Not particularly."

On the other side of the room, we heard Caroline declare loudly that her first word had been *'Caroline.'*

"Of course it was," I muttered under my breath.

Annie shot me a quick look. "Mine was *'goose,'*" she whispered.

I gave a snort. "I don't know what mine was."

"Okay... Do you want me to make one up?"

"No!"

Annie shrugged. "Alright..." She looked away and started chewing her fingernails.

I sighed and waited for the lesson to end.

As soon as it did, Ruby and I watched our classmates leave before shuffling over to Ms Sorenson's desk.

She looked up and smiled. "Hello girls."

I cleared my throat. "Erm, can we put a poster up in your classroom?"

"For The COOL Club," Ruby added.

"It's our *'God says'* teaser campaign," I explained.

"Ah, so *you're* responsible for those!" Ms Sorenson grinned. "We were discussing them in the staffroom."

---

[22] This had taken many forms, ranging from downright abuse *('Go to Hell!')* to more contemplative responses *('Do you have birthdays in Heaven?')*.

I bit my lip. I wanted to ask what was said and whether Ms Sorenson had considered Jesus yet.

"Which one am I getting?"

I held it up awkwardly. *'We need to talk. — God.'*

She chuckled. "I'd better be on my best behaviour then."

"It's not really like that," I said quickly. "It's not bad talking..."

"Perhaps I should ask him to teach some of my classes," she joked, giving us a wink.

I felt my cheeks turn red. It frustrated me that she wasn't taking it seriously. Perhaps I should have made one that read, *'Ms Sorenson, I do not want you to go to Hell. Where will you go if you die today? Choose Jesus before it's too late...'*

"There's a bit of space over there," she continued, pointing behind the door.

I nodded and went to pin the poster up, grieving over the fact that Ms Sorenson would probably never look at it again.

~*~

To our dismay, and despite the huge interest in our teaser campaign, nobody wanted to join The COOL Club. Ruby and I spent the whole of Wednesday lunchtime sitting dejectedly as people poked their heads in, saw us sitting there, and left in a hurry.

We overheard Georgina Harris say snidely, "See, I was right. I told you it was them."

"Not exactly very *cool!*" Darcy Bell said in reply.

We were about to give up when, five minutes before the end of the lunch hour, the door slowly opened and Annie Button wandered in looking lost.

I narrowed my eyes at her. "Did Caroline send you?"

"No... I followed the posters."

Ruby nudged me in excitement but I regarded Annie suspiciously. "You mean you've been sent to spy on us?"

She shook her head. "I just want to find out more."

Ruby leapt out of her chair. "That's great! What do you want to know?"

Annie shrugged. "I don't know... Like... about God and stuff?" She started to say something else but, at that moment, the bell rang.

"Well, I guess you'll have to come again next week!" Ruby said triumphantly.

"Alright." Annie gave a soft smile and walked out.

Ruby turned to me and grinned. "Isn't it amazing? Somebody actually came!"

I screwed up my nose and looked away. I already had to sit with Annie during Ms Sorenson's class. I didn't want to have to spend Wednesday lunchtimes with her too. "I don't know. Maybe the whole club thing was a bad idea after all."

Ruby ignored me and picked up her bag. "I can't believe somebody actually came! I wonder what we should talk about next week..."

I gave a half-hearted sigh and grabbed my belongings. "Let's go. We'll be late for Science."

Ruby followed me out of the classroom and down the corridor to the Science lab. Caroline had got hold of a pair of safety goggles and was trying to ram them onto Annie's face.

"Come on!" Caroline sneered. "Don't be such a kill-joy."

"I don't want to wear them," Annie protested.

Caroline laughed and commanded her friends, "Puss-Cat, Molly-Doll: pin her arms back!"

Kitty and Molly ran to Annie and pinned her against the wall. Annie squirmed but forced a smile as Caroline came towards her.

Caroline jammed the goggles onto her face and said, "There! They suit you!"

At that moment, Mr Riley, who was covering the lesson, walked into the classroom and yelled, "Annie Button! How dare you steal school property and wear them right under my nose!"

Caroline and her friends burst into hysterics as Mr Riley dragged Annie out of the classroom for a private scolding.

"Caro, that was hilarious!" Kitty whispered, as they pressed their ears up against the door. "He's threatening to call her parents!"

Caroline gave a smug grin. "I bet she's crying."

Ruby and I exchanged unimpressed glances and pretended not to be watching.

Mr Riley came back in, followed by a very sorry-looking Annie who was still wearing the offending goggles. As she made her way towards her giggling friends Annie caught my eye and shot me a sad smile. I shrugged and looked away.

For the rest of the week we watched from a distance as Caroline and the others' behaviour towards Annie grew increasingly unkind.

"Poor Annie," Ruby whispered after they threw her underwear out of the changing room window during P.E.

"Hmmm," I said uncomfortably.

We watched as Annie, under Caroline's orders, shimmied over to our horrified P.E teacher and confessed to throwing her pants out in order to try to impress Wayne Purdy.

"Do you think she's alright?" Ruby continued.

"Yeah. Some girls are just like that."

"Like what?"

"I don't know... Just mean to each other. They'll sort it out by the end of the week."

"I guess so."

But, on Friday lunchtime, as Ruby and I headed to the canteen, we saw Annie sitting alone on a bench. She looked up as we went past and said, "Hi Livi. Hi Ruby."

I tried to be kind as I asked, "Did you fall out with your friends?"

"No." She had a little nibble of her sandwich. "Caroline just said they wanted to eat as a four today."

I raised an eyebrow. "What about Ritchie?"

"He was too quiet. Caroline dumped him."

I paused and sat down beside her. "Don't you mean *Caro?*"

She blushed. "Only Kitty, Molly and Melody are allowed to call her that."

I stuck out my lip. "You mean Puss-Cat, Molly-Doll and... what does she call Melody?"

"Lauren."

Ruby and I looked at her in confusion. "Lauren?"

Annie nodded. "Because she looks like her friend from Peebles." She bit her lip and added, "Her friend's called Lauren."

I rolled my eyes. "Right."

"How about you?" asked Ruby. "What's your nickname?"

Annie gave a sad sigh. "The Shadow." She rubbed a hand across her face. "Because I just follow them around all day."

I nodded. "We get it."

Ruby gave her a gentle pat. "That's awful, Annie. They shouldn't—"

"Do *we* have nicknames?" I interjected.

"Yeah. Everybody has a nickname." Annie looked at Ruby. "You're Fruit Bowl."

"Because I collect banana stickers?" Ruby said in bewilderment. "That's hardly a whole fruit *bowl.*"

I gave her a withering look.

Ruby shrugged. "It could have been worse."

I looked at Annie. "What's mine?"

"Freaky Von Freakshow."

"See?" said Ruby.

I narrowed my eyes.

"Madame Maurel is L'Oignon which is French for 'The Onion,'" Annie went on. "Miss Fairway is Featherbrain, Ms Sorenson is The Beast—"

My jaw dropped open. "What?!"

Annie shrugged and repeated, "The Beast."

"But Ms Sorenson is the best teacher ever!"

Annie shrugged again. "Caroline's got them written down in a list in her pencil case."

"You need to find out," I ordered Ruby. "And write it all in her biography."

Ruby looked rather hesitant. "Okay..."

Annie gulped and rubbed her nose with her sleeve. Ruby and I looked at one another and I gave a slow nod.

"Hey, Annie," Ruby said kindly. "Do you want to be friends with us instead?"

To my surprise, Annie let out a loud sob and cried, "No!"

We looked at her in alarm.

"What do you mean, 'No'?" I said.

Annie sniffed noisily before whimpering, "I want to be friends with *them!*"

"But they're horrible!" I exclaimed. "And, for your information, we're really nice."

Annie shifted slightly. "I know you're nice. It's not that I don't like you. It's just... you're not as popular as them and my mum says it's important to be part of the in-crowd."

"Mums say stupid things," I said flippantly.

She nodded. "Does *your* mum say stupid things?"

"Probably not. She's dead."

"Oh yeah!" Annie blushed. "I knew that. I'm sorry."

I waved a careless hand. "It's fine. But, seriously, they don't like you."

"They did before Caroline came along."

"No they didn't. They were always leaving you out."

Annie turned away. Fat tears dribbled down her cheeks.

I exchanged an awkward glance with Ruby and wondered what to do.

Suddenly Melody trotted across the playground. "Oi, Annie!" she yelled.

Annie looked up hopefully. "What?"

"Caro says do you wanna come to the vending machines?"

Annie leapt to her feet. Without a second glance at us, she sprinted off with Melody.

"Well that's a bit pathetic," I muttered.

Ruby gave a sad smile and said nothing.

That afternoon, we were in Art where we overheard Caroline and her friends discussing an upcoming sleepover. I tried not to listen but couldn't help glancing across to see whether Annie was alright. She looked a little uncomfortable and I was torn between feeling sorry for her and standing by my previous assertion that she was, in fact, pathetic.

"We'll go to a nightclub, or something," Caroline said loudly. "We can borrow clothes from my dad's girlfriend, Irina. She's twenty two."

"That's so cool, Caro," Molly simpered.

"I know. She's like a big sister."

"My brother can get us fake IDs," Kitty offered.

"That will be great, Puss-Cat."

"I'll bring one of my dad's beers," piped up Melody.

"Lauren, I love you," Caroline drawled.

"Can I come?" Annie asked suddenly.

The others ignored her.

Annie tapped Caroline's arm and said, "Caroline?"

Caroline gave her a shove and yelled, "Don't touch me!"

"Sorry," Annie muttered. "I just—"

"What was that?" Kitty piped up. "Did you hear something?"

"Must be The Shadow," Caroline said coldly before pouring some paint onto Annie's work.

Annie gave a sob and grabbed her bag. Then she stood up and looked around. She paused before making her way towards mine and Ruby's table. "Am I still allowed to be your friend?" she asked through tears.

Ruby nodded earnestly as I cleared a space and patted the seat beside me. "Welcome to The COOL Club!"

~ 8 ~

Somebody needs to deal with Caroline

Despite being the ones who had rejected Annie in the first place, Caroline and her gang made it very clear that Annie's departure from the group had been taken as a grave betrayal.

"Traitor," Molly and Melody hissed as they passed us in the corridor on Monday morning.

"Can't believe you ditched us for *them*," Kitty said scornfully.

"Don't even look at her," Caroline commanded her friends. "She's dead to us."

Annie looked up and blushed.

"Ignore them," I whispered.

Caroline turned and gave me a sharp look. "Annie, I hope you realise your new friends have both tested positive for ringworm."

"Mmm worms!" the others repeated in sing-song voices.

Annie looked at me and Ruby in horror as the gang sauntered away.

"That's not true," I told her.

Annie nodded, although she didn't look entirely sure. She seemed pretty glum all morning, despite mine and Ruby's best efforts to cheer her up.

"You can come round my house sometime if you want," I offered during History.

"Or mine," Ruby added. "I've got a dog."

"We live opposite each other," I explained. "So you can come round both our houses in one day."

Annie gave a small smile. "Thanks."

I hoped she would forget about her old friends after that but she spent the rest of the lesson and most of Maths trying in vain to catch Caroline's eye. Then, at lunchtime, she kept glancing back and forth at Caroline's table.

"She's got a new *Tizzi Berry* lunch bag," she whispered as Caroline got her lunch out.

I rolled my eyes, as if to say, *'Who cares?'*

Annie didn't take the hint and kept staring.

The three of us watched as Caroline dug into her lunch bag and handed little packets to her friends. Kitty, Molly and Melody yanked open their gifts and started shrieking.

"What have they got?" asked Ruby.

"Tizzi Berry love hearts," Annie said sadly. "They keep your breath fresh for a week." She sighed before adding, "Apparently, Caroline's dad gives her fifty quid pocket money every week."

I eyed Caroline suspiciously. "If she's that rich, what's she doing at our school? There are plenty of private ones about."

"Her dad sent her here to toughen her up," Annie replied.

I raised an eyebrow. "She seems pretty tough already."

Annie shrugged. "Well, that's what she said."

I turned to Ruby. "How much of her biography have you done?"

"None," she muttered. "She refuses to speak to me."

I pursed my lips. "Do you know anything about her family?"

"No. She won't tell me anything. Not even the names of her parents."

"She lives with her dad and her dad's girlfriend, Irina," Annie piped up. "Irina's twenty two. Her mum lives in France with Caroline's stepfather... I think she said his nickname is Frog-Face."

I dropped my sandwich and grabbed Annie's arm. "What else do you know? Did she tell you any secrets?"

She shook her head. "That's about it. Apparently, Caroline goes to France every summer and she and her mum spend the whole time drinking wine and eating cheese."

"Wild."

At that moment, Melody came sidling up to us wearing a great big smirk. "Oi, Annie."

Annie looked up. "What?"

"Caro's got a present for you." Melody shook something behind her back.

Annie stood up a little awkwardly. "Really?"

"Yeah. Hold your hand out."

I looked across at Caroline's table where Caroline, Kitty and Molly were watching in amusement. "Don't do it—!" I warned.

But it was too late. Melody had already plonked Caroline's gift— a muddy fat worm— into Annie's outstretched hands.

"Mmm worms!" the gang sang loudly.

Annie screamed and flung the worm across the canteen where it landed on Miss Waddle's plate of sausages.

"Annie Button!" our Drama teacher roared. "Outside! Right now!"

Annie turned pink and followed Miss Waddle out as Melody ran back to Caroline's table in hysterics.

"That was so funny, Caro," she simpered.

"You did great, Lauren," Caroline told her smoothly.

I narrowed my eyes at them and grabbed my lunchbox. "Let's go," I said to Ruby.

We went outside where Annie was being berated by Miss Waddle.

"...Not to mention a blatant breach of health and safety!" our teacher finished angrily.

I tapped her on the shoulder. "Excuse me, Miss Waddle?"

Miss Waddle turned and gave me a fierce stare. "Livi Starling, did you have anything to do with this?" She waved the worm at me.

"No! It was Caroline MacBrodie."

"She knows I have a phobia of worms," Annie whimpered.

Miss Waddle eyed us suspiciously. "Caroline MacBrodie?"

The three of us nodded.

Miss Waddle looked like she was trying to compose herself as she took a deep breath and glanced away. "Well, I'll deal with Caroline," she said, absentmindedly stuffing the worm into her trouser pocket.

I opened my mouth and closed it again.

"Thanks, Miss," said Annie.

Miss Waddle gave us a terse nod and walked off.

I sighed. I knew there was no way Miss Waddle would *'deal with Caroline.'* Just last week Caroline had accused her of being *'the type of teacher who spends all her time trying to get affirmation from her students to compensate for never being popular at school.'* Miss Waddle had gone bright red and run into her props cupboard, re-emerging several minutes later with puffy eyes and the faint whiff of cigarette smoke. No, if anybody was going to *'deal with Caroline,'* it needed to be us.

That evening, distracted by the overwhelming desire to see Caroline humiliated in front of the whole school, I was making very slow progress with my homework when I received an unexpected phone call from Ruby.

"Hey Ruby. What's up?"

"Hey Livi. Come to the window!"

I ran to the window and waved.

"You know Caroline?" she said.

I rolled my eyes. "Yes, I know Caroline."

"I've got a plan."

"What do you mean?"

"Come round."

Without a moment's pause I hung up and ran straight over.

As soon as I reached her house Ruby threw the front door open and pulled me inside. She stopped to grab the family laptop before sprinting up the stairs. "Come with me!" she whispered, motioning to stay quiet as though Caroline herself could be hot on our heels.

I followed her up the stairs. "What's going on?"

Ruby ushered me into her bedroom and closed the door behind us, barricading us in with a pile of Violet's heavy art books.

"Ruby! What's going on?" I repeated.

"Caroline doesn't tell me anything," Ruby said indignantly. "So I thought I would do some undercover work." She sat on her bed and patted the space beside her.

I sat down and watched as she turned the laptop on. As soon as it loaded up, Ruby logged onto FriendWeb and checked her notifications. "Yes!" she exclaimed.

"What?" I demanded.

Ruby pointed to the message at the top of the screen. *'Hamish MacBrodie has accepted your friend request.'*

I looked at her in confusion. "*Hamish* MacBrodie?"

"Yup." Ruby gave a proud grin and explained, "I tried to add Caroline but she refused. So I went down her list of friends and tried the only other person with her surname. I figured he must be her brother or something."

My jaw fell open. "Ruby, you're a genius!"

"I know."

I leant over and clicked on Hamish's profile.

'Hamish MacBrodie likes football...' *'Hamish MacBrodie likes hamburgers...'* *'Hamish MacBrodie wants to go fishing this weekend...'*

I screwed up my nose. "We want to know about *Caroline*."

"Should I send him a message?" Ruby asked. "Ask him for information?"

I shook my head. "Too risky. He might tell Caroline."

Ruby nodded. "What should I do then?"

I rubbed my chin. "Let's go through his photos. See if there are any of Caroline."

"Good idea." Ruby clicked on a link and opened Hamish's photo albums.

We trawled through about two hundred photos, none of which contained Caroline.

"I guess they're not that close," Ruby said in disappointment.

"Which probably means he's really nice," I muttered.

"Oh, here!" Ruby had opened an album entitled, *'Loch Lomond with the family.'* "There's Caroline!" She pointed to a shot of Caroline perched on a little rowing boat. She looked rather sullen. In fact, as we scrolled through the photos, we saw she wasn't smiling in any of them.

"Do you think that's her dad's girlfriend?" Ruby wondered aloud, pointing out a frumpy-looking woman in a floral skirt and mismatched jumper.

I shrugged. "I thought his girlfriend was twenty two? That woman definitely looks older than that."

"Hmmm." Ruby raised an eyebrow and checked the date of the album. "It was last year. Maybe he's got a new girlfriend now?"

"Maybe. Or maybe Caroline's lying..."

We continued to scroll through the photos. They resembled the album of any ordinary family holiday: lots of sunshine and scenery and shots of people eating and endless moments which were obviously meaningful at the time but rather dull to anybody who wasn't there.

"They look like a happy family," Ruby said, pausing on a shot of Caroline, Hamish, the frumpy woman and a tall man on top of a mountain.

"Apart from Caroline," I said. "She looks utterly fed-up."

Caroline wasn't even looking at the camera. The tall man— presumably her father— had an arm around her and seemed to be urging her to smile. I peered at him and wondered what he was like. He hadn't been tagged so we couldn't see his name or anything else about him.

"Maybe he's not on FriendWeb?" Ruby suggested.

"Obviously!" I said scornfully. "It's a bit uncool when parents join FriendWeb."

Right on cue, a message popped up in the corner of the screen. *'Belinda Rico would like to send you a virtual hug!'*

Ruby winced and deleted the message. "What next?" she asked quickly.

"I guess we just keep an eye on Hamish's profile and see if we can pick up any more clues."

Ruby nodded and turned back to the album. She went through the photos a second time and scrutinised them very carefully.

"What are you looking for?" I asked.

She paused on a shot of the loch at sunrise. "Just wondering..."

I rolled my eyes. "The Loch Ness Monster isn't there."

She looked up with a sheepish grin. "You never know."

~*~

For the first time since the start of term, I couldn't wait to get to Ms Sorenson's lesson.

"I've been thinking about my biography," I told Annie as we headed to our desk. "Perhaps you could refer to me as a *'feisty heroine.'*"

She giggled. "Okay."

We pulled out our folders and looked at one another.

"Right," I said. "Let's do this. Ask me anything you want."

Annie thought for a moment. "What's your favourite ice cream flavour?"

"Strawberry."

She wrote it down. "Now you ask me something."

"Okay!" I tapped my pen against my teeth. "Why are you scared of worms?"

She blushed. "Because I ate one once. I thought it was spaghetti."

I gave an impressed nod. That could make an interesting anecdote for her early years. "What else are you scared of?"

"Well, I don't like fireworks," she said slowly. "Because I know someone who was hit in the eye by one... And I hate fish eyes because they creep me out... And garden gnomes..."

"We used to have some garden gnomes," I told her. "Ruby's family have them now."

Annie shuddered. "I've hated them ever since one winked at me."

"Never go into Ruby's bathroom then."

She gulped. She looked as though she was about to say more but then she stopped and shrugged. "And a few other things," she finished quietly.

72

I smiled and wrote it all down.[23]

"What about you?" she asked. "What are you afraid of?"

I stuck out my bottom lip. "Not much. Maybe polar bears."

She looked at me in surprise.

"They eat humans," I explained. "And sometimes even their own cubs."

Annie nodded. "Apparently they sound a bit like elephants when they're angry."

"I know. I've perfected their sound."

"Really?"

I took a deep breath before giving my best *Bipolar Polar Bear* impression.

Annie's jaw fell open.

Most of our classmates started laughing but Ms Sorenson looked up and smiled at me so I didn't care too much about the ridicule of my peers.

"That was amazing," Annie whispered.

I gave a humble shrug. "Have you got any special talents?"

She thought for a moment. "Not really. But I've got a birthmark in the shape of a dolphin on my shoulder."

I raised an eyebrow. "Cool."

"Yeah. My mum says dolphin tattoos are really popular. So I'm lucky because I've got one for free." She beamed.

I chuckled to myself and said, "That's nice." I made a note about Annie's birthmark before glancing across the room to see how Ruby was doing. As far as I was aware, she and Caroline had spent the lesson in silence so far.

Suddenly, Ruby blurted out, "Have you got any brothers?"

Caroline turned to her and glared.

"Or sisters," Ruby added quickly.

After a pause, Caroline replied, "I've got two brothers."

"What are their names?"

"Lucas and Pierre." Caroline sniffed and looked away.

---

[23] As it happens, Annie is frightened of far more than worms, fireworks, fish eyes and garden gnomes. Over the next few days, I learnt that she's also afraid of toe socks, moustaches (especially Mr Riley's), the pi button on her calculator and the word *'lush'* which Caroline says a lot. I expect Caroline knew it freaked Annie out because several times that week she came up behind us and hissed it in her ear.

"Oh! Not…" Ruby caught herself just in time and shook her head. It would have ruined everything had she asked, 'Not Hamish?'

Caroline gave her a funny look. "They're *half* brothers," she said curtly. "I couldn't cope with whole ones. They live in France."

"With your mum?"

"Yes."

Ruby gulped. "Have you got any *other* brothers?"

"What?" Caroline kept glaring. "Do you think I'd say I had two brothers if really I had three? How dumb are you?"

Ruby blushed and looked across at me, as if imploring me to help. I just shook my head.

"She's lying to you," I told her after the lesson ended. "We know Hamish is her brother. You've seen his photos on FriendWeb."

Ruby chewed her lip. "Why would she lie about names?"

"Because 'Hamish' sounds strange?" Annie suggested.

"But why would she say her dad has a twenty two year old girlfriend and her mum lives in France with a man called Frog-Face if really she's got a nice normal family?" Ruby looked completely stumped. "It doesn't make sense."

"She's just a mean liar," I said. "She's trying to make herself sound exciting. She's probably never been to France in her life."

"Hamish didn't have any French holiday photos," Ruby agreed.

"Exactly! She's probably not a model either."

Ruby scratched her chin and said, "Weird."

"It's not weird," I insisted. "Caroline MacBrodie has a very boring life and you're going to expose her in her biography by writing the truth."

Ruby nodded. "Ms Sorenson probably *wants* us to tell the truth," she reasoned.

"Of course she does! And you'll get extra points for all your research."

"I guess that's what real biographers have to do."

"Precisely!" I rubbed my hands together and said with glee, "Caroline MacBrodie, prepare to be utterly dealt with!"

Annie looked particularly vengeful as she said through narrowed eyes, "Now we'll see who the worm is…"

Ruby gave a nervous laugh. "I'll try my best."

~ 9 ~

Strawberry people

It was Saturday morning and I had my face pressed against the living room window. At youth group the previous evening Joey had invited me to go to Filey with him and his parents and I'd been up half the night shaking with excitement.

As soon as I saw their car pulling into our street I yelled, "I'm going out now!"

Jill glanced up as I sprinted to the door. "Your shoelaces are undone."

"There's no time!" I exclaimed, dashing out of our house and into the Cashbottoms' waiting car.

"Good morning Livi," Janine said from the passenger seat.

I slid in beside Joey. "Hi."

Joey's dad turned and gave me a friendly smile. "Wonderful to see you again, Livi," he boomed.

"You too, Mr Cash— Ronnie."

As we pulled out of the estate, Joey announced, "I've got something for you!" He handed me a rolled-up piece of paper.

"What is it?" I asked in amazement.

"I drew a portrait of you."

"Really?"

"Yup. Open it!"

My heart beat wildly as I unrolled his drawing but, immediately, my joy turned to horror as I stared at it. Although the majority of my face looked reasonably normal, he had given me massive bulging eyes which took up almost half the page.

"Do you like it?" Joey asked. "Doesn't it look just like you?"

I felt like I was going to throw up. If Joey's drawing was right, my eyes were bigger than my hands. I nodded and muttered a feeble, "Thanks."

"You should put it up in your house," Joey suggested. "So everyone sees it when they walk in."

I shuddered as I imagined people fainting at the sight of my monstrous googly eyes.

"Are you going to?" he pushed.

"Let the girl think for herself!" Ronnie called from the front. "She can do whatever she wants with it."

I sucked in my cheeks and looked away. What I *wanted* to do with it was tear it into tiny little shreds and feed it to Dennis. What I actually did with it was fold it up very carefully and tuck it into my jacket pocket. I spent the whole journey trying not to cry as I wondered whether I really looked that ugly.

By the time we arrived in Filey I felt truly dreadful. I really didn't fancy wandering around in public with my freakishly big eyes and wondered whether to ask if I could just wait in the car until it was time to go home.

Before I could summon up the courage, Janine turned in her seat and asked, "Do you like fish and chips, Livi?"

I gave a little nod.

"Great! Shall we get some for lunch, Ronnie?"

Joey's dad gave a hearty, "Indeed!" and pulled into a parking space.

"Wait till you eat these fish and chips!" Joey said as we piled out of the car. "They're amazing."

I forced a smile and followed Joey and his parents into the fish and chip shop, nodding when Ronnie asked if I wanted a can of cola and shaking my head when Joey asked if I wanted to try an oyster. Once we had our food I ate my fish and chips in silence, not daring to look at anyone the whole time. I couldn't stop thinking about Joey's horrendous drawing and practised squinting in an attempt to make my eyes look smaller.

When we'd finished our lunch Joey's mum gave his dad a nudge and said, "How about we let Joey and Livi have some time alone?"

Ronnie chuckled. "Of course! They won't want us oldies cramping their style!" He shot Joey a wink. Then he gave us some money for ice cream and told us to be back at the car in two hours.

Joey gave me an eager grin. "Shall we go and look for rocks?"

I squeezed my eyes shut and nodded.

"I know a really good spot!"

I nodded again and followed him down the promenade towards a particularly stony area of the beach.

"See!" he said. "There are loads here."

I peered through the slits in my eyes.

Joey picked up a black rock and handed it to me.

"Thanks." I pretended to be interested in a nearby rock and picked it up.

Joey was filling his pockets and I tried to keep up as he scuttled across the beach but I was squinting so much that I kept tripping over.

Eventually, to my relief, Joey said, "Do you want to stop now?"

"If you want," I said through narrowed eyes.

Joey pointed to a nearby bench. "Let's go and sit down."

"Okay." I followed him, keeping my eyes down the whole time.

We sat in awkward silence until Joey said, "It's nice here, isn't it?"

I turned to him and squinted.

He gave me a funny look. "Livi, are you okay? Is something wrong with your eyes?"

"I don't know!" I said hotly. "This is how I was born."

Joey went red. "I didn't mean to offend you... I just meant, why do you keep squinting?"

I felt myself getting choked up as I blurted out, "You think my eyes are massive!"

He gaped at me. "What?"

"Your picture," I stammered. "You drew me with horrible big eyes. I looked like an owl or a frog or something!"

Joey shook his head. "No! You don't understand. I drew your eyes really big because they're my favourite bit. That's what cartoonists do. They exaggerate the best bits."

My jaw fell open. "You mean I don't look ugly?" I asked weakly, dragging my sleeve across my dripping nose.

"Of course not!" he exclaimed. "You're really—" He went bright red as he finished quietly, "Pretty."

My heart almost leapt into my throat. "Thanks," I whispered.

"Is that why you've been so quiet?"

"Yeah."

"Phew!" He gave a huge sigh of relief and started laughing. "I was scared you'd gone off me."

I blushed. "No... I haven't gone off you."

"Good." Joey sat back and gave another sigh. A few seconds later he asked, "Can I hold your hand?"

"Hold my hand?" My stomach churned as I tried to work out what to do. "I'll be back in a minute..." I ran behind a nearby ice cream stand and quickly phoned Ruby.

She answered after the first ring. "Hey Livi! What's up?"

"Joey wants to hold my hand," I whispered. "Should I do it?"

Ruby giggled down the phone. "I don't know. Do you want to?"

"I think so... But I just wanted to check it wasn't wrong."

"What does Jesus say?"

"I don't know! I haven't read the whole Bible yet!"

"I mean right now. Did you ask him?"

I frowned. "Well, no. But I figured you could just tell me."

"Well, I don't know!" Ruby laughed.

I exhaled slowly. "Okay, thanks," I said before hanging up.

I trotted back to Joey and gave a timid smile.

He grinned and said, "Well?"

I shrugged. "If you want." I sat beside him and tentatively held my hand out, feeling myself blush as he took hold of my fingers.

We stared straight ahead, sitting in silence for several long minutes as our anxious fingers did the talking. His hand was soft and warm and I was conscious of not wanting to squeeze it too hard. My heart thundered in my chest the whole time and it felt as though everybody in the world was staring at us, aware that we were holding hands for the very first time.

Just as it was starting to feel a bit more comfortable, normal even, Joey turned and asked, "Can I kiss you?"

My jaw dropped and I let go of his hand. Other than the odd practise with my teddy, Sausage-Legs, I have never been kissed. I glanced at Joey's expectant face and muttered, "Er... Hold on." Then I sprinted behind the ice cream stand and rang Ruby again.

"Hey Livi!" she sang. "So, did you hold his hand?"

"Yeah. He wants to kiss me."

"Hmmm."

"Should I?"

"I don't know!"

"What would *you* do?"

"Me?" Ruby gave a little hum. "I don't want a boyfriend until I'm old enough to get married."

"That's crazy!" I exclaimed. "That's years away."

"Well, in our last family meeting we were discussing boyfriends because Violet's about to go to Art College so she's expecting some interest from boys and Oscar made a really good point. He said anything that helps your relationship with Jesus is good and anything that hinders it is bad."

"Oscar's four!" I scoffed.

"Exactly."

I sniffed. "It's only a kiss."

"Why are you ringing me then?"

"Because I don't know what to do!"

"Well... Ask Jesus."

I hung up and frowned. For some reason, I didn't want to ask Jesus. I was afraid he would just say 'No' without thinking about it. It didn't feel fair that he would stop me having fun. Then again, I had always assumed my first kiss would be very magical and completely spontaneous— not shivering on a bench with a pocketful of rocks. What if I regretted it later?

I wandered back to Joey who was waiting with two ice creams. He looked rather bemused. "Well?"

"Sorry," I said awkwardly. "I don't think I'm ready yet."

"That's okay." He handed me an ice cream and shrugged. "Although, for future reference, next time should I invite Ruby along too? It would save a lot of time."

I blushed and looked away. "Sorry," I repeated.

"I got you strawberry," Joey continued. "I was trying to guess what you'd like and you seem like a strawberry kind of person."

I looked at him in amazement. "I *am* a strawberry kind of person!"

He held up his own ice cream. "Me too."

I licked my ice cream and gazed out at sea. "I like Filey," I said.

Joey nodded. Ice cream dripped down his chin in a way that on anyone else would look revolting but on him, for some reason, looked kind of cute. "Filey makes me *smiley!*" he warbled in a silly voice.

I giggled and then fell silent.

We sat quietly for ages until, all of a sudden, Joey looked at his watch and said, "Oh! It's time to go now."

"Has it been two hours already?" I asked in disappointment.

"Yeah." He stood up and pulled me to my feet.

We headed back to the car, alternating between holding hands and just banging them against each other.

As I was trying to figure out whether this made us a couple or not, Joey turned to me and smiled. "So," he began awkwardly. "Are we, you know... going out with each other? Like, can I put it on my FriendWeb profile?"

I nodded keenly. I wanted nothing more than to publicise whatever we were on FriendWeb.

We were halfway home when my phone beeped with a message from Ruby. I pulled my phone out of my pocket and shielded it carefully as I read the text.

'Well? What did Jesus say?'

I frowned and shoved it back in my pocket.

Joey caught my eye and beamed. I quickly looked away. In the front, Janine and Ronnie were discussing Joey's older brother who, from the sound of it, was dating somebody they didn't approve of. I bit my lip and wondered what they thought of *me*.

Suddenly, Joey reached into the pocket of the seat in front of him and pulled out two shiny hoops. "Do you want these?"

"What are they?"

"They're Jesus Jangles. They have crosses all over them so that you can carry Jesus' death and resurrection with you wherever you go."

He handed them to me and I peered at them, marvelling at the way the little crosses sparkled in the sunlight.

"They were probably Julie's," Joey continued. "But she's got loads so she won't mind."

I put them on. "I think I've seen Grace Moore wearing some."

"Probably. Everybody wears them." He paused before adding, "Girls, I mean. Obviously *I* don't."

I giggled and shook my arm, enjoying the sound of them clanging together.

"They look good on you."

I blushed. "Thanks."

I looked up in time to see Janine and Ronnie exchanging smiles in the front of the car.

My phone beeped again.

My stomach churned as I wondered whether it was Ruby, pestering me to reply.

"That was your phone," said Joey.

"It won't be important," I insisted.

I pretended to examine the Jesus Jangles before feigning interest in the passing scenery as the homes and hills and lives of countless strangers flashed before my eyes. I wondered how many other girls had become *something* with a boy that day. And how many of them felt as strange and scared about it as me.

"There's a sheep," Joey pointed.

"Oh yeah..."

"And some chickens."

I gave an awkward nod as I stared out of the window, praying silently. *Jesus, is it okay if Joey's my boyfriend? You don't mind, do you? You don't seriously want me to wait until I'm old enough to be thinking about marriage?* Before waiting for an answer, I looked down at the Jesus Jangles. *If you don't want Joey to be my boyfriend, make one of these bracelets disappear.* I gazed at them intently but nothing happened.

I looked up and caught Joey's eye. He grinned and put his hand in the space between us. I paused for a moment before grinning back and sliding my hand into his.

~ 10 ~

As bright as a Button

"So, are Jesus and the Pope the same person?" Annie enquired.

Ruby and I turned to her in surprise.

The three of us were perched atop tables in Miss Dalton's classroom as we conducted that week's COOL Club meeting. We had a Bible open to the middle of Luke's gospel where, up till Annie's question, we'd thought we were making perfect sense.

"No!" said Ruby. "Jesus is God. The Pope is just a man."

"Jesus is God?" Annie blinked at us. "Don't you mean the Son of God?"

Ruby looked a little flustered as she tried to explain, "Well, yes. But God is sort of three in one: Father, Son and Holy Spirit."

"Three gods?"

"No. One God in three parts."

Annie gave a slow nod. "Ohh. Okay then."

She looked at me and smiled but I just shifted awkwardly. I was still trying to get my head round the trinity myself.

The door opened and Violet, dressed all in red, walked in. "I'm joining your club," she announced.

My heart sunk. Now we were less cool than ever.

"We're reading the parable of the prodigal son," Ruby told her sister.

Annie beamed. "I'm learning about Jesus."

"Oh good," Violet replied. "Let me help."

The door opened again. I looked up expectantly but this time it was Rupert Crisp in search of the Chess Club.

"Ah, *COOL* Club," he said when he realised his mistake. "Well, that's what happens when you follow a poster with your glasses off!"

He turned to go, but not before Violet cornered him with the words, "What's the most important piece on the chess board?"

Rupert looked at her. "The king, of course."

"And who's the king of your life?"

Rupert raised his eyebrows and came towards her. "I am."

"Then you'd better prepare to be checkmated," Violet continued smoothly.

Ruby let out a frighteningly loud guffaw and I almost fell off the table. She gave me a sheepish smile as she explained, "We recently made an agreement to always laugh at each other's jokes."

Before I could say anything, Violet turned and frowned. "That wasn't a joke, Ruby."

"Oh."

"I'm deadly serious."

"Sorry."

I rolled my eyes. "*Anyway,* let's keep going with our study."

Ruby nodded and turned back to the Bible. "So, even though the son had gone away from his father, the father wept with joy on the son's return," she told Annie.

"And that's like us," I added. "However far we've gone, we can always go back to God."

I started to say something else but got distracted by Rupert laughing as he said, "God created the universe? Oh I don't think so!"

I looked up. Violet's cheeks had gone as red as her skirt and she was almost salivating as she argued with Rupert over God's existence.

"Shall we read a bit more..." Ruby suggested. She flicked through the Bible but kept glancing up at Violet and Rupert who were getting more and more heated in their debate.

In the end, we put the Bible down and watched.

"Pascal's Wager," Rupert said pompously. "Not to believe in God is an unlosable bet. If God exists and I'm a good person, he'll let me into Heaven when I die. If he doesn't exist, I haven't wasted my time serving an imaginary deity." He smirked. "Win win."

Violet rolled her eyes. "That's only true if the God who may or may not exist fits perfectly into your mould."

"What mould?"

"The mould that says 'good' people go to Heaven."

"Are you saying good people *don't* go to Heaven?" Rupert asked with a sneer.

"I'm saying that God is not made in your image!" Violet scoffed. "You might think that you're good but you'll never meet his perfect standards. You're guilty as charged and will go to Hell unless you accept Jesus as your Saviour."

"You're telling me somebody could be utterly moral and yet still be sent to Hell because they don't follow Jesus?" Rupert frowned and shook his head. "I can't believe in a God who would send millions of innocent people to Hell."

"Neither can I," Violet replied coolly. "But could you believe in a God who would allow countless *guilty* people to choose Hell despite the fact that he has provided a way for them to be saved?"

Rupert looked at her in confusion. "What?"

I chewed the inside of my cheek.

Annie and Ruby were looking equally lost.

"I'm a scientist," Rupert continued. "I deal with facts."

"Science doesn't disprove God," Violet retorted. "Science belongs to God."

Rupert laughed. "See, that's exactly the kind of thing I would expect to hear from an ignorant, deluded individual such as yourself. Science does *not* belong to God! Do you know anything about metaphysics?"

Violet sniffed. "No."

"How about the M-theory?"

Violet raised an eyebrow. "The what?"

Rupert grinned. "Checkmate."

Violet exhaled heavily. "You might be better than me at chess but you'll never outsmart God."

Rupert strode over to the door and threw it open. He saluted Ruby, Annie and me before saying, "I believe we have Science this afternoon. I'll see you there for what I hope will be an enlightening experience for us all." He turned to Violet. "And you, lady in red. It's been a pleasure!"

Violet slammed the door behind him. "Many foolish people are sure that God does not exist," she warned us. "Yet they are confident they know exactly what the God who doesn't exist is like."

I bit my lip. My head was reeling. I hadn't completely followed Violet and Rupert's debate but, one thing was certain, Rupert definitely didn't leave any closer to God. How were we supposed to convince people who had such strong arguments against him? Rupert was clearly well informed when it came to scientific theories. Were we really, as he'd put it, *'ignorant, deluded individuals'?* I started to worry that I didn't have enough information. I couldn't even explain the trinity to Annie. How would I answer if I ever got into a debate with a serious intellectual?

Ruby was looking equally stunned. We exchanged uneasy glances and looked away.

In the silence that followed, Annie piped up, "Anyway, tell me more about Jesus."

~*~

For the whole time I've been at this school we are yet to have a permanent Science teacher. This week's lesson was being covered by Mr Rennison, one of the Music teachers.

He held the lesson plan at arm's length as he read, "Use a Bunsen burner to test for acids and alkalis..."

Everybody cheered at the mention of using the Bunsen burners. Our class had officially been banned from using them ever since Sheena Ali set fire to a table last term. Whoever had left Mr Rennison the lesson plan had clearly forgotten.

As several people nudged one another in wild excitement, Mr Rennison looked up and asked, "Am I missing something?"

"Not at all, Sir," Caroline said smoothly. "This class just has a particular fondness for testing acids and alkalis."

Mr Rennison blinked. "Alright then. Get on with it."

Our classmates sprang to their feet and ran towards the pile of Bunsen burners in the corner of the lab. Within minutes, all manner of items were being burnt and Mr Rennison spent the whole lesson running around with the fire extinguisher.

As Ruby went to fetch some equipment for our table, Annie tapped me lightly on the arm. "Livi, I've been thinking about what you and Ruby said and I want to do it."

I raised an eyebrow as I wondered what we had said. I thought back to that morning's Food Technology lesson in which Ruby and I had fantasised about how weird it would be if the entire world suddenly turned into cake.

"You want to live in a house made of cake?"

"No!" She giggled. "I want to do what the pedicure son did. I want to go back to God."

"You want to become a Christian?"

"Yup."

I looked up as Ruby returned with the Bunsen burner and a handful of test tubes. Unlike the rest of our classmates, Ruby was taking the lesson very seriously and had decked herself out in a white lab coat and a pair of safety goggles.

"Ruby!" I hissed. "Annie wants to become a Christian!"

Annie beamed and nodded.

Ruby dropped the equipment. "Really?"

"Yup," Annie said proudly. "I was thinking about it when we were watching Rupert argue with the girl in funny clothes."

"My sister," Ruby muttered.

"Yeah, her. Listening to them argue about God made it all make sense."

"*That's* what convinced you?" I said. "You do realise Violet didn't win that debate?"

"I know." Annie gave a happy shrug and explained, "But in that moment I realised there's so much I don't know. I need Jesus to help me figure it all out. And, if I believe in God, like Rupert said, it's win win!"

I wasn't sure I understood her reasoning. "So... You want to follow Jesus?"

She nodded.

"You believe he died for your sins?"

"Yup!"

"And rose from the dead?" Ruby added.

Annie grinned and kept nodding.

"Then great!" I said. "Let's do it!"

And so, by the glow of a Bunsen burner, in a Science class led by a Music teacher, Annie Button gave her life to Jesus.

All the way home, Ruby and I kept beaming at one another as we celebrated Annie's conversion.

"It happened so easily!" Ruby exclaimed. "Like, we didn't have to try at all."

"I know!" I said in awe. "It was so cool." I thought for a moment before admitting, "I wish Jill would get saved as easily as Annie." I wanted to add that I had made a vow to save her by the summer but I feared that voicing it aloud would somehow make it even more impossible.

Ruby shot me a sympathetic smile. "I wish Jill would get saved too."

"She's just not interested," I said with a sigh. "She gets angry if I mention Jesus or God or church or praying. I can't even say *'Bless you'* when she sneezes."

"Why not?"

"She says people shouldn't impose their beliefs on anyone else."

Ruby gave a little smirk.

"What's so funny?"

"It's just that's quite a strong belief and she's imposing it on you."

I gaped at her. She was a genius! "That's what I should say to her!"

Ruby squirmed. "Don't say *I* said it," she begged.

"Don't worry!" I assured her. "I won't." I had every intention of taking full credit for this little piece of ammunition.

As soon as I walked into my house, I made a beeline for Jill.

She was sitting on the sofa reading a magazine. She looked up as I joined her. "Hi Livi."

"Hi," I replied. I paused for a moment as I wondered how to begin. "Do you like these?" I waved my new bangles in the air. "They're called Jesus Jangles. They have crosses all over them so that you can carry Jesus' death and resurrection with you wherever you go."

Jill wrinkled up her nose. "Sounds a bit weird."

"Everybody wears them."

"So? If everybody jumped off a cliff would you do the same?"

"No... But I'd have a peek to see what all the fuss was about."

Jill sniffed and went back to her magazine.

"Annie became a Christian today," I continued merrily.

"Who?"

"My friend, Annie."

Jill grunted and kept reading.

I tutted and wondered how to provoke her further. I coughed before saying casually, "Oh, by the way, I've kind of got a boyfriend now. Joey from my *church.*"

I said the word *'church'* really loudly but she just gave a funny smile and said, "Good for you."

I blinked. "Are you actually alright with that?"

"Yes. I'm pleased. You're finally doing something normal."

"What?"

"Every normal teenage girl wants a boyfriend," Jill said shortly.

I wrinkled up my nose. "You want me to be like everyone else? What happened to *'If everybody jumped off a cliff...'?*"

Jill shrugged and ignored me.

"So... You're okay with me having a boyfriend but you think these are weird?" I shook the Jesus Jangles in her face.

She shoved my hand away. "Yes, Livi! I do!"

I growled before pushing even further. "Why do you have such a problem with me talking about God?"

Finally, Jill looked up and said stiffly, "I just don't think people should impose their beliefs on anyone else."

I gave a triumphant grin. "That's a strong belief. Do you impose it on anybody?"

Jill opened her mouth and closed it again. She scowled at me before turning back to her magazine.

I left the room with a smug sigh. *Checkmate.*

The dingy life

"Hey Livi. How's tricks?"

I almost dropped the phone. "Dad?"

"How have you been? I've missed you."

I felt my insides squirm. This was the first time I'd spoken to my father in months. I sat down to keep myself from falling and squeezed my eyes shut as I said in a whisper, "I'm fine."

"Good." He paused before announcing, "I'm getting married."

My jaw fell open. "What?"

"Her name is Erica. She teaches yoga. That's how we met."

I grimaced at the idea of my dad doing yoga. "Married?" I repeated helplessly.

"It's a little fast, I know!" He chuckled. "But Erica said she has to make big decisions immediately otherwise she'll never make them at all."

I pursed my lips. Impulsive Erica the Yoga Instructor didn't sound like Mother Material. "Is she—? Do you—?" My mind raced as I scrambled for what to say. "What's she like?"

"She's great," Dad said simply.

I chewed the inside of my cheek as I tried to imagine this lady who had won my father's heart. I couldn't imagine him settling down with a wife. "Does she have any children?" I asked tentatively.

"No. She doesn't like kids."

"Oh."

"She breeds chinchillas though."

I didn't reply. Impulsive Erica the Chinchilla-Breeding Yoga Instructor *definitely* wasn't Mother Material. I wondered what I was supposed to say. *'Congratulations...'? 'I'm so happy for you...'?* My heart hung like a rock as I said, "Well, thanks for telling me."

"Of course. I knew you'd want to know."

"Yes..."

"I'd love it if you could meet her before the wedding. That way it won't be awkward on the day."

"Meet her?" I spluttered, my head reeling. "I guess..."

"The wedding is in two months so we were thinking you could pop across to Hull this Saturday."

"Two months?" I squeaked. "This Saturday?"

"Yeah. Erica's in the middle of a course on Mental Discipline but she says she can squeeze you in before her Meditation seminar on Saturday afternoon."

I nodded slowly. I hated her already.

"We can have cockles at the marina!" Dad continued.

"Cockles?"

"It will be great! Call me when you get to the station and we'll come and get you. I'd better go now. Erica needs to call her masseuse."

I hung up and put my head in my hands. It had been an ordinary day and I had been looking forward to watching a bit of ordinary television before going to bed and dreaming ordinary dreams. Suddenly, I'd been catapulted back into a nightmare that I'd hoped was over forever and it seemed that nothing would ever be ordinary again. It had been hard enough forgiving my dad when I thought I didn't have to see him anymore. But just hearing his voice had caused a whole load of unwanted feelings to come bubbling to the surface. I gulped hard to keep myself from crying. I was torn between utter frustration at having such a useless father and a tiny, ridiculous spark of hope that maybe, *just maybe,* Erica would be somebody special.

I heard Jill coming out of the bathroom so I hurriedly wiped my eyes and fixed a happy expression on my face as she came down the stairs.

"My dad just called," I said casually.

She looked at me in shock.

I gave a carefree shrug and added, "He's getting married."

Jill took a deep breath before asking, "Are you alright?"

"Yeah, fine," I insisted. "I don't have a problem with him."

Jill pursed her lips and looked away. I heard her call my father something rather rude.

I felt this would be an ideal opportunity to show Jill how to take the Christian approach so I said boldly, "You need to forgive him."

Jill looked up, her eyes blazing. "How dare you! You know nothing, Livi. Absolutely nothing. Don't you dare tell me to forgive him!" She stormed into the living room and slammed the door.

I bit my lip and grabbed the side table to steady myself. *Why, God?* I begged as the tears began to fall. *I'm not ready for this.*

~*~

I hadn't intended to tell Annie many details about my parents but I started crying in Ms Sorenson's lesson after she asked me when I had last seen my father. I ended up telling her everything although I begged her not to write it all in my biography.

"So, you'll have a stepmother?" she asked curiously as we gathered in Ruby's bedroom on Tuesday evening.

"Yeah, I guess so," I whispered. I sighed and looked away. I didn't want to add that I was holding onto the vain hope that she would be everything I had ever wanted in a mother.

"How do you feel?" asked Ruby.

I shrugged and pulled at the tassels on her rug. "Don't know."

As they waited for me to say more, the room filled with awkward silence and I kicked myself for bringing such complication into what ought to have been a fun evening showing Annie round our houses.

Originally, we had intended to divide our time up between Ruby's house and mine. But Jill had been in a particularly bad mood ever since my father's phone call and I hated the idea of Annie meeting her when she was in such a state. So, against my better judgement, I'd ended up telling Annie that my sister had ringworm. This meant we had to stay at Ruby's for the whole evening, other than one brief visit to mine so that Annie could use our gnome-free toilet.[24]

"Do you want us to pray for you?" Ruby asked.

I started to shrug and then said instead, "Yeah."

Ruby cleared her throat.

---

[24] During the said visit, Jill emerged from the kitchen carrying a folder emblazoned with the CTC logo. Annie leapt backwards in fright and said, "Don't touch me!" Jill looked down at her folder and, believing Annie's reaction to be that of a militant vegetarian, insisted, "I don't have any chicken on me." Annie just gaped at her and said, "I hope your worms go away soon!" Jill gave me a quizzical look as I hurried Annie out as quickly as possible.

Before she could begin, I interrupted with a moan. Something else was bothering me. "It was good for me to forgive my dad, right?"

"Yeah," said Ruby.

"Well, I told Jill she needed to forgive him and she yelled at me."

She shifted uneasily. "Maybe you shouldn't have said that."

I gave an irritated sniff and picked at my fingers. "Then how do I convince her?" I muttered.

Ruby sighed. "I don't know."

Annie looked from me to Ruby and, clearly feeling out of her depth, asked if I wanted her to plait my hair.

"Maybe later," I mumbled.

She nodded and started plaiting her own.

We sat in silence until Ruby asked, "Shall we pray now?"

I gave a quick nod and looked down.

Ruby took a deep breath and began to pray. "Father God, thank you for being our wonderful loving Father and for having such great plans for Livi..."

I sniffed again and sucked in my cheeks. I wasn't feeling all that thankful right now.

When Ruby had finished, Annie closed her eyes, put her hands together, and said very seriously, "Hey Peter, it's Annie. Please help Livi this weekend. Amen." She opened her eyes and beamed.

I looked at her in confusion. "What did you mean when you said, 'Hey Peter'?"

Annie blinked at me. "I was talking to God."

"God's name isn't Peter."

"Yes it is."

I was about to laugh but glanced quickly at Ruby, just in case I'd missed something. She was looking as confused as me. "Peter?" we asked in unison.

"Yeah." Annie shrugged. "That's what they call him at my grandma's church."

I leant over and whispered to Ruby, "What is she talking about? Is it some kind of cult?"

"Just stay calm," she whispered back.

"It's his name," Annie insisted. "Everybody has a name."

"You can't call God 'Peter,'" I told her.

"Why not?"

"Because!" I waved my hands wildly. "You just can't. It's a rule."

"A rule?" Annie was wide-eyed. "I didn't realise there were rules."

Erica was reasonably pretty, in a stern kind of way— tall and skinny with jet black hair and pointy eyebrows. She wore a long maroon jacket and knee high boots. I expected she was rather bendy. I wasn't sure whether to hug her or shake her hand. In the end, I half embraced her and, in return, she gave me a pat on the shoulder which contained all the enthusiasm of someone who has never wanted a daughter in her life.

"Hi Liv," she said coolly.

"It's Livi," I corrected.

She gave me a patronising smile. "That's what I said."

My dad stood beside her, grinning as though it were some grand reunion.

I wondered if Erica knew what a rubbish father he had been. But she just gave me a pointed look and said, "Your dad has really missed you," as if it was me, rather than him, who had behaved like a complete idiot and then vanished without a trace.

I shot my dad a quick glance but he just said, "I'm so glad we're back in touch."

Tears stung the backs of my eyes as I bit my lip and looked away. I wished he would at least *pretend* to be sorry.

"Shall we go and get something to eat?" he continued, putting one arm round me and the other round Erica.

I nodded dumbly and allowed myself to be escorted out of the train station and across the city centre to Hull marina.

I stole the odd glance at Erica as we walked. She started to tell my father about an upcoming conference entitled *'Couples' Communication.'* "We absolutely *have* to go," she said. "Good communication is a must for a healthy marriage."

My dad began to protest that there was a very important football match on that afternoon but she just snapped, "You're coming, Charlie!" and he nodded and fell silent.

We reached the marina where my father led us to a café called *'The Dingy Life.'*[25] It was a dreary little place containing a handful

---

[25] It was actually called *'The Dinghy Life'* but the *'h'* had been stolen.

of empty tables surrounded by plastic white chairs and tacky red tablecloths covered in sticky stains.

"You'll like it here," my dad assured me.

I had barely glanced at the menu before he ordered cockles and chips all round.

I wrinkled up my nose but said nothing. Then I gave Erica a sideways glance and asked politely, "What are your chinchillas called?"

In my daydreams they'd had nice names like *'Poppy'* and *'Daisy.'* But, in reality, they had stupid names like...

"Anarchy and Antinomy," she replied smoothly.

I gave a slow nod and finally abandoned all hopes of ever acquiring a decent mother. I glanced out of the window and pretended to be interested in the boats that lined the edge of the marina. I could see my dad twitching nervously out of the corner of my eye. He kept clearing his throat as he drummed lightly on the table. I couldn't make out Erica's expression and I didn't particularly want to.

Despite the fact that none of us were speaking to one another, when the waitress returned a few minutes later she put down our food as though we were any ordinary family.

I had one tiny moment to revel in how it felt to hear somebody say, *"Pass this to your mum,"* before Erica exclaimed, "Oh she's not mine! Does this body look like it's been through childbirth?"

I rolled my eyes. She wasn't quite an evil stepmother. I mean, I didn't fear for my life.[26] But she was something of a cow. I watched in disgust as my father leant over and fed her a cockle. I was torn between hating him all over again and yet feeling a sense of pity for a life that I didn't envy in the slightest.

"Oh Liv," Erica said abruptly. "Before I forget, I'd rather you don't call me *'Mum.'"*

I had no intention of calling her *'Mum.'* I'd been thinking of much worse names. "Well, I'd rather you don't call me *'Liv,'"* I shot back.

She raised her eyebrows. "What should I call you then?"

I gave a snort. "Call me *Livi,* because that's my name!"

She gave me a funny look. Then she sat back in her chair and said carelessly, "It's a strange name. Did you choose it, Charlie?"

"No," my dad replied. "It was her mother's name."

---

[26] Although the cockles looked somewhat poisonous, kind of like infected eyeballs. I wanted to take one home and see if it freaked Annie out.

94

"She named her after herself?" Erica asked in surprise. "That's rather vain, isn't it?" She gave a little laugh.

I glared at her. "What about *your* name? *Erica*... It's kind of a boy's name with an '*a*' tacked onto the end. What's that all about?"

She took a long sip of her drink and said nothing.

"Erica's parents died in a car crash," my dad said, as if that explained everything.

In the silence that followed, Erica excused herself and went off to the toilets. I sighed and started picking at a seam on my trousers.

My dad gave me a wave across the table. "Hi!"

"Hi," I said awkwardly.

"Thanks for coming."

I nodded.

"I'm really glad you and Erica could meet."

I nodded again.

"Erica was really looking forward to it."

I gave him a withering look. "I don't think she likes me."

"Of course she does!" my dad insisted. "If it helps, she's just a bit jealous of you being the other woman in my life."

"Well, that's alright then," I muttered.

"I'm glad you like her."

I sucked in my cheeks and said nothing.

We sat in silence until Erica returned from the toilets.

She carried a handful of blue stones. "I picked these up from the bathroom," she told my father. "We should get some for our centrepieces— it will be great for the feng shui."

My dad nodded.

"I've got a rock collection," I said loudly. "You can borrow some if you want."

Neither of them replied and, as Erica took her seat, my father scooped up a forkful of cockles and tipped them into her mouth.

I screwed up my nose as the two of them dribbled cockles over the tablecloth. I watched them for ages and wondered why my father had even bothered phoning me in the first place. Erica clearly wasn't interested in me. And, judging by the fact that he had barely spoken to me through the entire lunch date, neither was he. I squeezed my eyes shut and counselled myself, *Keep forgiving him. Do the right thing. Make God proud.* I felt I was being very mature about it. Only time would tell whether I had successfully let my father go or whether one day a fury of pent up emotion would come screaming out of me like a bomb.

Erica was telling my dad about her plans to set up an alternative health retreat centre. He was nodding along as though it was all very enlightening.

It dawned on me that if I was going to be *really* holy then I ought to tell them about Jesus. I paused for a moment, unsure whether I wanted my dad to become a Christian. I feared it would somehow undermine all the hurt that he had caused. But, desperate for God to see I was really trying to please him, I took a deep breath and said, "We have this club at school called The COOL Club."

They looked up from feeding one another cockles.

"It stands for *Children Of Our Lord*," I continued. "Because I'm a Christian."

My dad smiled. "I'm glad you've found a nice hobby."

"It's more than a hobby! It's life and death!"

Erica gave me a thoughtful look. "I have a wonderful book called *'Release the god inside you.'*"

"That sounds rubbish," I muttered.

"I had some Mormons knock on my door the other day," my dad added.

"That's not the same," I insisted. "Anyway, do you want to meet Jesus?" I had wild visions of them falling on their knees before God, followed by me rolling them out to be baptised in the marina.

"Why? Did you bring him with you?" Erica looked at my dad and they both chuckled.

"Yes, actually," I said. "He's everywhere."

"I find Christianity particularly stifling," Erica retorted. "We don't need people telling us what to do. Do we, Charlie?"

My dad shook his head.

I bit my lip. Part of me wanted to say, *'Fine! One day you'll see but maybe by then it will be too late!'* But another part of me feared that God would hold me responsible for not trying harder to save them.

I spent the rest of the meal, if you could call it that, tracing a finger along the grubby tablecloth and willing myself not to cry.

Once lunch was over, my father and Erica walked me back to the train station. I saw Erica screw up her nose when she saw that my train had been delayed by five minutes so I said, "You don't have to wait with me."

"Of course we'll wait!" my dad insisted.

Erica gave a curt nod.

We stood in silence until my train finally rolled in.

Immediately, Erica turned and said briskly, "It was lovely to meet you."

I said nothing.

"So, we'll see you at the wedding?"

I nodded slowly. "I suppose... Can I bring a friend?"

Erica grimaced. "Don't bring your sister. I know all about the..." she waved her hands around, "...sordid history."

I looked at my dad.

"You can bring Ruby," he said.

"She's not too wild, is she?" Erica asked him. "I don't want too many kids running around."

"Oh, Ruby's very wild," I said hotly. "She'll dance right down the aisle and flash you."

Erica looked at me in horror.

"She's joking," my dad assured her. "Ruby's very quiet."

"Oh good." Erica breathed a sigh of relief and forced a smile. "Then, yes. Of course you can bring a buddy."

I exhaled heavily. "Okay. Bye then." I gave a careless wave and ran onto the train.

I had barely found my seat before I saw them put their arms around one another and walk away.

Tears trickled down my cheeks as the train pulled out of the station. My chest throbbed with such rage towards my father. Just when I thought I had forgiven him. Now I would have to do it all over again! I wiped my eyes and hunted in my bag for some chewing gum to take away the horrible taste of cockles.

In the seat behind me a baby was whimpering and her mother was gently trying to soothe her back to sleep. I closed my eyes as I tormented myself with thoughts of Indifferent Erica, the God-Hating, Cockle-Eating, Stone-Stealing, Soon-to-be-Stepmother. Of all the people in the world, why on earth had my father been so stupid as to fall for *her*?

It wasn't long before I started thinking about my mum. *I wish she hadn't died,* I said to God. *Why did she have to?*

Fields and streams and roads rolled past the window but God stayed silent.

Is my mum in Heaven? If she is, please give me a sign.

I felt sick as I wondered whether my mother had ever prayed to Jesus. *Did she accept you, Lord? In her dying moments? Or perhaps in secret when nobody was watching?* The fear that she had never known him and had ended up in Hell troubled me immensely. *Oh God, why didn't you let her live long enough for me to save her?* I let out a silent sob and dragged my sleeve across my face.

Behind me, the baby had started to howl. I wondered whether she would grow up to know Jesus or whether that helpless bundle of flesh would one day find itself in Hell. It dawned on me that everybody in the world was a powerless baby once. And, before God made them, they were nothing. When it all comes down to it, the brightest minds in the world are nothing but dust. Even Rupert Crisp, with his superior intellect, was completely at God's mercy when it came to his eternal destination.

The train jolted suddenly and I tensed in fright, fearing a collision. I glanced round the carriage just in case these were the people I would die with. I wondered if I ought to stand up and make an announcement so that people could be saved before they met their death, but then I remembered Dad and Erica's mocking response and frowned. *What's the point in telling people about Jesus if they don't want to know?*

When God still didn't reply, I added furiously, *Here I am, trying to tell people about you, yet you hardly seem pleased at all.* I rubbed a weary hand across my face and wondered why God was ignoring me. I hoped he wasn't punishing me for holding hands with Joey. *Am I doing something wrong? Don't you care?*

Still nothing.

I took a deep breath before venturing, *Peter? Are you there?*

But all I could hear was the helpless bundle of flesh crying her eyes out behind me.

~ 12 ~

The art of being fine

Annie's dad is a psychoanalyst, with a very slight emphasis on *psycho*. He has a habit of stroking his chin and rocking from side to side whenever anybody's speaking. I spent less than an hour in his presence round Annie's house and developed an instant aversion to him.

Annie had invited me over so that we could work on our biographies together[27] and I arrived with a brand new notebook ready to gather as much information as possible. Had I known that Annie's father was a therapist, I would have been a little more guarded in my arrival. But, arriving entirely unawares, I rang the doorbell five times and pressed my face against the frosted glass.

Moments later, the door opened and I found myself nose to nose with Mr Button.

The eager grin dropped from my face as he regarded me very solemnly. "You must be Livi?"

"Yeah," I muttered.

He stepped back and let me enter. "And how are you today, Livi?"

"Fine," I replied.

"Fine?" he repeated.

I blushed and wondered whether I was meant to expand on that.

He eyed my notebook and stroked his chin as he asked, "Do you keep a journal?"

"Just doing homework," I said quickly.

Annie came galloping down the stairs. "Hey Livi!"

I looked up in relief. "Hey Annie."

---

[27] Ruby had wanted to join us but had been obliged to visit one of Violet's prospective Art Colleges with the rest of her family.

"This is my dad," she said proudly.

I forced a smile.

"That's his office." Annie pointed to a little room across the hallway. A sign on the door read, 'Dr Gerard Button.'

At this point, I hadn't yet learnt that he was a therapist so I said, "You're a doctor? Do you operate on people in there?"

Mr Button peered at me. "I'm a psychoanalyst."

I still didn't know what that was but nodded politely.

"He understands peoples' hidden thoughts," Annie explained. "Like a mind reader."

I felt myself blushing as my jaw dropped open.

Mr Button exhaled slowly. "I do not read minds, Annie," he said. "I help my clients deconstruct the hidden agendas of their subconscious selves in order to bring completeness to any fragmented parts."

I bit my lip and squirmed. I had no idea what he'd just said but it sounded mighty intrusive.

Annie grinned at me. "Cool, huh?" She pointed to my notebook. "Do you want him to write it down?" Before I could reply, Annie took my notebook from me and instructed her father, "Write down what you just said. Livi's writing my biography."

Mr Button gave a thoughtful nod. "Livi's writing your biography?"

I took my notebook back. "It's alright," I said. "I can remember."

Just then, Annie's mother came out of the kitchen and greeted me with a squeal. "Oh, you must be Livi!"

I looked at her in surprise. Judging by the bright pink jumpsuit, face plastered with make-up and exuberant grin, she was nothing like Annie's father.

"Come into the kitchen!" she said cheerily. "I've made soup for lunch."

Annie linked arms with me and led me down the hallway.

I entered the kitchen rather cautiously, curious as to what a psychoanalyst's kitchen might look like. To my surprise, it was just like any other kitchen. If anything, it was a little messy. I perched beside Annie at the table and gave her a nervous smile as her mother served our lunch.

"Did you find our house easily?" Annie asked me.

I nodded and looked down. I didn't want to admit that I had got utterly lost and spent the last twenty minutes crying in a bus shelter.

"I'll just take this up to Old Budgie," Annie's mum said suddenly, walking out of the kitchen with one of the bowls of soup.

I looked up in confusion, wondering whether they had a bird on the loose, but, in case my curiosity betrayed some dark subconscious secret, I didn't dare ask.

Across the table, I saw Annie's father watching the way I buttered my toast. Just knowing he was observing me, possibly creating theories over how I ate, made me feel incredibly self-conscious. I completely lost the ability to eat in a normal fashion and kept dribbling soup down myself.

"It's lovely to have you here, Livi!" Annie's mother said as she returned from feeding the budgie. "Annie's told us all about you."

My stomach sunk. I stole a quick glance at Annie's father and wondered what he knew but his calm expression gave nothing away.

"Livi can do animal impressions!" Annie announced.

I shook my head. "No I can't."

"Yes you can!" Annie exclaimed. "Do your *Bipolar Polar Bear!*"

I shook my head again, petrified that Mr Button had already secretly written me off as a crazy person.

"I can't do any animal impressions," Annie's mother said thoughtfully. "But I can do a cockney accent. Do you want to hear it, Livi?"

I gulped. "Okay."

Mrs Button handed her soup spoon to Annie and stood up. She gave an unnecessary curtsey before launching into a raucous rendition of *'Consider yourself'* from *'Oliver.'*

I wasn't sure whether it was deliberately bad or whether she expected me to applaud. Annie was grinning so I tried to be polite by smiling too.

Mr Button watched her very seriously the whole time. Since he was a master of the mind, I wondered why he didn't find his wife's behaviour odd. It struck me that her wackiness might be a carefully constructed ruse in order to see whether I would join in. Perhaps this was the way they vetted their daughter's friends.

Mrs Button finished with a roar and sat down. "I used to want to be an actress," she said as she took her spoon back from Annie. "My stage name was going to be *'Lindsay Celebrity.'* But my father completely crushed me. He told me I had less talent than a nine year old boy."

Having recently seen an amateur production of 'Oliver,' I could see her father's point. I gave what I hoped was a sympathetic smile and turned back to my soup.

All of a sudden, Annie pointed to me and declared, "Livi's one of the reasons I'm a Christian now!"

I felt my cheeks burn. "You don't need to point at me," I said awkwardly.

Annie beamed and continued to her parents, "And we've got this club called The COOL Club. Haven't we, Livi?"

I wanted to curl up and die.

Annie's mother was staring at us with a wide-eyed grin. "Oh Annie!" she said happily. "You're in the cool club. How nice."

Annie's father stroked his chin and said nothing.

As soon as lunch was over, Mr and Mrs Button arose from the kitchen table and went into Mr Button's office.

"What are they doing?" I whispered to Annie.

"My mum's therapy session. She always has therapy at two o' clock."

"Your dad is her therapist? Is that allowed?"

Annie shrugged. "He doesn't charge her."

I wondered whether to write this down. "Do you want me to put that in your biography?"

Annie gave another carefree shrug. "I don't mind. Do you want to see my room?"

"Yeah!"

"Come on then!" Annie gathered up the soup bowls and threw them in the sink.

I followed her as she trotted through the hallway and up the stairs.

Just like her father, Annie had a little plaque on her bedroom door. Hers, however, read, 'Beware of the hedgehogs.'

I smiled to myself as Annie pushed the door open. I immediately realised that I should have taken more notice of the sign. My jaw dropped at the sight that met my eyes: Hedgehogs. Hundreds and hundreds of hedgehogs— stuffed hedgehogs, but hedgehogs nonetheless— all staring at me with teeny beady eyes and pokey snouts. They were everywhere. She had five whole shelves full of them, not to mention many more crammed under her bed, in her shoes, and in a neat little line along her window sill. She had every colour imaginable for every occasion under the sun.[28] There was even a pair of giant hedgehog slippers poking out of the wardrobe. My head spun as I walked round her room and took it all in.

Annie threw herself onto her bed and beamed. "By the way, I like hedgehogs."

I laughed. "I gathered that."

She pulled one off a shelf and handed it to me. It was comprised of slightly matted blonde threads inside a stocking and had buttons for eyes.

"Looks interesting," I said. "Where's it from?"

"Me and my mum made it," she said proudly. "Out of my hair."

I dropped it. "What?"

"I used to have hair down to here." Annie pointed to her hip. "But, one day, I got chewing gum in it and had to have it all cut off. I was crying and crying the whole time I was at the hairdressers. Then my mum suggested we take my hair home and make it into a hedgehog! Cool or what?"

I handed it back to her. "I suppose..." I chewed my bottom lip as I glanced round the rest of Annie's room. There was a pile of magazines on her bedside table. The top one had a photo of a man looking in a mirror. I picked it up and pointed to the title. *"Psyched up?"*

"It's my dad's," Annie explained. "I was looking for pictures of brains for our History homework because Mr Holborn said people used to cure headaches by cutting holes in their brains." She held up a half-chewed photo of a brain[29] and said, "See?"

I giggled and flicked through the magazine. Articles with convoluted titles such as, *'Cutting off narcissistic supply,'* and, *'The art of self-deception,'* jumped out at me. I wondered how many magazines I would have to read before I could match Mr Button's mind reading prowess. As I skimmed through it, in search of a cartoon section, something gloriously awful caught my eye. "Oh my goodness!"

Annie leant over. "What?"

I pointed to an advertisement at the foot of the page. "Look!"

Annie gasped. "That's Caroline!"

It sure was. Right under the slogan, *'All dry, no cry. Sweet dreams from tots to teens,'* was a picture of a sleeping Caroline

---

[28] I even saw one which held a sign bearing the words, *'Happy 40th birthday, you old hog.'*

[29] By the looks of it, Annie had drilled a hole through it with a screwdriver.

MacBrodie tucked under a blanket, her backside protruding just enough to show off a gleaming white nappy.

"This is amazing!" I could hardly contain my excitement.

Annie nodded. "We have to tell Ruby!"

I grinned and grabbed my phone. She had barely answered before I yelled, "Ruby! Guess what?"

"What?"

"You know Caroline said she was a model..."

"You mean she isn't?"

"Oh, she is!" I looked at Annie and we burst out laughing.

"What's so funny?" asked Ruby.

Annie took the phone from me and bellowed, "Caroline wears nappies!"

"What?"

I took the phone back and, through snorts, managed to tell Ruby all about the advertisement.

"Are you serious?" she exclaimed. "She's in a magazine wearing a nappy?"

"Yup! And she's sucking her thumb!"

"That's hilarious."

"Let's pin it up at school!" Annie suggested in my ear.

"No," I said. "Don't tell anybody. Let's keep it all secret for the big reveal." I paused before adding pointedly to Ruby, *"Her biography."*

"Right," she said seriously.

"We'll cut it out for you," Annie said, reaching for some scissors.

I took them off her. I didn't want her mangling it like she had with the photo of the brain.

"I'd better go," said Ruby. "We're about to have a tour of the laundry rooms."

"Say hello to Violet!" Annie yelled in my ear. "Are you having fun?"

Ruby gave an exaggerated yawn before hanging up.

I put my phone away and carefully cut the advert out. I tucked it into the back of my notebook, securing it with a paperclip. Then I turned to a fresh page and made a quick sketch of Annie's room, scribbling in circles to indicate the multitude of hedgehogs.

Annie started giggling. "I can't believe Caroline wears nappies!"

"Well, she doesn't *actually*," I began.

Annie looked at me in confusion.

"Oh alright, she's does," I said with a smirk.

Annie gave a contented sigh. "What should we do now?"

I shrugged. "I don't mind."

"Do you want to see our garden?"

I had already seen it from her bedroom window but, for want of something better to do, I said, "Yeah, sure."

"Come on then!" Annie grinned and leapt off her bed.

I took one last look at the throng of staring hedgehogs and followed her out.

"This is Old Budgie's room," she said, pushing open the door of the room opposite hers.

I raised an eyebrow, amazed that their pet would have a whole bedroom to itself, and eagerly peered in. I immediately jumped back in surprise. By the window sat a gaunt old man in a dressing gown slurping a bowl of soup that was probably stone cold by now.

My stomach churned as the man looked up and gave a toothless smile.

Annie ran over and hugged him. "Hey Old Budgie!" she sang.

He slowly raised a hand and patted her on the cheek. "Lovely Annie," he muttered hoarsely.

I lingered in the doorway. His room smelt funny and, having never known anyone so old and decaying, I wasn't sure how to conduct myself. It crossed my mind that perhaps this was yet another test from Mr and Mrs Button and they were secretly watching me from the office and waiting to see if I would freak out. I looked for hidden cameras and pretended to be fine.

Annie returned to me. "He's going to die soon," she said as she closed his door.

I looked at her, aghast. "He'll hear you!"

"He knows," she insisted. "He's planned his funeral already. He wants me to sing '*My Way*.'"

I gulped and wondered what songs I ought to have at *my* funeral.

As we wandered back down the stairs, Annie whispered, "We have to be quiet when we go past Dad's office. He doesn't like his clients hearing me."

"Even though his client is your mum?"

Annie nodded and put a finger to her lips.

"What are his other clients like?" I asked. "Do you ever see them arrive?"

"Sometimes." Annie smiled. "There's one lady who stops outside our front door and counts to ten before she rings the bell.

And there's a man who has a really loud stammer. And a woman who always wears the same outfit. But most of them look completely normal."

"How long do they come for?"

"Some of them have been coming for years and years." She waved a hand in the air.

"What's wrong with them?"

Annie shrugged. "All different things."

I exhaled slowly as I wondered how Mrs Button's session was going and whether Mr Button had cracked a smile yet. I imagined the two of them spending hours locked in his office poring over all the miserable details of her troubled past. As we crept past the office and headed into the garden I couldn't help but feel curious.

"What happened to her?" I asked quietly.

Annie blinked at me. "Who?"

"Your mum. Why does she need so much therapy?"

Annie cocked her head to one side and thought for a moment. "They spent years trying to work out why she hated herself. It turned out she was feeling guilty about her parents' divorce. After that, they dealt with her shame at never being as popular as her sister. Then she got over her fear of confined spaces after they realised it was linked to a time when she got trapped in a toilet cubicle. But then she developed an attachment to therapy. So now they're working on that."

I nodded and glanced at the garden. It was quite neat, with vegetables growing down one side and a little old shed in the corner. At the back of the lawn was a small plaque which read, 'R.I.P. Nana.'

I looked at Annie in alarm. "Your grandma isn't buried under there, is she?"

"No," she replied cheerily. "Nana was the name of my gerbil."

I breathed a sigh of relief and wrote it down.

"We also had a tortoise but it ran away."

I gave an impressed nod. "I'm not allowed any pets."

"I'd rather have a brother or sister," Annie admitted. "At least you've got a sister."

I screwed up my nose. "Yeah."

"Or would you rather have parents?"

I blushed and looked away. "Dunno."

Annie must have realised she'd said something wrong because she hurriedly changed the subject by pointing to a nearby tomato plant. "Last night I dreamt I was eaten by this tomato plant. My dad said it meant I was carrying anxiety over the effects of puberty on my body."

I grimaced and made a mental note never to share any of my dreams with Annie's father.

Suddenly, Annie turned quite pale. "A worm!" she squealed, clutching my arm in terror.

I looked at the ground. "Oh yeah."

Annie shook as the worm, which was wriggling at a speed of less than a metre an hour, made its way slowly towards us.

"Do you want to go back inside?" I asked.

She nodded and sprinted to the door.

I followed her into the hallway where she ran to the stairs and sat with her head between her legs.

"Does your dad ever give *you* therapy?" I asked. If he did, he certainly wasn't doing much for all her phobias.

"Oh, no!" Annie exclaimed. "That would be unethical."

I glanced at the closed door of Mr Button's office. Mrs Button's session had run over. "Oh."

"How about you?" Annie asked curiously. "Would you like some therapy?"

I shook my head. "No way! I'm completely fine."

Several minutes later, Mrs Button emerged from her therapy session looking a little teary. She went straight into the kitchen to make herself a cup of tea.

Mr Button followed her out. "Hello," he said to us. "Are you having a nice time?"

Annie nodded happily but I regarded him rather warily. I hated the idea that with one glance in my direction he might be able to gain access to my deepest thoughts, dark desires and all manner of mysteries in the labyrinth of my unconscious.

"We're fine," I said.

He nodded before repeating, "Fine?"

I wrinkled my brow. "Yes. Completely fine."

~ 13 ~

I'm Violet

God and I hadn't spoken in over a week. I hoped it wasn't a deliberate snub on his part and tried not to take it personally, yet I couldn't shake off the niggling fear that he was angry with me. I suspected it was something to do with my relationship with Joey. But, if that was the case, then it really wasn't fair. I had made it plain that God could make one of my Jesus Jangles vanish as a sign if he wanted me to end things. Yet, every night, I had surrendered the bangles to him only to find them still lying on my bedside table the next morning.

I had tried once or twice to raise the matter with him but could never quite find my voice. Instead, I kept an eye out for things I could do to win back his approval. This included praying for my dad and Erica whenever I thought of them, silently adding *'Jesus'* to my classmates' names every time a teacher called the register and praying through the Lord's Prayer each time I brushed my teeth.

I thought I was doing alright until Saturday night's episode of *'Freaky Human'* which had a new feature called *'Art in Heaven.'* One of the items happened to be a single grain of rice on which someone had written the entire Lord's Prayer.

My jaw dropped as the camera zoomed in on the teeny, tiny, perfect writing. "How did they do that?" I wondered aloud.

As if to answer my question, the presenter chuckled and said, "I expect it required a very thin pen and a lot of devotion!"

Something churned inside me. I had thought that spraying toothpaste across the bathroom mirror whilst rattling through the Lord's Prayer twice a day was a sign of my growing faith. Now I wasn't so sure.

As soon the show ended I snuck a handful of rice up to my bedroom along with the thinnest pen I could find. With hindsight, I should have started small and been content to try to get my *name* on there but I wanted to prove I could be just as devoted as anybody else by recreating the Lord's Prayer grain. God would surely be proud if I managed it.

By midnight, I had a pile of spoilt rice and a throbbing headache. I flung the rice in the bin and hung my head in shame, the Lord's Prayer going round and round like a taunt as I went to brush my teeth.

For the whole of the next week I set my alarm half an hour earlier so that I could get up and read the Bible. I figured that if I started my day off right then God was bound to bless the rest of it.

Unfortunately, most days I pressed the snooze button more than a few times until I ended up getting up even later than normal. Those days were characterised by a deep sense of shame as I feared God would be disappointed in me for not trying hard enough.

In order to spur myself on, I made a big sign and put it beside my door: *'What have you done for God this week?'* Beneath it, I made a chart with little boxes that I could colour in to keep track of how often I prayed and how much of the Bible I had read. Perhaps, if I finished it by the summer, I would get to save Jill as my reward. I could hardly believe that, despite my best efforts, she still wasn't seeing sense.

I tried to reason with her at breakfast on Monday morning.

"If you were standing in the middle of the road and a truck was going to run you over, you'd want me to tell you to move, right?"

She looked at me a little suspiciously. "Yes..."

"Well, this is the same. If you keep standing where you are then you're going to go to Hell. You need to run to Jesus."

Jill sighed. "Stop it, Livi."

"But I'm trying to help you. I'm trying to show you that God cares!"

She gave a cold laugh. "God doesn't *care!*"

"He does!"

"Then why is this world such a mess?" she demanded. "Why are so many people starving and dying and losing the will to live? Why do earthquakes and tsunamis wipe out whole villages? Why do so many people die young? Where's your own mother, Livi?"

I felt my cheeks grow hot as Jill glared at me. I glanced down and poked my cereal. "I don't know," I muttered.

Jill turned her back on me and switched on the kettle. Tears pricked the backs of my eyes as her words made a nest in my ears. *'Where's your mother, Livi?'* By the time her tea had brewed the nest had sprouted wings and taken up residence in my heart.

After a very long silence, Jill gathered up her things and said a hasty goodbye before leaving for work. As the front door clicked behind her I bit my knuckles and poured my breakfast down the sink, wondering why I was trying so hard to convince my sister of something I wasn't even sure I believed myself.

Halfway to school, I took a deep breath and turned to face Ruby. "If God cares so much, then why are so many people losing the will to live?"

Ruby stopped and stared at me. "I don't know," she said. "But I know God is good."

"But what about starving children? What about earthquakes and tsunamis? What about... my mum?"

Ruby chewed her lip and thought for a moment.

Before she could reply, Violet, who had wandered up beside us, gave a haughty sigh in my ear. "Oh look! It's the old suffering question," she said snootily. "People believe a lot of lies about God. And it stops them finding out what he's really like."

I looked at her. "What?"

Ruby gave a soft smile. "Our mum always says that you don't really know someone till you've walked a mile in their shoes. Well... you can't walk a mile in God's shoes, can you? His feet are too big. But..." Her smile widened. "You *can* ask for a ride on his shoulders."

"If you get off your own high horse," Violet added snidely.

I bit my thumb as I looked from Ruby to Violet.

Violet gave a condescending sniff before ending with, "Basically: God is God. And you're not."

I mulled it over all day. I supposed they had a point. At any rate, I had nothing better. So, that evening, after spending a torturous six minutes[30] praying for Jill's salvation, I went into her bedroom and declared, "You believe a lot of lies about God. Don't you want to find out what he's really like?"

Jill gave me an affronted look and told me to get out.

I let out a moan. *God, why isn't this working?* I wondered if I needed to set my alarm even earlier.

---

[30] I ran out of words very quickly.

~*~

By Wednesday's COOL Club meeting, I was feeling incredibly dejected. Jill was far from saved and, despite putting up a fresh batch of posters around the school, we were yet to have any new interest from our schoolmates. By now, I was praying the Lord's Prayer at least a dozen times a day, yet I felt further from God than ever. I decided I would need to try even harder.

"Let's take this into the canteen," I said, the moment our meeting began.

Although Ruby and Annie looked rather taken aback, Violet rubbed her hands together with glee and said, "Great idea, Livi!"

I looked at her a little warily. "I'll do the talking," I told her. I didn't want her to mess things up.

She sniffed. "Fine."

I leapt off the table and led the way out of the building and across the playground. It was my private mission to save at least one person by the end of the lunch hour. As soon as we entered the canteen I took a deep breath and headed straight for some of the girls in our class. Georgina Harris and Darcy Bell gave me a funny look as I plonked myself down beside them. Opposite us, Connie Harper and Sheena Ali stopped mid-sentence and stared at me. Violet took the seat next to me and gave a crazed grin. Behind us, Ruby and Annie lingered uncertainly.

I forced a smile as I said, "We were just wondering..." I waved a hand at myself and the others.[31] "Do you want to know about Jesus?"

They gave me a baffled look. "Not really," said Georgina.

I pursed my lips and asked, "Do you believe in God?"

"Yes," she said. "I just don't like organised religion." She screwed up her nose and added, "Or organised clubs."

Ruby gave a tentative smile but I quickly interjected, "When you say you believe in God, what do you mean? Do you pray much?"

Georgina shrugged. "Sometimes."

"I pray sometimes too," Connie Harper said from across the table.

"When?" I enquired.

"Oh, you know, when someone's ill or things are hard."

---

[31] Violet continued to grin crazily, Annie let out a shy giggle and Ruby blushed.

I sniffed. "I wouldn't like a friend like that."

Connie blinked at me. "What?"

"I wouldn't want a friend who just wanted to use me whenever they were in trouble."

Connie gave a splutter and looked at her friends. Georgina rolled her eyes and Sheena glared at me.

"Shall we go?" Darcy muttered.

The four of them grabbed their things and marched off.

I frowned. "I thought I was making a good point."

"You were..." Ruby said quietly behind me. "But you made it quite meanly."

I gave a huffy sigh and moved on to the next table. A bunch of first years were looking at me rather warily.

"Hey guys," I said. "We're from The COOL Club. Have you heard of us?"

They all shook their heads apart from one girl who said, "You put those funny God posters up, didn't you?"

"We did. What did you think of them?"

"They're alright."

"Well, you see, we're Christians and—"

"I'm a Christian," another of the girls piped up.

I looked at her in excitement. "You are?"

"Yeah, I was christened."

"Oh but that's not enough," I said. "Do you follow Jesus?"

"What do you mean 'follow Jesus'?"

"Is Jesus your Lord?"

"Lord?" She laughed in surprise and her friends giggled. "No!"

"Who is he then?"

"I don't know. I'm not saying I believe it all but I'm still a Christian."

"How?"

"My parents ticked it on the census. So I'm sort of a Christian but not a practising one."

I took a deep breath and willed myself to stay calm. "I'm not practising either," I said stiffly. "I'm doing it for real."

The girls looked at one another and giggled again. I feared they were way too immature to take The COOL Club seriously so I made my excuses and left.

As I strode through the canteen, Ruby, Annie and Violet followed behind me, trotting slightly to keep up.

At one point, I heard Annie ask, "Can I go and get a drink?" but I pretended not to hear. There wasn't time for distractions.

My chest felt all knotted and angry as I scoured the room, desperate for a breakthrough. I approached another table where a solitary sixth form boy was eating a sandwich and reading a book entitled, *'Stars and their Properties.'*

I cleared my throat. "Excuse me?"

The boy looked up. "Yes?"

"Do you think it's right to live for fame and fortune?"

"What?"

I pointed to his book.

"Oh." He smirked. "This is a Physics textbook."

I blushed and quickly composed myself. "What are you living for?"

The boy shrugged before admitting, "Fame and fortune."

I felt a surge of courage as I repeated, "Well, do you think that's right?"

He raised an eyebrow. "I think people should be free to do whatever they want as long as it doesn't hurt anyone."

"I think so too," I countered. "But what if it hurts God?"

"Why should it hurt God?"

"Because he has feelings. And if you live in a way that rejects him then it hurts him."

He sniffed. "That's your truth, maybe. I have my own."

"There's only one truth," I said hotly. "God exists whether you believe in him or not."

The boy paused before grinning. "Ah well, I'll plead with him in the end. He'll still let me into Heaven."

I gave him a sharp look. "You can't dismiss God and then expect him to repay you on your terms."

He frowned at me. "Are you saying I'm going to Hell?"

I shrugged. "If you don't want to spend your life on earth with Jesus, why would you want to be with him for eternity?"

"Look, I just came in to eat my lunch and read my book. I don't have time for this." The boy picked up his stuff and walked out.

As I yelled, "You're a sinner!" after him, I saw Ruby staring at me with a mortified look on her face.

"What?" I said indignantly. "It's true!"

"Perhaps," she replied. "But you're not being very nice."

I turned to move on, almost bumping into Fester as I went. "Hey Sir. Can we tell you about Jesus?"

Fester raised an eyebrow. "Not right now, Livi. I've got some marking to do." He gave a curt nod and strode off.

"Oh well, Fester," I muttered. "You've had your chance."

Just as I was about to pounce upon Aaron Tang and Freddie Singh at a nearby table Violet grabbed me by the arm and said awkwardly, "Livi, would you mind toning it down a bit? You're being kind of weird."

"What?"

"You're being weird," she repeated. "It's embarrassing."

My jaw fell to the floor. "*I'm* being weird?" I exclaimed. "And *you're* embarrassed?"

She nodded.

Beside her, Ruby and Annie gave sheepish shrugs.

I swallowed hard and grabbed a nearby chair to steady myself. *What's happening to me?*

"Are you alright, Livi?" Ruby asked gently.

I shook my head. "I need to go and lie down."

I ran all the way back to Miss Dalton's classroom and lay flat out on the floor. Ruby and Annie almost tripped over my face as they came running in behind me.

"Livi!" they cried. "Are you okay?"

I shook my head. "I'm Violet."

Ruby kept quiet as Annie came over and put a hand on my forehead. "You're not Violet," she said slowly. "You're *Livi.*"

I let out a moan and closed my eyes. Even though I was already lying down, I felt like I was about to fall. Tears streaked down my cheeks as I rolled over and curled into a ball. "I don't understand!" I cried through tears. "How am I meant to save them?"

~ 14 ~

Just a kiss

I felt pretty lost for the rest of the week. I shuddered every time I remembered how militant and *weird* I had been on Wednesday lunchtime and made a vow that I would never *ever* behave like Violet again. And yet, my eyes were wide open to the apathy towards God in the hearts of Jill and my classmates and I couldn't shake off the desperate panic that I had a personal responsibility to save them. How was I meant to do this without fulfilling the stereotype of a judgemental and pushy Christian? If I wasn't going to shout about my faith, it seemed that the only alternative was silence. All week, every time I heard Jill using God's name as a swear word, I simply bit my lip and said nothing. Then I'd feel a pang of guilt for not challenging her, mixed with a simmering anger at God for not revealing himself to her more plainly.

By Saturday morning, I was thoroughly miserable and at a loss as to what to do. But I was determined to push it out of my mind as Joey had invited me over to his house and I didn't want to be poor company. I spent a full hour fretting over what to wear[32] and counselling myself, *Remember to be cool.*

As I left the house, Jill called after me, "Have fun with your boyfriend."

I felt my insides squirming as I muttered, "Thanks," and quickly pulled the door shut.

As I waited for the bus to come, I caught sight of my reflection in a car window and worried that I was too dressy after all and would give off the appearance of having tried too hard. All the way to Joey's house I felt a combination of anticipation and fear as I

---

[32] I didn't want to look too casual nor did I want to repeat any of the outfits Joey had ever seen me wear in case I would start looking too ordinary or mundane. So I opted for a fairly smart skirt and one of Jill's polo necks, hoping it would make me seem sophisticated.

wondered what had become of me. Less than six months ago I had no need of either God or a boyfriend. Suddenly I was pretty consumed with both. Yet, rather than feeling exuberant about my faith in God or my status as Joey's girlfriend, it seemed that both relationships brought nothing but turmoil: the more I tried to please God, the more I found myself failing; the closer I got to Joey, the more I feared him losing interest in me.

As I walked up Joey's winding drive, I had a sudden irrational desire to run away.

Joey was waiting for me at the front door.

I fixed a grin on my face and ran the last few steps. "Hey!" I said, stopping to give him an awkward hug.

"How are you?" Joey asked as he led me down the hall and into the den.

I forced a cheery smile. "Yeah, good."

"Have you done anything exciting this week?"

My stomach churned but I played it cool as I pretended to mull things over. "Can't think of anything. It's been a pretty normal week... I've been normal... How about you?"

"I had a great week! I got a new drawing desk for my bedroom. It's bright green."

"Cool! Can I see it?"

He shook his head. "My parents don't let me have girls in my room."

"Why not?"

He shifted awkwardly. "It's just... I don't know."

I grinned and said in my best super-villain voice, "Are they scared I'll try to *seduce* you?"

It was meant to be a joke but, to my mortification, Joey turned bright scarlet and fell off the sofa. "No..." he muttered weakly. He gave me a hopeful smile and added, "Although, we *could* kiss if you want?"

Now it was my turn to blush. I shook my head. "Not yet."

He looked disappointed as he shrugged and said, "Well, just tell me when you're ready."

I sucked in my cheeks and turned away. Part of me wondered whether to just get it over with and let him kiss me. I didn't want him to think there was something wrong with me. And, the longer I waited, the more it felt like a big deal. I took a deep breath and turned back to face him. "Have you kissed anybody before?"

He started to say something and then stopped and shook his head. "No," he confessed.

116

I breathed a sigh of relief. "Me neither."

He grinned. "So it will be really special when we do."

I nodded slowly.

"You wanna?" He kept grinning.

I gave him half a nod but, as he came towards me, the words *'really special'* echoed round my brain. If my first kiss was *'really special,'* did that mean every kiss from that point onwards wouldn't be? What if I had another boyfriend after Joey? Would I regret not saving my *'really special'* first kiss for him? I thought about Ruby not wanting a boyfriend until she was old enough to get married. It seemed perverse and sensible both at the same time. I stared hard at Joey and wondered whether he ever thought about marriage. I recoiled as I realised with a grimace that if we ended up getting married I would have to keep my own surname.

Joey was staring at me. "Are you alright?"

"Yeah. I was just thinking."

"About what?"

"Lots of things... Growing up... Getting married."

He fell off the sofa all over again.

"I don't mean now," I spluttered. "Or even us... Not that I'm saying I don't... But, I mean, of course we're not..."

I gave myself a good shaking as Joey gaped at me.

"I was just thinking about kissing," I explained awkwardly. "And whether we would regret it."

He frowned. "It's just a kiss. It's not..." He went bright crimson and started coughing.

"I know. I know it's not a big deal or anything... I just..." I sighed again and looked down at my hands. "What if we break up?"

He eyed me suspiciously. "Are you going to break up with me?"

I shook my head. "No way!"

"Well, I'm not going to break up with you. So what's the problem?"

I shrugged. "What would make you break up with me?"

"Nothing!" he exclaimed without a pause. "Why? What would make *you* break up with *me?*"

I chewed my lip as I considered it. "I suppose if God told me to."

He raised his eyebrows. "Has he told you to?"

I glanced at my Jesus Jangles. "I don't think so," I whispered.

He gave a triumphant beam. "Good."

I started picking at some loose thread on one of the cushions. I couldn't figure out whether I was just being really silly. Joey clearly

117

didn't think it was a big deal. And what's a kiss anyway? People kiss all the time. People kiss complete strangers. Yet, whatever way I looked at it, I couldn't shake off the nagging feeling that somehow I would end up regretting it. "I'm not ready yet," I muttered.

He rolled his eyes. "Okay. Do you want some cake?"

"Cake? Alright."

"Come on then." He grabbed my hand and led me out of the room and down the hallway.

We wandered into the kitchen where Janine introduced me to a full room of middle-aged women as *'Joey's special friend.'*

I immediately dropped Joey's hand and gave a shy wave.

A lady in a purple dress smiled and said, "Oh, how lovely."

Somebody else said, "Ah yes, we've heard all about you!"

I felt myself blushing and looked at the floor.

To add to my embarrassment, Joey announced to his mother, "Livi wants some cake."

I tried to protest but Janine said. "Of course! Carrot or chocolate?" She pointed to two platters on the table.

I pretended it was a difficult choice in case Janine had made them herself but, in truth, the sound of a cake made of carrots made me feel rather nauseous. I must have slightly overdone my enthusiasm as Janine ended up cutting me a slice of both. "No, I just want chocolate..." I tried to protest.

But Joey elbowed me and whispered, "Take both."

Janine looked at me. "Do you want both, Livi?"

I gave a slow nod and stared at my feet, hoping none of her guests would think I was greedy.

Due to his chocolate allergy, Joey had no choice but to have a slice of the carrot cake. He cut himself an extra large piece and said, "Let's go."

I nodded and followed him out of the kitchen.

As we padded down the hall, I heard one of Janine's friends say, "Children grow up so fast, don't they!"

We went back into the den and closed the door behind us.

I slid the piece of carrot cake onto Joey's plate before turning my attention to the massive slice of chocolate cake. I dipped my finger into the buttery brown icing and said, "Yum."

Joey watched me enviously. "I wish I could eat chocolate."

I gave him a sympathetic smile and tried to be discreet as I shoved it into my mouth.

"Mark prayed for me to get healed the other day," he continued mournfully. "It didn't work."

"We could try again," I suggested.

Joey looked at me.

"It's worth a prayer," I said. "There's no harm in trying." Secretly, I'd had the sudden thought that maybe God could use it to give me a sign. If he approved of our relationship then he could put my mind at rest by healing Joey.

Joey shrugged. "Go on then."

I took a deep breath. "I don't know how to do it," I admitted. I put a tentative hand on his shoulder and murmured, "Jesus, please heal Joey of his chocolate allergy... Amen."

"Amen!" Joey sang.

I held my plate out, my heart pounding as I wondered whether my prayer had worked. "Try it," I squeaked.

I watched as Joey pinched some cake between his fingers and put it in his mouth. He chewed slowly and swallowed. Then he looked at me and grinned.

"Well?"

Joey took a deep breath and looked as though he was about to say something but, at the last moment, he shook and began a violent sneezing fit instead.

I waited for him to settle down. "Are you okay?"

Joey nodded and dragged himself off to the kitchen, sneezing all the way. I heard him whimper to his mother, "I ate some of Livi's chocolate cake."

Janine scolded him. "Joseph Teddy!"

I grimaced as I heard Joey explaining to the room full of guests, "We thought I was healed."

I sat back in frustration and picked at the carpet. For a tiny moment I had truly thought Joey was better. Was the lack of healing a sign? Or was it just a poor prayer? Or was God busy doing something else entirely? I fiddled with my Jesus Jangles as I prayed, *What does this mean, God?*

Joey came back into the den carrying another plate of carrot cake. He threw himself on the sofa and said, "Oh well."

"Oh well," I echoed. I paused before asking, "Was your mum cross?"

"She didn't mind. Susan looked a bit shocked though."

"Who's Susan?"

"The lady in the purple dress. Her son died a few years ago. Lots of people prayed but he still died. So she stopped believing in God. I don't think she likes it when people talk about faith stuff. I usually try not to mention Jesus around her."

I immediately thought about my salvation rampage on Wednesday and blushed. "How *do* you tell people about Jesus?"

"I kind of don't," he replied with a shrug. "Unless they ask. I don't like offending people."

"But aren't you worried they'll go to Hell?"

He shrugged again. "I don't really think about it."

I was aghast. "How can you not think about it?"

He rammed some carrot cake into his mouth. "I just don't," he said with his mouth full.

I stared at him as he took another bite.

"I'm not like Mark," he continued, bits of cake spraying out of his mouth. "He likes telling people about Jesus.[33] I just think people can figure out for themselves what they want to believe."

"But I thought you had a club," I said weakly. "ALIEN."

"We do. But I just go for the biscuits. I don't run it."

I let this sink in. "So, maybe I'm making too big a deal out of it?" I wondered aloud. "Like... People should just believe what they want? Should I stop trying to tell them?"

"I don't know. Hey, do you want to play with this?" He held up something blue and shiny.

"What is it?"

"A robotic fighting hamster."

"What does it fight?"

"Anything. Watch." He set the toy on the floor and grabbed a nearby piece of paper, which happened to be a recent church bulletin. Then he pressed a button on the hamster's back and it charged at the paper. Within five seconds it had ripped it to shreds.

I raised an eyebrow. "That's kind of cool."

Joey grinned. "Let's make it fight something else."

"Okay." I looked round the room but couldn't see anything suitable. "How about my sock?" I took it off and handed it to Joey.

He took it a little awkwardly and placed it in front of the hamster. "And destroy!"

We cheered as the hamster ran to my sock and started devouring it.

After feeding the hamster both of my socks, Joey ran round his house gathering as many disposable items as possible. Over the next few hours we didn't talk much but we did feed the hamster

---

[33] This is true. Mark's always bragging about the number of Jesus flyers he's handed out. This past week, I've had a vain fantasy of one day rocking up beside him on the street and handing out twice as many.

until it ran out of batteries. I had meant to come home by the middle of the afternoon but the hamster was such fun that we lost track of time and I ended up staying all day.

As he walked me to the bus stop Joey pointed to a nearby field where a number of tents had been erected. We could hear the sound of carnival music and the smell of fried onions wafted over us as we crossed the street.

"The Hollyhocks Festival is on this weekend! We should go."

"Okay!" I said. "How about tomorrow afternoon?"

Joey wrinkled up his nose. "We're visiting my sister... What about the morning?"

"We've got church," I reminded him.

"Oh yeah." He gave a cheeky grin. "Well, we could miss it just once, couldn't we?"

I paused. Was that allowed? "What about next Saturday?" I ventured.

He shook his head. "It will be over by then."

I bit my lip. "You wouldn't mind missing church?"

"I'd rather go to the festival." When I looked at him, he continued quickly, "It's not that I don't like church. Obviously I do. It's just, I was brought up with it, you know. So it sometimes gets a bit boring."

I let out my breath. "I guess we could miss church just once."

"Cool! I'll see you tomorrow."

"Okay."

Joey turned to go and then stopped and shot me a curious glance. He leant over very carefully and slowly put his face towards mine. Inches from my face, he paused and raised his eyebrows.

I gave a little nod and shut my eyes as he pressed his lips to mine. It lasted all of one second and my cheeks began to burn as we stumbled back and stared at each other.

"Bye," he said in a whisper.

I nodded dumbly and stuck my hand out for my bus.

It wasn't till I got home that I saw I had nearly fifteen missed calls from Ruby.

"Where were you?" she asked when I rang. "We were meant to be going to the cinema."

I hurriedly checked the time. I'd been at Joey's for six hours. "Whoops," I said. "I forgot."

"How? What were you doing?"

"I was at Joey's. We got really into this fighting hamster that he's got. It kind of destroys whatever you give it..."

"Oh."

"Sorry."

She sighed. "It's okay. Do you want a lift to church tomorrow?"

I paused. "Erm, I'm not going this week."

"How come?"

I took a deep breath and tried to sound evasive as I said, "I'm just going to hang out with a friend."

"You mean Joey?"

"Yeah... There's this festival thing in a field near his house."

"What kind of festival?"

"I don't know. But it looks cool."

Ruby didn't reply for a moment. Eventually, she asked, "So, are you and Joey really serious?"

"Sort of. We were talking about marriage and things today."

She gasped. "You're going to marry Joey?"

"No... I just meant we were talking about marriage in *general*."

"Oh."

I forced a laugh. "You should have seen the fighting hamster."

"Hmmm... Well, I'll see you Monday then."

"Okay. See you Monday."

"Have fun at the festival thing."

"Thanks... Have fun at church."

Ruby sounded like she was going to say something else but, in the end, she just muttered, "Bye."

I scowled and hung up. I was fairly certain Ruby disapproved of me missing church in favour of seeing Joey and the feeling that she was judging me irritated me. Yet, she hadn't actually *said* she disapproved which made me even angrier. I shoved my phone into my pocket and headed into the living room.

Jill barely looked up from the television as she asked, "Did you have fun with your boyfriend?"

I frowned. "Yes."

She smiled and carried on staring at the screen. "Good."

I sunk into the sofa and picked at my nails. Although I probably ought to have been relieved, it bothered me that while Ruby showed signs of concern over my love life my sister didn't seemed fazed in the slightest. I watched Jill out of the corner of my eye and realised with a sinking heart that she would probably be far more alarmed at the idea of me praying for Joey's chocolate allergy than she would at the news that I had just given away my first kiss.

~ 15 ~

Checking facts

Ruby didn't ask me how the festival had been so I made a point of not mentioning it either.[34]

We walked to school a little faster than usual on Monday morning and I felt a combination of irritation and guilt as I cast sideways glances in her direction and wondered what she was thinking. I hoped she had forgiven me for losing track of time on Saturday. And I hoped she didn't think I had turned into one of those girls who forget about their friends once they have a boyfriend.

I caught her eye and forced a smile. I wanted to tell her that she was still my best friend but I wasn't sure how to bring it up without risking making things even more awkward.

She smiled back and said, "Church was good yesterday."

I bit my lip and wondered what I should say in return. *'The festival thing was good...'? 'I missed you...'? 'Joey sometimes finds church boring...'?* In the end, I just muttered, "Cool."

I figured it was probably best to act like everything was normal and resolved to get through the day without mentioning Joey at all.

Unfortunately, I didn't bank for an unforeseen confrontation with Caroline MacBrodie and her gang during morning break.

Ruby, Annie and I were wandering aimlessly down the corridor when we passed Caroline, Kitty, Molly and Melody loitering by the water fountain discussing boys.

---

[34] For the record, it had been wet and expensive and we'd wasted all our money trying to hook a duck to win a cuddly toy. What with buses being unreliable on a Sunday and Joey needing to leave early to go to his sister's house, we'd ended up with less than an hour together. I spent most of that time petrified that Joey would want to kiss me again and kept pausing to plaster my lips with chocolate flavoured lip balm as a deterrent.

Caroline was bragging about her latest boyfriend, a college student named Ryan.[35] "It's a proper serious relationship," she said snootily. "High school boys are so immature."

I stifled a laugh as Kitty simpered, "Oh Caro. You're so cool."

Ruby and Annie kept on walking but, against my better judgement, I glanced up and caught Kitty's eye.

She nudged her friends before asking with a grin, "Do you have a boyfriend, Livi?"

"Obviously," I replied coolly.

They looked at me in surprise.

"Have you kissed him?" Molly demanded.

I squirmed. "None of your business."

"That means she has!" Melody squealed.

I gave a coy shrug but Caroline tutted and said, "No it doesn't."

I opened my mouth and closed it again. I was aware of Ruby beside me and wasn't sure I wanted her to know about mine and Joey's kiss.

I tried to stand my ground as Caroline looked me up and down. "What's his name?"

"Joey."

"Joey what?"

I blushed. "None of your business."

Caroline gave an ugly sneer. "He doesn't exist."

Her friends looked at me in disdain.

"Yes he does!" I insisted.

Annie tried to come to my aid by saying, "He does. I've seen his photo on FriendWeb. He can stand on his head."

Caroline and her gang sniggered.

I wanted to add that he was really rich but the words caught in my throat.

"I bet he's ugly," Kitty hissed.

I rolled my eyes and turned to walk away but, before I did so, I heard Caroline mutter, "Some people are so deluded."

I turned back and glared at her. "I'm not the one who's deluded! I'm not the one who pretends to be something I'm not!"

Ruby grabbed my arm. "Livi, don't!"

I caught her eye and nodded. She was right. I couldn't give away what we knew. I forced a cough before saying, "Well, I'd love to stay and chat but we have some work to do on our biographies."

---

[35] This is the fifth boy she's supposed to have dated in about as many weeks. I would eat an egg if one of them actually existed.

Caroline gave an exaggerated scowl. "Och! I hate that lesson. *Personal and Social Development.* It's so pointless."

"It's not pointless!" I retorted. "But perhaps you're not personally and socially developed enough to understand it. And, for your information," I added loudly, *"The Beast* is the coolest teacher in school."

I turned to storm off but my grand departure was ruined by me almost colliding with Ms Sorenson who had just emerged from the staffroom.

I felt my cheeks burn as she stared straight at me. "I'm a beast?" She looked a little bemused.

"No, no, no!" I said wildly. "I just... It was..." I glanced at Caroline and bit my lip.

Caroline sneered as if to say, *'Go on then.'*

I looked back at Ms Sorenson. I wanted to say, *'It's Caroline's nickname for you,'* but that would ruin the impact of her reading it in Ruby's biographical account. I thought about mine and Ruby's research on FriendWeb and the nappy advert which was still tucked into the back of my notebook. I couldn't waste all our hard work. I had to hold my tongue.

Ms Sorenson was looking at me expectantly.

"Sorry," I mumbled. "I didn't mean it."

She gave me a long look before smiling to herself and saying, "Alright." Then she nodded curtly and left.

I felt my whole body burn with shame as I watched my favourite teacher, the least beastly teacher in the world, walk away.

At the water fountain, Caroline's gang shrieked with laughter.

"Would you believe it?" Caroline jeered. "Freaky Von Freakshow covered my back!" She grinned at her friends as they cackled like deranged hyenas.

I narrowed my eyes at them and breathed heavily out of my nose. *You'll see,* I thought darkly as they linked arms and went sauntering down the corridor.

Once they were out of earshot Annie turned to me and said, "I need to write about Joey in your biography, don't I?"

"I guess so," I muttered, rubbing my head weakly. I blinked quickly to keep myself from crying and wondered whether I ought to run after Ms Sorenson and try to explain. Maybe I could say I had actually meant to say *'The Best'*?

"Is he your first boyfriend?" Annie continued obliviously.

I gave a slow nod.

"Should I say *'boyfriend,'* or do you call him something else... Like your *'romantic companion,'* or your *'sweetheart,'* or something?"

I almost choked. "Boyfriend is fine," I squeaked.

Annie nodded and started to write in her notebook. "How do you spell *'Joey'*?"

I took her notebook and wrote it down for her. While I was at it I also wrote down *'Cashbottom.'* She stared at it but, to my relief, she didn't seem able to pronounce it and didn't comment.

"You're so lucky to have a boyfriend," she whispered. "Do you love him?"

I felt myself blushing as I coughed and spluttered, "I don't know!" I fiddled with the hem of my skirt, trying desperately to pretend that it wasn't a big deal.

"So... *Have* you kissed him?" Annie went on.

"Sort of," I said, avoiding Ruby's gaze. I didn't add that it was only once and not for very long and nowhere near as special as I'd hoped. "Don't put that in my biography though," I added, unsure if I wanted Ms Sorenson to know.

I stole a glance at Ruby. She wore a funny smile and I braced myself as I waited for her to ask whether I had checked with Jesus about my relationship with Joey.

I had already rehearsed what I would say: *'For your information, I've told Joey I'll break up with him if God makes me. I've asked for plenty of signs but God hasn't given me one yet so don't judge me till you have all the facts.'*

But she didn't ask.

~*~

The next day, I approached Ms Sorenson's lesson with a little trepidation. I was frightened she would have had time to mull over my *'Beast'* comment and might be waiting for me with a punishment. I crept past her desk as quickly as possible as I shuffled into the room behind Ruby and Annie.

To my relief, she looked up and smiled. "Good afternoon, Livi."

I gave a shy smile in return and ran to my seat.

Once everyone had sat down, Ms Sorenson got our attention with the words, "Your biographies are due in two weeks time."

The class murmured in surprise.

Kitty put her hand up. "Don't we have till the end of term?"

Ms Sorenson gave her a quick look. "No."

I stared at Annie in amazement and wondered what our teacher had up her sleeve.

"But Miss," Kitty whined. "I don't know anything about Rupert yet."

Beside her, Rupert looked a little affronted as he snapped, "That's because you haven't spoken to me all term."

Kitty blushed as Ms Sorenson gave her a pointed look and said, "Miss Warrington, I suggest you give careful thought to how you spend your time in the next couple of lessons." She looked round at the rest of the class. "That goes for all of you. To be entrusted to tell another person's story is a very big responsibility. I won't take kindly to anybody who thinks they can treat this task lightly."

Most of our class shifted and avoided her gaze but I looked at Annie and grinned. We were more than ready to write each other's biographies. I had even made a start on her front cover: a picture of her name spelled out in buttons.

"Now, get on with your work," Ms Sorenson finished. "And please check your facts carefully. I was once introduced as coming from Dubai which, I believe, is nearly five thousand miles from Ireland with a landscape nothing whatsoever like Dublin."

My classmates laughed and pulled out their work.

I nudged Annie. "Ms Sorenson is from Ireland!"

"Didn't you know that already?"

"How would I know?"

She giggled. "Couldn't you tell from her accent?"

"No..." I felt myself blushing. "But you all have accents up here so I didn't think about it."

Annie laughed even louder and said, "You're so funny, Livi! Did you really think Ms Sorenson was from Yorkshire?"

"Shhh!" I hissed. I didn't want Ms Sorenson to hear and think I'd not only gone round calling her a beast, but an English one at that.

"Her surname is 'Sorenson.'" Annie put on a mock Irish accent and grinned. "That's an Irish name."

"No it's not. I looked it up online. It's from Scandinavia."

Annie burst out laughing again. "That's not even a real place!" She pounded the desk with her fists.

I rolled my eyes and glanced across at Ruby.

I was just in time to hear her ask Caroline, "Can I please check my facts... What are your brothers' names?"

Caroline gave her a sharp look. "I've already told you," she snapped. "Lucas and Pierre."

Ruby gave a slow nod. "And... are they their real names or... nicknames? Like, do they have French names when they're in France and Scottish names when they're in Scotland?"

Caroline looked at Ruby as though she were something brown and smelly on the heel of her shoe. "What?"

Ruby blushed. "Never mind." She coughed. "Your dad's girlfriend is called Irina, right?"

"Mirela."

"But I thought—"

Caroline gave an irritated sigh. "He's got a new one."

Ruby glanced across at me and we exchanged knowing looks. Caroline was obviously lying.

Caroline followed Ruby's gaze and glared at me.

I looked down and pretended to be consumed in my work.

For the next hour, I alternated between writing Annie's biography and stealing the odd peek at Ruby and Caroline. They had fallen back into their usual silence and Ruby stared straight ahead, looking incredibly frustrated. I felt rather sorry for her although I tried to shoot her encouraging smiles to assure her it would all be worth it once she'd written Caroline's biography.

As the lesson drew to an end, I looked across in time to overhear Ruby saying stiffly, "Okay, Caroline, you haven't asked me anything about my family and our biographies are due in soon. I know you don't care about my life, but I'm going to tell you anyway." Caroline opened her mouth but Ruby continued quickly, "My dad is called Stanley. He's an optician. My mum is called Belinda. She likes baking cakes. My older sister is called Violet. You might have seen her around school dressed all in one colour."

Caroline snorted. "You're related to Rainbow Drip? Why doesn't that surprise me?"

Ruby gulped but went on as though Caroline hadn't said anything. "My little brother is called Oscar. He was a medical miracle."

"You mean he was a mistake?" Caroline sneered.

"No! I mean my mum had ovarian cancer and everybody thought she was going to die but she didn't. Then Oscar was born."

I looked up in surprise. Why hadn't I known that?

Caroline sniffed. "Big deal."

Ruby coughed. "I was born feet first, my earliest memory is of my doll's head falling off, I used to do ballet but I kept getting tangled up in my tutu, I collect banana stickers, I don't like wasps, itchy jumpers, or loud hand dryers and my dog is afraid of people eating apples." She finished with a nod and looked away.

Caroline looked her up and down and sniggered.

Ruby had gone bright red, as though she was trying not to cry. I tried to catch her eye but she had buried her head in her work.

As soon as the bell rang, Annie and I packed up our things and joined Ruby at her desk.

I waited for Caroline to leave before saying casually, "I didn't know your mum nearly died."

"Oh yeah." Ruby shrugged.

"Why didn't you ever tell me?"

"Well, it never really came up. Plus *your* mum actually did die so I didn't want to upset you by saying mine hadn't."

I blinked at her. "So... what else don't I know about you?"

Ruby cocked her head to one side. "I once fought an angry goose and won."

My jaw fell open. "Ruby Rico! You're wilder than you seem."

She smiled. "I guess everybody is more than they seem."

I nodded. "For example, did you know Ms Sorenson is Irish?"

Ruby gave me a funny look. "Yeah. She has an Irish accent."

I blushed and shot a glance in our teacher's direction. She looked up from her filofax and grinned.

"I *know*," I insisted to Ruby in a whisper. "I was just checking you had all the facts."

She giggled and led the way to the door.

Before we left, I took a deep breath and turned to our teacher. "Ms Sorenson, I honestly don't think you're a beast..." I swallowed hard as a lump caught in my throat.

She kept smiling at me. "It's alright, Livi," she said calmly. "I check my facts carefully too."

I breathed a huge sigh of relief and turned to go.

"Oh and by the way..."

I looked back.

"You're quite right about my surname. My grandfather was from Denmark."

My heart gave a little flutter as she winked.

Annie looked rather perplexed. "That's not what you said," she hissed at me as the three of us linked arms and left the room. "You said some other place."

I grinned. "Maybe everything is more than it seems."

129

~ 16 ~

The key to Caroline's story

We were in the middle of Maths when I received a text from Joey. *'Are you going to church on Sunday?'*

I bit my lip, afraid that he might ask if I wanted to miss it in favour of another festival. I sent a quick reply, tucking my phone out of sight so that Fester wouldn't notice. *'I think so. Why?'*

I kept my phone on my lap, shooting regular glances at our teacher as I waited to see whether Joey would text again. I was also careful to angle my phone away from Ruby and Annie who were beside me and forced myself to play an active role in their conversation about banana stickers and hedgehogs so that they wouldn't notice how distracted I was.

"What's your favourite kind of hedgehog, Livi?" asked Annie.

"Er... I don't know," I said. "Small ones, I guess..."

"I like small ones too!" Annie exclaimed. "And really big ones."

"I've got four stickers with hedgehogs on," Ruby added, patting her treasured portfolio. I nodded along as she pointed them out.

A few minutes later, my phone lit up with a new message. I glanced down and hurriedly read Joey's response. *'Oh good. I'm not going to be at youth group cos we're having a meal out for Mum's birthday. I just wanted to check I'd see you on Sunday.'*

I breathed a sigh of relief. I was about to text back when my phone started to ring. I gasped as the words *'Unknown caller'* danced across the screen. Of course, my phone was set to silent, but it soon started to vibrate and, in my haste to turn it off, I accidentally accepted the call.

Ruby and Annie looked up as the mystery caller began muttering faintly in my hands.

I gave them a sheepish shrug before ducking under the table and answering in a whisper, "Hello?"

It was my dad. "Livi! How's tricks!"

I almost banged my head. "Oh... Hi."

"What are you doing?"

"I'm in Maths," I whispered. "I can't really talk."

Dad laughed. "I'm just ringing to ask a question about the wedding."

My heart pounded as I wondered foolishly whether he was going to ask me to be one of the bridesmaids. I tried to sound casual as I replied, "Oh?"

"Would you be able to hand out sandwiches after the ceremony? Erica booked a catering team but they're a little short."

A bubble of anger popped inside me. "I suppose so," I said through gritted teeth.

"Great! If you wear a white shirt you'll blend right in."

"A white shirt?"

"Yes. Your school shirt should be fine."

I sucked in my cheeks as a lump formed in my throat. I was about to tell him that I wouldn't be attending his stupid wedding after all when I was interrupted by the sound of somebody tapping the table above my head.

"Livi, quick!" Ruby whispered, just as Caroline MacBrodie drawled, "Mr Lester, I thought you might like to know that Livi is under the table making a phone call."

I scrambled out from under the table as fast as I could and shoved my phone into my bag.

Fester looked at me. "What were you doing, Livi?"

I swallowed hard and shrugged, frightened that I would cry if I tried to say anything.

"Were you on your phone?"

I took a deep breath. "Yes Sir. Sorry. It was a family thing." I bit my lip and looked down.

Caroline snorted. "Something requiring your immediate attention, I presume?"

I narrowed my eyes at her. "Yes."

Fester looked at me strangely and gave a slow nod. "Get on with your work, girls," he said.

Caroline raised her eyebrows and stormed back to her seat. For the rest of the lesson she could be heard muttering about the lack of discipline in state schools and its correlation with joblessness in later life.

I sunk down in my chair and sighed.

Ruby and Annie looked at me curiously.

"Who was on the phone?" asked Ruby.

"My dad." I scowled. "He wanted to ask me to be a waitress at his wedding."

Ruby frowned and Annie stuck out her bottom lip in pity.

Fester came sidling up to our desk. "Is everything alright, Livi?"

I avoided his gaze. "Yeah."

"Was it Jill on the phone?" He sounded concerned.

I looked at him and grimaced. I didn't want to admit to the true nature of my phone call but, if I told him Jill had rung me in the middle of a lesson, he might worry that something was wrong with her and take it as an invitation to make contact.

"It was my dad," I said. "But please don't ask me about it. Everything's fine."

Fester raised his eyebrows. "Oh. Alright." He gave a curt nod and returned to his desk.

"Wow!" Annie gasped. "He didn't tell you off or anything!"

I closed my eyes and rubbed my head. I didn't want to have to tell her about Fester's previous role as Jill's boyfriend. I *definitely* couldn't have *that* in my biography.

"How did you do it?" she continued in awe.

"I don't know. He must just be in a good mood."

Annie gave an impressed nod.

Ruby was looking at me in concern. "Are you alright?" she whispered.

I flicked the table leg. "Families are so rubbish."

She patted me. "Do you want us to pray for you?"

I pouted. I wasn't sure what could be done. "If you want."

Ruby bowed her head and started to pray.

Beside her, Annie closed her eyes and prayed solemnly, "Hey Peter, please help Livi not to feel sad about her dad's wedding. Amen." She opened her eyes and beamed at me.

I exhaled heavily out of my nose. "You really shouldn't call God 'Peter.'"

She giggled. "But that's his name!"

I shook my head. Her carelessness bothered me. "No it isn't!"

"It's what they call him at my grandma's church!" Annie paused before adding, "You should come and see."

I was about to refuse but, to my surprise, Ruby nodded and said, "That's a good idea!"

I looked at Ruby in alarm. I wasn't sure I wanted to go to a church where they made up names for God. What else might they do? "Are you sure?" I muttered.

"Why not?"

I cocked my head to one side. "When?"

"This Sunday?" Annie suggested.

"Yeah!" Ruby agreed.

I sucked in my cheeks. Joey wouldn't be at youth group on Friday. If I went to a different church on Sunday then I wouldn't get to see him all week.

I was about to make my excuses when Annie sang, "Hooray! We should have a sleepover at mine on Saturday night!"

Ruby grinned.

My stomach squelched. A sleepover? I couldn't miss that either!

The two of them looked at me expectantly.

I gulped and wondered whether it would be inappropriate to ask if Joey could come to the sleepover.

Ruby gave me a curious look. "You don't have to come if you don't want to."

"Oh I want to! I just..." I thought fast. I needed to portray disappointment at the idea of missing King's Church without going overboard. "I just like going to *our* church, that's all."

Ruby didn't look convinced. "You mean because Joey will be there?"

"No! I liked it before I started going out with Joey, didn't I?"

She shifted awkwardly. "Sorry."

"It's okay." I forced a smile and considered my words carefully. "The idea of a different church is strange because I really like our church... But I suppose I can miss it just once."

Annie beamed. "Yey! Let's plan our sleepover!" She began listing the various activities that her house offered.[36]

Suddenly, Caroline's shrill voice wafted over from the other side of the room. "I pity people who are so dependent on their families that they can't even get through a Maths class without feeling the need to call them!"

I pursed my lips as I looked across at her.

Caroline caught my eye and sneered.

"I know what we'll do at our sleepover," I muttered to Ruby and Annie. "We'll work on Caroline's biography."

---

[36] Photo shoots with her stuffed hedgehogs, talking to a dying old man and spying on her father's clients to name but a few.

~*~

Hamish MacBrodie had updated his FriendWeb page. Ruby, Annie and I sat cross-legged on Annie's bedroom floor, Annie's laptop open before us as we hunted for fresh information about Caroline.

"That's new," Ruby announced, pointing to a recent post about Hamish's football club. "And that hamster photo is new too." She continued scrolling through various posts and pictures. "That's new... That's new... That's— Ooh!"

We all leant closer.

Under the heading, *'Blast from the past!'* was an old family photo of a bunch of people at a wedding. Squatting on the front row, an elfish-looking young girl wearing a hideous tartan dress had been tagged as Caroline.

Ruby clicked the photo and a full-sized version filled the page. I was about to mock Caroline's dress when Ruby gasped and pointed to the screen.

In the comments section Hamish had posted, *'Uncle Malcolm looks a bit shifty. Must have been eyeing up the bridesmaids!'*

Underneath, Caroline had written, *'Shut your face, idiot! Tell tales on your own father.'*

I raised an eyebrow.

"So... Hamish is her *cousin?*" Ruby said slowly.

"Malcolm..." I grabbed the laptop off Ruby and quickly typed *'Malcolm MacBrodie'* into the search engine.

Seconds later, a number of links appeared on the screen. The top one read, *'Peebles businessman, Malcolm MacBrodie, sentenced to four years for fraud.'*

We shrieked and hurriedly opened the webpage.

It was an archived newspaper article from several years ago.

My heart pounded as I read aloud, *"Earlier in the month, a jury returned a unanimous guilty verdict for local businessman, Malcolm MacBrodie, who had been tried for multiple counts of fraud. Sentencing him this afternoon to four years in prison, Judge Justice Finney told the defendant, 'You were motivated by greed and selfishness and felt invincible as you sought to cheat the system, but you have become unstuck and must pay accordingly.' MacBrodie, formerly of investment firm Strongs and Hold Ltd, was rumbled after a former mistress, his Romanian secretary Sorina Banciu, contacted police with information as revenge for MacBrodie ending their six month fling. It soon transpired that*

MacBrodie's affair with Ms Banciu was only the tip of the iceberg as a further five former employees testified to intimate relations during his trial. MacBrodie's wife of seventeen years was said to have been devastated by the revelations of his secret life. She returned to her native town of Beauvais in France earlier in the year and is believed to have since remarried. Their daughter, who cannot be named for legal reasons, is being taken care of by relatives..." My jaw dropped open as I gaped at Ruby and Annie.

Ruby looked a little stunned. "I can't believe we found that."

"And she made fun of me when my dad got a speeding ticket!" Annie said hotly. "She is going to be so sorry!"

I looked at the date of the article. It was just over four years old. I shook my head as I pieced it all together. Caroline's father had just been released from jail and they'd moved to Leeds to escape his past. He didn't send her to a state school to toughen her up; he sent her because he'd lost all his money. And the wild holidays in France probably weren't so wild now that her mother had a brand new family over there. "Those photos from Loch Lomond..." I muttered. "They weren't Caroline's parents. That's when she was staying with relatives."

Ruby let out a long sigh. "No wonder she looked so miserable."

"Then maybe she really does have French brothers," Annie added. "Perhaps she wasn't lying about that."

I kept staring at the screen. "Isn't this crazy? The key to her story! Just in the nick of time!" I read over the article once more. "Crazy," I repeated.

Ruby sucked in her cheeks. "How am I meant to write about it all?"

"My dad could help," Annie suggested.

I gave her a dubious look. When I had arrived, her father had stared long and hard at me, his calm expression giving nothing away as he asked, "How are you today, Livi?"

I had replied, "I'm fine."

He'd repeated, "Fine?"

And I'd said, "Yes, I'm *fine,*" before running up to Annie's room.

"He'll be able to tell us Caroline's secret thoughts," Annie explained.

Ruby raised her eyebrows. "I guess that could be useful."

Annie leapt off her bed. "Let's go!" she yelled as she threw open her bedroom door.

Ruby and I followed her out, exchanging bemused smiles.

We were about to go down the stairs when Annie said suddenly, "We should check he's not got a client." Without warning, she pushed Old Budgie's door open and a waft of impending death swept over me.

Annie ran into her great uncle's room and trotted over to the window. "Hey Old Budgie!" she sang.

Old Budgie, who was looking even frailer than last time, looked up from his bed and coughed. I forced a smile as he gave a timid wave and greeted us with a hoarse whisper. "Hello girls."

"Hello," Ruby and I said politely.

Old Budgie opened his mouth, as though about to say something else, but instead just took a very long slow breath. He looked like he was going to keel over at any moment and Ruby and I gripped one another tightly in dread.

"There isn't a car outside," Annie declared from the window. "And most of them come in cars. Unless it's the sweaty man who jogs here. Or the lady who comes in a taxi. Or the woman who gets dropped off by her husband and always shouts at him as he drives away." She pursed her lips. "Hmmm." Without warning, she ran out of Old Budgie's room and trotted down the stairs.

Old Budgie stared after her and gave me and Ruby a gummy grin.

I nodded and quickly closed his door, exchanging an uncomfortable glance with Ruby as we followed Annie down the stairs. We lingered in the hallway as Annie pressed her ear up to her father's office door.

She beckoned us and asked in a whisper, "Can you hear anything?"

Ruby and I tentatively pressed our ears against Mr Button's door and shook our heads.

Annie shrugged and gave a loud knock.

Moments later, Mr Button opened the door. "Annie, I've told you not to disturb me when I'm in my office!" he scolded. "I could have had a client in here."

"We knew you didn't," Annie insisted. "We listened at the door and couldn't hear anything."

Mr Button stared at me and Ruby and I felt myself blushing.

I cleared my throat. "We have a psychology question, please."

He gave me an odd look. "A psychology question?"

I nodded. "What would be the secret thoughts of a person who had to spend four years living with relatives because their father was in jail and their mother had moved to France?" I paused before clarifying, "It's not me."

Mr Button took a deep breath and stroked his chin. "They would probably feel very rejected," he said. "And perhaps exhibit some reactive behaviour, either in the form of extreme withdrawal or extreme aggression."

I looked at Ruby and Annie. "Aggression!" we said in unison.

"Such a child would undoubtedly carry a lot of guilt," he went on. "They would consider themselves the reason for their family's dysfunction."

"Even though it's her parents' fault?" Ruby asked in surprise.

Mr Button nodded. "Children need to see their parents as good. So, when something happens that doesn't make sense, they often make sense of it by blaming themselves."

I gave an impressed nod. Mr Button certainly knew his stuff. He was looking at us all curiously but I figured there was no point in hanging around. "Well, thanks," I said. "We'll let you get on with your work."

He gave a thin smile as we ran back up the stairs.

"You could have a psychoanalyst's report at the back of the biography!" I suggested to Ruby once the three of us had returned to Annie's room.

Ruby nodded slowly. She looked rather apprehensive as she opened her notebook and bit the lid off her pen.

"Write this:" I dictated. *"Caroline's life was a disaster from start to finish."*

Annie giggled.

Ruby paused before writing it down. "Seems a little harsh," she said as she read it over.

I shrugged. "It's true though. Oh, and don't forget to add this." I grinned and held up the nappy picture.

I didn't sleep well that night since the three of us had opted for sharing Annie's bed and they were both wriggly sleepers. We had to keep the light on too, as Annie had a fear of the dark, and I couldn't relax with all her stuffed hedgehogs staring at me. I also couldn't stop thinking about all our research for Caroline's biography and, as cleverly constructed phrases filled my mind,[37] I half wished I'd

---

[37] *'From riches to rags: the secret behind Caroline's scowl,'* and, *'As shocking as a plate of cold haggis.'*

been paired with her myself. On top of all that, I was rather anxious about our impending visit to Annie's grandma's church.

Just before she fell asleep, Annie muttered drowsily, "Goodnight Livi. Goodnight Ruby. Goodnight Peter God."

I exchanged a worried glance with Ruby.

"What's your grandma's church called?" I asked Annie.

"St Mary's on the Hill," she whispered back.

I chewed my lip. It sounded normal enough. "And *everybody* calls God *'Peter'*?"

"Yup," Annie said dreamily. "It's his name. You'll see."

I blinked at the ceiling. "What do we do if it's a really weird church?" I whispered to Ruby.

"We run."

I gulped.

Annie had already fallen asleep. My stomach churned as I wondered what lay in store for us the following morning. I was torn between pitying Annie for being so daft and fearing that she might know something I didn't.

~ 17 ~

St Mary's on the Hill

Annie's grandma, who Annie addressed as *'Granny Button,'* had the same piercing stare as Annie's father. She picked us up at nine on the dot, clad in a mauve dress suit and hat. She held a Bible in one hand and an umbrella in the other. The sky was blue and showed no signs of rain but it was clear she was the type of woman who always came prepared.

I felt myself blushing as I trundled down the stairs in my jeans and sweater. I'd got so used to wearing everyday clothes to church that it hadn't occurred to me to bring anything smart. I hadn't even brushed my hair, having rolled out of bed a mere ten minutes earlier. Nor had it crossed my mind to bring my Bible. It was some consolation that Ruby hadn't brought a change of clothes either and we clung to one another for support as Granny Button looked us up and down.

After a slight pause, she said, "Right." Although, from the look on her face, she meant, *"Wrong."*

Before I could dwell too long on my lack of preparation, Annie[38] grabbed our arms and said, "Let's go!"

Ruby and I nodded and closed the front door behind us. The three of us trotted along with muted excitement as Annie's grandma led the short walk to St Mary's on the Hill.

It was a traditionally grand and imposing church building, set on a mount and surrounded by a dilapidated graveyard. It looked as though it must have been beautiful once but its former glory was hidden behind a weakening roof and a neglected batch of ivy which grew up the weathered walls.

---

[38] Who looked a little like a human-hedgehog hybrid in her Sunday best— a pair of smart brown dungarees, furry grey leg warmers and a small brown hat.

As we walked through the graveyard towards the church entrance Ruby whispered in my ear, "I think it's one of those smelly churches."

I turned in shock and asked what she meant.

But there wasn't time for her to answer. Once inside the building, it was apparent that St Mary's on the Hill was a very serious church. Unlike at King's Church, everybody was sitting in silence as they waited for the service to begin. At the front, above a marble altar, was a gigantic carving of Jesus mounted painfully on a wooden crucifix. Bright red marks seeped out of his hands and feet and the crown of thorns on his head sparkled sharply in the sunlight. I winced at the sight of it. Up and down the walls were a line of beautiful stained glass windows filled with images of sombre-looking saints and cherubim. I decided that, if I ever got rich, I would have such a window in my bedroom.

I felt a little uncomfortable striding through the building in my jeans but tried to smile when Annie caught my eye as I didn't want her to know that I'd never been to that kind of church before. Beside me, Ruby was gazing at the crucifix. We followed Annie's grandma to a pew near the front and quietly took our seats. I glanced at Annie and she grinned. I gave her a quick smile in return and looked at Ruby. Ruby caught my eye and nodded pleasantly. It felt odd just sitting there staring at one another. But nobody else was speaking so we had no choice but to sit in silence as the building slowly filled up around us.

After what felt like ages, a little bell rang out and everybody got to their feet. It sounded like the dinging at the start of a wrestling match and I stood up, craning to see what was going on. Moments later, a procession of people came in carrying candles and long sticks. They walked down the aisle followed by a man wearing robes. The robed man reached the front and stood in front of the altar. He was old and austere-looking and I had no idea if he was a priest or a vicar or even a bishop but I didn't want to break the silence by asking. One thing was for sure: although he wore a fancy costume, he definitely wasn't a wrestler. We stood as he said a prayer. Then we sat down as he said another one. Then we stood again as he started to swing incense up and down the aisles.

Ruby nudged me and whispered, "See? Smelly."

I gripped the pew in front to steady myself. The incense was making me feel faint.

The congregation began to sing a hymn, accompanied by the overpoweringly nasal sound of a loud pipe organ.

I tried to join in but much of it appeared to be written in olden language and it was all a little dreary.

Down the pew, Annie's grandma sang in a high-pitched warble, her chin wobbling frantically.

I exchanged a bemused grin with Ruby before looking down.

The hymn went on for a long time and I started to tire of standing but it didn't seem like the kind of church where you were allowed to sit as you pleased.

I glanced round at the congregation and took note of how serious everybody looked. There were quite a lot of old ladies, all singing as shrilly as Annie's grandma. Nobody had their hands raised and I was very glad Stanley wasn't there to dance down the aisle.

The hymn finished and everybody sat back down. I breathed a sigh of relief but, the next thing I knew, we were standing again.

The man spoke in a monotone fashion and, every now and then, the congregation chanted in response. I tried to nod along as though I understood but it was all washing over me and I found it hard to keep up. We were standing and sitting faster than a game of *Musical Bumps* and I kept glancing at Annie as I wondered how on earth she knew what to say.

She caught my eye and beamed.

I gave half a smile back and tried to concentrate as the man read a short passage from the Bible.

Unlike Ruby and me, Annie seemed perfectly comfortable with the rituals and the reciting and the constant rising. I wondered if I had been missing something all this time. Perhaps this was the *proper* way to do church: in a proper building with a proper script. I turned carefully in my seat and considered the parishioners one by one. An old man behind me wore a serious suit and a long white beard and looked incredibly holy as he nodded through the reading. For one daft moment, I wondered if he was Jesus.

Just before I could lean over to ask him, the man at the front finished with the words, "This is the word of the Lord."

The congregation recited, "Thanks be to God."

"There!" Annie said loudly. "Thanks Peter God."

I looked at her in surprise and burst out laughing.

A few people turned to stare. Annie's grandma looked rather affronted.

I bit my lip and tried to hold back my giggles but wasn't entirely successful.

On my left, Ruby started to shake. The tips of her ears went bright red and her face contorted wildly as silent tears streamed down her cheeks.

Annie frowned as she whispered, "What's so funny?"

"Thanks *be to* God," I said between titters. "Not *Peter!*"

Annie's eyes widened and she clasped a hand to her mouth to keep herself from squealing aloud.

I gave another chuckle and quickly looked down to compose myself. Then I made the mistake of looking up at Ruby and the urge to giggle rose up all over again. In my effort to restrain myself from laughing, I lost control of my senses and emitted a loud snort from my nose.

A lady in front of us jumped.

"Be quiet, girls! This is God's house!" Annie's grandma hissed in my ear.

I shifted uncomfortably and covered my mouth with my hands. My whole body hurt from fighting the urge to let rip.

All around us, people were throwing shocked glances in our direction and I was petrified that the man at the front might stop his address to tell us off.

I squeezed my eyes shut and commanded myself to be sensible. It wasn't funny anymore. In fact, it was painfully embarrassing. I tried to distract myself by thinking of something sad but the more I fought to be serious the greater the urge was to laugh. I fixed my eyes on the huge crucifix above the altar and told myself, *Think of Jesus dying on the cross. This is very, very serious.* I took deep breaths and avoided Ruby and Annie's gaze. But, every time I thought about how inappropriate it would be laugh, I started to shake all over again.

After he had read a few more things, the man said, "This is the word of the Lord," once more.

I shoved both hands into my mouth as the congregation repeated, "Thanks be to God."

Without thinking, Annie joined in with a hearty, "Thanks Peter God," and Ruby and I collapsed into hysterics again.

After that, there was another hymn so we were able to let out little giggles under the guise of singing badly.

Next, everybody lined up to do something called 'communion' which Ruby quickly explained in my ear as, "Eating bread and drinking wine to remember Jesus dying for us."

I looked at her in confusion. "What?"

"I'll explain later. Just copy everyone else."

I nodded and joined one of two orderly queues down the aisle. I craned my head to watch as we shuffled slowly to the front of the church where two couples were holding shiny bowls and silver chalices.

At the head of our line was the man I had mistaken for Jesus. As each person reached the front, he said something to them and handed them a piece of something small and white from his bowl. I couldn't tell what it was but it didn't look like any bread I had ever seen before. It looked more like flattened chunks of snow. I wondered where it had come from; perhaps from a special church shop or even from Heaven itself. I couldn't wait to taste it.

As each person received their snow bread from the man, they said something to him in reply but, try as I might, I couldn't catch what it was.

The closer our line got the more glorious and mysterious the bread appeared until I found myself salivating.

Eventually, I reached the front.

The Jesus-man raised a piece of snow bread and said, "The body of Christ, broken for you."

I gave an inaudible mumble in reply and took the bread from him. It felt rather papery between my fingers, almost like a little cardboard tiddlywink. I paused to marvel at the tiny cross etched onto it before popping it into my mouth, stepping sideways so as not to hold up the line. The moment the bread touched my tongue, the whole thing seemed to collapse in on itself. I had barely processed how it tasted[39] when it stuck to the roof of my mouth. I frowned and tried to be discreet as I unwedged it with my thumb. Then I approached one of the chalice holders, wondering what Jill would say when I told her I'd had a glass of wine that morning.

I was afraid the lady might ask to see some ID, or at least check that I knew what I was doing, but she just smiled serenely and handed me the glass. "The blood of Christ, shed for you."

I gave another garbled murmur and raised the chalice to my lips. It smelt like vinegar and I was so nervous that I took a huge gulp and ended up swallowing it the wrong way. I spluttered and retched and tried not to draw attention to myself but the people around me gave me funny looks when wine started dribbling out of my nose.

As I staggered back to my seat, I heard Annie whisper to her grandma, "I think Livi's choking on Jesus."

---

[39] A cross between an ice cream wafer and a piece of paper.

Annie's grandma looked across at me and tutted. "You're not bringing your friends again," she said to Annie.

I screwed up my nose and looked down at my feet, all previous desire to laugh gone.

Once communion was over, the congregation stood as the man said a prayer. Then we sat down again and he began a long, monotonous sermon.

I puffed out my cheeks and tried to concentrate but I kept getting distracted by the sight of the leftover bowls of snow bread at the front. I wondered whether I'd be able to take some home with me once the service was over. I thought it would be a fun game to see how long I could hold one on the edge of my tongue until it melted.

The sermon went on for quite some time and my bottom grew numb as I wriggled impatiently on the uncomfortable wooden pew.

Ruby looked rather tired beside me.

I stifled a yawn. If this was God's house, it was a little boring. The whole experience was so very different from Sunday mornings at King's Church and I had no idea what to make of it. I looked up at the giant crucifix as I prayed silently, *God, is this really how church is meant to be? You like ours better, right?*

The robed man finally completed his sermon and, after another hymn and a bit more standing around, he concluded the service with a prayer. Then he walked back up the aisle and out of the building with his procession of candle holders and stick bearers.

I was about to ask Ruby if it was finished when I saw that she had fallen asleep. I stifled a giggle before giving her a nudge.

She awoke with a grunt and exclaimed, "Wah?!"

"Shhh!" hissed Granny Button.

Ruby blushed as she told one of the few lies I have ever heard her utter: "I wasn't asleep. I was praying."

Annie's grandma sniffed and turned away.

I gave Ruby a bemused grin but she pursed her lips and muttered, "I actually *was* praying before the incense lulled me to sleep."

Around us, the congregation rose in silence and started to make their way out of the building. I grabbed Ruby's arm as we followed Annie and her grandma up the aisle. The robed man was standing at the door shaking the hands of the parishioners as they left. I approached him a little warily, unsure whether shaking his hand was a formal requirement or a divine privilege.

He took my hand in both of his. "Nice to see you."

Afraid that there was a script to follow like with the bread and wine, I looked down and mumbled something unintelligible.

The man looked at me. "Pardon?"

"I don't know what to say in this bit," I confessed.

To my relief, he gave a hearty chuckle and said, "Bless you."

"You too," I squeaked before trotting away.

Ruby didn't even stop to shake his hand. She just blushed at him and ran to catch up with me.

We found Annie outside, perched on an old headstone. "So that was my grandma's church!" she said gaily. "Did you like it?"

I forced a smile. "You should come to ours sometime."

"Okay!"

"Ours is quite different," Ruby said carefully.

"Very different," I agreed. I glanced around before adding, "Better."

A few nights after our visit to St Mary's, I had a very vivid dream. I was standing at the bank of a river where many streams met at my feet. Some of the streams flowed really fast, almost like they were being driven by a fierce wind. Others trickled along a lot more slowly, perhaps with debris or large rocks reducing the flow. One or two even looked close to drying out. Nevertheless, all the streams flowed into the same wild river. Just as I was wondering where would be the safest place to swim, somebody in white, surrounded by a light so bright that I couldn't see him, said in a loud voice, "I really love my bride."

I turned and almost fell into the river.

Immediately, I awoke with a start and switched my lamp on, the sensation of falling pulsating through my body. The light flickered, casting shifting shadows up and down my walls and, for a brief moment, I felt as though somebody was watching me.

I gripped my bed sheets in fright. "Jesus, is that you?"

As I rubbed my eyes and looked around, I started to come to my senses. I let out a sigh. It was plain that there was nothing there except for old Sausage-Legs gawping at me from the shadows.

~ 18 ~

God wants to speak to you

There was a tall man standing with Eddie and Summer as we arrived at youth group on Friday evening. He looked vaguely familiar and, to begin with, I wondered if he was off the telly. I began to indulge in a wild daydream about a famous actor coming undercover in search of teenage believers for a new documentary. It would be called *'The COOL TV Club.'*

But, when I asked Ruby about him, she giggled and said, "He's from church! He plays drums in one of the worship bands."

"Ohh," I said.

Beside me, Joey grinned and went to put his hand in mine.

Without thinking, I pulled my hand away and feigned a sneeze. We hadn't held hands in a church setting before and the thought of it made me feel a little shy. I feared that everybody else would be just like Ruby, determined not to date until old enough for marriage. I wasn't sure what Eddie and Summer would think to see us holding hands like a common couple.

Joey waited for me to settle down before reaching for my hand again.

I quickly faked another sneeze and stole a glance at Summer who, to my relief, was locked in a conversation with Grace Moore.

Joey looked at me in confusion. "Are you alright?"

"Maybe I caught your chocolate allergy," I said feebly.

Before he could reply, I pointed to Eddie who had just got everybody's attention. "We're starting now."

As the group shuffled into a circle, Nicole came up to me and whispered, "Is it true you and Joey are going out?"

"Yeah, sort of." I shifted awkwardly. I didn't know whether to be proud or whether to try and hide it.

She smiled and nudged Grace Fletcher. "I told you."

Grace Fletcher gaped at me. "I never would have guessed."

I wasn't sure whether this was a compliment or not so I gave a quick shrug and sat down, avoiding eye contact with Joey in case he tried to grab my hand again.

Once everybody was settled, Eddie indicated the tall man beside him and said, "Some of you will know my brother, Stevie. He thought he'd join us tonight."

The tall man gave a wave.

Before Eddie could continue, Violet put her hand up and asked, "Are we going to have some time at the start in case anybody has some news to share?"

Having never before asked that question, it was clear that Violet herself had some news to share.

Summer gave her a smile. "Would you like to tell us something, Violet?"

She nodded. "I got into my favourite Art College."

"Oh well done!" said Summer.

The rest of the group congratulated Violet.

She grinned and added, "Also, it's my birthday in a few weeks time and I'm having a party which will now double as my leaving party. We're hiring a hall because I'm going to be eighteen so I want it to be special. I've already asked Jim and Angela if I can borrow the overhead projector from church for my slideshow on surreal art. You're all invited!"

I sucked in my cheeks and turned to Joey. I couldn't think of anything worse than a party planned by Violet and I wanted to make it clear that, although I was friends with Ruby, I could take or leave the rest of her family.

To my surprise, he leant over and said to Ruby, "I think it's time for The Glory Seekers to make a comeback!"

Her eyes widened. "Yeah!"

I watched as they high-fived one another.

"Hey, Mark!" Joey yelled across the circle. "The Glory Seekers are reuniting for Violet's party!"

Mark grinned. "Awesome."

I gave a tentative cough. "What's 'The Glory Seekers'?"

"Our old band!" said Joey.

"Oh."

"I'm free tomorrow if you want to rehearse?" called Mark.

Joey nodded and turned to Ruby.

"Sounds good to me," she replied.

Violet looked across and gave them an approving nod. "Yes, you can play at my party," she said. "But don't sing *'Jesus be a lozenge.'* I hate that song."

I felt my cheeks go red as Joey and Ruby exchanged glances and burst out laughing.

"That's the best song!" Joey told me. "It has the line, *'Jesus be a lozenge; clear out all my junk!'*"

"Cool." I looked away as he and Ruby started reminiscing about all the songs on their old set list.

"Livi, are you free tomorrow?" Ruby asked me suddenly. "Do you want to come?"

I gave a relieved nod. "Thanks." I poked Joey. "Is that okay?"

"Of course. You've not heard me play guitar before, have you?"

I shook my head and forced a smile.

"Right then," Summer said loudly, cutting through the conversations that had erupted round the circle. "We're going to start with something a bit different today."

We stopped talking and looked at her.

"Does God speak to us?" she asked.

I joined in with the eager nodding.

"Of course God speaks to us!" Violet said haughtily.

"How does he speak to us?"

A few people put their hands up.

"Through the Bible," said Rory.

Most people put their hands back down.

"Absolutely." Summer nodded. "How else?"

"He puts things on our hearts," said Nicole. "He helps us see things differently."

Grace Moore put her hand up. "Sometimes he speaks to us through other people. Like in words of knowledge."

"Which is what?" Summer pressed.

Grace thought for a moment. "It's when the Holy Spirit tells you something that you wouldn't naturally know."

"Fantastic!" Summer looked pleased. "Grab a partner and we'll do a bit of that today."

The group burst into excited chatter as we broke into pairs. I stared at my lap in dismay. I had no idea how to hear God properly. So many of my questions to him seemed to fall to the floor unanswered. There was no way I could get through this exercise without looking stupid. I looked up to see both Ruby and Joey gazing at me.

"Who do you want to pair up with?" asked Joey.

I looked from him to Ruby and felt myself blushing. If I had to be completely honest, I kind of wanted to go with Ruby. I wouldn't have to pretend that I knew what I was doing. But I didn't want to let Joey down.

Before I could reply, Ruby said with a shrug, "It's alright. I'll go with Nicole."

"Okay," I squeaked.

Joey grinned as Summer prayed for us all. "I got a new fighting hamster this week," he whispered.

I pretended to be pleased although, inwardly, I feared that his interruption rendered Summer's prayer void since we hadn't been polite enough to even listen to it.

When she'd finished praying Summer looked round and said, "Take a moment to ask God for a word or picture for your partner."

My heart pounded as I sat with my eyes shut, willing God to say something to me. *Please, please, please speak to me, God...* For a very long moment nothing came and I almost went into a panic. Then, suddenly, the faint image of a rabbit formed in my mind. I had no idea what it meant and made a frantic attempt to attach a meaning to it[40] but every idea felt more and more ridiculous.

I waited for a while longer but I didn't get anything else and, eventually, Summer got our attention and told us to share what we'd received with our partners.

Joey looked at me expectantly. "You go first."

I squirmed as I muttered, "I could have just made it up but I saw a picture of a rabbit. I don't really know what it means..."

He gave thrilled cry. "That's amazing! My latest cartoon strip is of a rabbit!"

"Oh, okay." I still wasn't sure whether it had just been my imagination but Joey seemed pretty happy about it so I pretended to smile along. "Did you get anything for me?" I asked.

He screwed up his nose. "Just the word, 'Father.' Like, God wants to remind you that he's your Father and sometimes you forget. But I guess you know that already."

My stomach churned as I gulped and said, "Yeah... Thanks."

Summer got our attention again and asked how we had found the exercise. I didn't want to admit that I wasn't sure whether it was really God speaking or just our imaginations so I stayed quiet

---

[40] *God says you bounce like a rabbit..? God says you're cute like a rabbit...? You have the ears of a rabbit...? You eat carrots like a rabbit... Carrots... Carrot cake..? God says keep eating carrot cake...?*

149

and listened as some of the others shared what they felt God had told them. Most striking was Violet reporting that Grace Moore had given her the word, *'Litherop.'*

"That's the name of one of the halls of residences at my Art College," Violet explained. "It's like God's saying he's prepared a home for me!"

I stared at Grace Moore in astonishment. Surely that couldn't have been her imagination?

Summer was beaming. "Isn't Jesus wonderful?"

As the others nodded, Bill put his hand up and admitted, "I don't think God said anything to me."

I breathed a sigh of relief. At least I wasn't the only one.

"That's alright," Summer assured him. "It sometimes takes time to recognise his voice."

"Was I meant to hear a voice?" Bill looked rather alarmed.

"No, not necessarily," Summer said quickly. "God speaks in lots of different ways. As you get closer to him, you'll start to be more sure when it's him."

"Remember that God will never contradict the Bible," Eddie chipped in. "So make sure you weigh revelations with Scripture and, if you need to, with someone else. God is always loving and he never brings confusion." He paused and looked round at us all. "It's like getting to know any friend. You build up a history together and develop your own ways of communicating. It doesn't have to be in concrete words. Sometimes God uses pictures, or feelings, or little promptings. He even speaks to us in dreams."

I suddenly remembered my recent dream and put up my hand. "I had a weird dream..." I said. I shared my river dream with them before asking, "Was it from God?"

"It sounds like it." Eddie grinned.

"What does it mean?"

"Well... The Church is sometimes referred to as Jesus' bride."

"Which church?"

"There's only one."

"There are loads of churches!" I exclaimed. "Last Sunday, for example, Ruby and I went to our friend's grandma's church and it was really slow and boring."

I didn't add that it wasn't at all how church was meant to be and that God must surely like ours better. I'd made the mistake of saying that to Jill and she'd snorted and replied, "You've been a Christian less than six months and already you're an expert?"

"They didn't do church like we do it," I said instead.

"Maybe not," said Eddie. "Expressions of Christianity will differ throughout the world but we're all part of one Church."

Grace Moore put her hand up. "I think Livi's dream means the Church is made up of many streams and some are flowing faster than others. But we're all part of the same river and God loves us all."

A few people looked from Grace to me in intrigue. I sucked in my cheeks as I wondered what I would need to do to be as wise as Grace. I bet she read her Bible every day and never even looked at boys.

"But it was *really* boring," I insisted. "And we did this strange thing where we had to queue up to eat bread and wine. Except it wasn't real bread—"

"We do that sometimes," said Summer.

"We did it two weeks ago," Violet piped up.

I blushed. That was the week I'd gone to the festival with Joey.

Nicole grinned at me. "I went to one of those churches once. It smelt really funny."

"I know!" I agreed. "I nearly fainted."

Ruby gave a fervent nod. "A smelly church," she whispered.

Joey put his hands together and sang piously, "Hallelooooojah!"

We giggled.

Eddie got our attention. "Be careful when you think your understanding of God is the only way," he cautioned. "Or even the *best* way. God is a God of reconciliation. He longs to draw all people back to himself and all people back to one another— beginning with the Church. One of Jesus' last prayers was for his people to be united. We've been divided for far too long."

"But we *can't* be united," I argued. "Each church is so different."

Eddie laughed. "Unity is not uniformity."

I felt a little lost as I chewed this over. *'Unity is not uniformity.'* "But then how do we know what to *do*?" I asked. "What's right? What does God *want*?"

As the rest of the group started to mumble, Eddie's brother piped up, "We need to keep it simple. Seek Jesus."

I frowned. "But that doesn't really answer how to do church—"

"Keep it simple," Stevie repeated. "We make things so complicated. How are we going to reach a broken world if we're too busy bickering amongst ourselves over whether to sit or stand or eat bread in a certain way? I tell you, life's messy enough as it is. For goodness sake, let's keep church simple!" We watched as he scratched his elbow and went on, "I, like many people out there, looked at the Church and the last thing I saw was an answer to my problems. I was a lost cause, like you wouldn't believe!" He started to list things on his fingers. "I smashed up a car, I dealt drugs, I cheated on every girlfriend I ever had. I even stole a truncheon from a policeman..."

My mouth fell open. He was a real live criminal! I never would have guessed. I'd assumed the majority of people at King's Church had been Christians most of their lives, especially anybody connected with Eddie and Summer's family since they seemed so good and holy.

"I hated God," Stevie said. "And I spent a lot of time trying to convert this one to follow me in hedonism!" He gave Eddie a friendly shove. "But they got me in the end."

"How did they convince you?" Grace Fletcher asked eagerly.

My ears perked up, ready to record a blow by blow account of his conversion. If God could save *him, surely* he could save Jill.

Stevie grinned. "They just loved me."

I screwed up my nose. That sounded a bit soft.

"I started to experience Jesus through them," Stevie continued. "Whatever I did, they kept on loving me. They never gave up on me. Their love was fiercer and stronger than all my flaws and I couldn't fight it."

I stifled a yawn. I'd hoped for something a little more dramatic.

Joey nudged me and stuck his hand out, challenging me to a thumb war.

I stole a quick glance at Summer. She appeared enthralled by Stevie's story and wasn't even looking in our direction. I gave Joey a nod and gripped his hand with mine. Then I looked him in the eye and mouthed, *"Go!"*

He smirked and yanked his thumb out of reach.

We jostled around, careful to keep our hands hidden behind our knees as we fought to capture each other's thumbs. I made sure to glance up occasionally so that it wouldn't look like I had stopped concentrating. In truth, I was growing bored. We were supposed to be discussing the proper way to do church but it seemed Eddie's brother had gone off on a tangent about his own life story which didn't really shine any light on the matter. Nor was it particularly helpful in my quest to save Jill.

I stifled another yawn as he finished with the words, "Love is the most powerful weapon. It's the one thing the devil can't use. And love always wins."

At that moment I faltered slightly and Joey's thumb clamped down hard on mine.

I winced and tried to pull away.

Joey grinned. "I win!" he whispered.

"I wasn't trying," I hissed back.

"Well, we'd better end there for tonight," Eddie said from across the circle. "We seem to have run over!"

I gave a hearty nod and arose with the rest of the group, forcing a smile as I joined the others in thanking Stevie for sharing his testimony.

Summer approached me just as I was leaving. I feared that she had seen mine and Joey's thumb war after all and was going to tell me off for not concentrating through Stevie's story. But she just said, "Thanks for sharing your dream, Livi."

I shrugged. "That's okay." She kept beaming so I asked, "Was it really from God?"

"I believe so."

I gave half a smile. "Cool."

"God wants to speak to you," she continued. "I think he has lots to tell you."

I felt both thrilled and terrified at the prospect. "What do I need to do?" I asked desperately. I dug my nails into my hands as I waited for her to say, *'Read the Bible more,'* or, *'Save a few people,'* or even, *'Break up with Joey.'*

But she just grinned and said, "Listen."

I bit my lip and looked down. Maybe she didn't realise how much of a hopeless Christian I was behind the scenes. I gave a quick nod and turned to go.

"Oh, Livi?"

I turned back. "Yes?"

"Eddie's taking the twins to visit their grandparents after church on Sunday. Do you want to have lunch with me?"

"Okay..." I said. Inwardly, my heart started to pound as a nagging voice whispered, *'No, don't have lunch with Summer! She'll find out you're not as clued up as you pretend to be. Then she'll tell you off for dating Joey and ask you why you're so behind on all your Bible reading. Do you really want people interfering with your life?'* I pushed such thoughts aside, fearing that if she was so good at hearing from God, she might be able to tune in and read my mind.

She beamed. "Great. I'll see you on Sunday."

~ 19 ~

The freedom to choose

"Can I join your band?"

Ruby, Joey and Mark looked up from tuning their instruments.[41]

We were in Mark's stuffy garage where Mark had offered me an old crate to sit on. I'd spent the last half an hour watching from the side as the three of them cleared a space to rehearse and discussed which songs to play at Violet's party.

Finally, Ruby replied, "Of course! What do you play?"

"Er..." I paused and sucked in my cheeks. "The tambourine?"

Joey screwed up his nose. "Can you learn the violin?"

"By next month?" I exclaimed.

"Grace Moore learnt the flute pretty quickly."

I frowned. I wanted to make some snide comment like, *'Well, maybe she should be your girlfriend then!'* but I was afraid he might agree.

"You could make our posters?" Ruby suggested.

"Aw!" said Joey. "I've already designed a cartoon."

I pouted at him.

"Sorry," he said.

"It's fine." I sniffed. "I'll just watch."

The three of them shot me awkward smiles before turning back to their music.

I sat back in a sulk and watched as they began their rehearsal.

Their first song was about whether Jesus brushed his teeth.

'Did you wash every day?
Did you shave your beard?

---

[41] Joey had his guitar, Mark had a bass with a rainbow-coloured strap, and Ruby had a funny-looking stick which I learnt was called a piccolo.

Did you blow your nose?
Did you look kind of weird?'

I fanned myself with an old newspaper and pretended to look interested as Joey glanced across and waved.

Next was a song about Jesus feeding the five thousand. It opened with the words, *'Have you ever seen so many men eating fish?'* I pursed my lips as I imagined a swarm of fish devouring hundreds of people.

The three of them rehearsed non-stop for what felt like an eternity and barely acknowledged me the whole time. I alternated between feelings of boredom and self-pity as I wondered whether I should at least *try* to learn the violin.

At one point Ruby called across to me, "Are you okay, Livi?"

I nodded and shifted clumsily on the crate.

"The next song is one of my favourites," she said. "Listen!"

I forced a smile. "I am."

Ruby turned back to the boys and gave a firm nod.

Joey played a few chords as Ruby cleared her throat and sang, *"Jesus doesn't care about how bad you think you are. He died because he loves you even though you're very scarred..."*

Joey strummed more exuberantly as Ruby led them in the chorus. *"Jesus doesn't care, Jesus doesn't care. No matter what you've done before, Jesus doesn't care..."*

I raised an eyebrow as Mark and Joey echoed softly, *"Jesus doesn't care... Jesus doesn't care..."*

Ruby picked up her piccolo and did a little solo before beginning the second verse. *"Jesus doesn't care about how far away you've been. He died to bring you close to him, he wants to make you clean. Jesus doesn't care, Jesus doesn't care..."* She paused before belting out, *"NO! Jesus really, truly doesn't care!"*

They finished with a mighty roar and grinned at one another.

I screwed up my nose before saying tentatively, "You might want to rethink that song."

They looked at me. "Why?"

"Well..." I suppressed a smirk. "It sounds like you're saying *Jesus doesn't care.*"

"Ohh," said Joey. "We didn't think of that."

I giggled. "How about... Jesus *always* cares?"

They looked at one another as they considered it.

I waved a hand. *"Jesus always cares, Jesus always cares... Even when you're feeling lost, Jesus is always there...?"*

155

"That sounds good!" said Ruby.

Joey and Mark nodded.

"Oh, and the song about loving the leper..." I said. "It kind of sounded like you were saying '*leopard*.'"

They laughed in astonishment.

"And, in '*Jonah and the Whale*,' you might want to change the line about the '*man-eating fish*.' It gets kind of confusing when you sing it straight after the song about Jesus feeding the five thousand."

"Livi, you're amazing!" Joey exclaimed. He ran over and gave me a hug.

I almost fell off my box. "Thanks."

"Let's go though each song again," Mark suggested. "And Livi can help us make them better."

Joey and Ruby nodded and said, "Yeah!"

The rest of the rehearsal flew by. Mark found me an old deck chair to sit in and I dragged it right up to the front of the garage where I made myself comfortable in the role of director. Most of the songs were rather nice and gushy. I felt something a little more challenging would help to spice things up so I quickly jotted down a new song entitled, '*Don't go to Hell*.' It began with the words,

'Can you hear him calling to your cold and crusted heart:
"Come to me before it's too late
Believe in me, don't make me wait
You will be really sorry
Really sorry if you don't."
For the world and its desires will fade away
And what will you tell him when it's judgement day?'

I hoped that Jill would be present at Violet's party and take note. I made three copies and passed them round and Joey nodded and started strumming on his guitar. By the end of the rehearsal, something resembling a song had emerged.

"Great work, guys!" Mark said as he and Ruby made final adjustments to their set list. "This gig is going to be awesome."

Joey flung his guitar down and came trotting over to me. "Our songs are so much better now that you're in the band!"

A wave of delight rushed through me. "Thanks."

He grabbed my hand. "What are you doing tomorrow?"

"Tomorrow?" I looked at him. "Well... I was going to go to church."

"Yeah, me too," he said, although he didn't sound too sure. "Unless you'd rather hang out?" He stared at me, wide-eyed and hopeful.

I bit my lip as I considered his eager grin. I was about to say yes when I remembered my arrangements with Summer. "I can't. Summer asked me to go round hers for lunch. She'll notice if I'm not at church."

He pouted. "You don't have to go to hers. You can say you're double-booked."

I pursed my lips as I thought about it. "But what if she finds out? I think I should see what she wants."

He sniffed. "She's going to tell you to break up with me."

"She can't. I can do what I want."

"What will you do if she says, *'I'm really disappointed in you'?*" He put on a mock frown and wagged his finger at me.

My stomach churned. I hated the idea of Summer being disappointed in me. "I don't know... What *should* I do?"

"Tell her to mind her own business! It's *your* life and you've got to guard it... with your life."

I nodded. "Alright."

The following day, armed with Joey's instruction to guard my life with my life, I perched awkwardly at Eddie and Summer's kitchen table while Summer made us some sandwiches. She had bought smoked salmon especially but, at the sight of my worried expression, she said, "I also have cheese or ham, if you'd prefer?"

I nodded. "Yes please."

"Which? Cheese or ham?" She looked at me. "Or both?"

"Er... Both," I said uncertainly.

She smiled and reached into the fridge.

I glanced round the room. Above the table was an elaborate painting of the Garden of Eden. It was filled with luscious green plants and bright flowers that twinkled in the sunlight. Hundreds of animals surrounded a couple who were dancing, naked and unrestrained. In the middle of it all stood a massive tree laden with juicy-looking fruit. I gazed at the picture in awe, scanning the plethora of animals for new impressions to perfect. There was a dazzling peacock lounging by a stream and I made a mental note to research their noise when I got home.

Summer looked up from making our sandwiches. "I'm glad you were free today, Livi."

I fixed a resolute expression on my face.

"What have you been up to this week?"

I felt myself blushing as I replied, "I'm halfway through the New Testament and I run a Christian club at school and yesterday I wrote a song about Hell for The Glory Seekers."

Summer stared at me for a moment. I braced myself for her prying into my relationship with Joey but, instead, she asked, "Do you know that God is pleased with you?"

"What?"

She joined me at the table with our lunch. "On Jesus' baptism, before he'd even done anything, God declared that he was pleased with him. Did you know that?"

I shook my head and kept staring at her as she handed me my sandwich. "Thanks," I muttered.

"Do you know what that means for you?" Summer continued.

I shook my head again.

"It means you never need to do anything in order to get God's approval."

I sucked in my cheeks. "Okay."

"Most people think Christianity is all about dos and don'ts..." Summer paused before adding, "Mostly *don'ts*. But Christians ought to be known for their freedom, not their constraints, don't you think?"

I gave a cautious nod and took a nibble of my sandwich.

"Do you feel free?" Summer went on.

I looked at her in confusion, wondering whether this was a roundabout way to tell me off for dating Joey. "I don't know..." I said hesitantly. "What do you mean?"

"Do you know that God is pleased with you, no matter what you do?"

"I don't know," I repeated. "What if I don't read the Bible enough? Or if I don't pray for ages? Or if I don't save many people?" I paused before adding, "I get so stressed out about that."

"About what? About saving people?"

I nodded. "Yeah. People don't listen. It's annoying. It's like they *want* to go to Hell or something."

Summer gave me a curious look. "Do you like trying to save people?"

"No. But God wants me to, doesn't he?"

"God wants to make himself known through you," she said. "But it's him who does the saving. Just love people and keep on loving them even when they don't respond in the way you'd like."

158

I brushed past the sentimental reference to love and asked, "But how do I convince them? There's this boy at school called Rupert who's really clever. Violet had an argument with him and he started talking about all kinds of scientific theories and things. What should I tell him?"

"Don't try and win with words. It ends up being a battle of who's the cleverest. Leading someone to Christ is about reaching the heart."

I looked at her in dismay. "How do I do *that?*"

Summer grinned and pointed to my sandwich. "What does your lunch taste like?"

"Er... It's nice, thanks."

She nodded. "Describe it to me."

"Er..." I wondered whether she was testing my gratitude. "It's kind of cheesy and a little bit hammy. I can't really explain it... Do you want some?"

She grinned again. "Sometimes words aren't enough. Don't just tell people that Jesus died for them. They need to taste for themselves that the Lord is good."

I frowned. "How?"

"Love them."

I stifled a groan. I didn't have time for something as soppy as love. There had to be more cunning means. "But I want to save my sister by the summer," I blurted out. "And I don't know how. Why won't God make her believe?"

"God doesn't make anybody do anything," Summer replied. "Love isn't love without the freedom to choose." She pointed to the painting of the garden. "Why do you think God put the forbidden tree right in the middle?"

I shrugged and glanced at the picture. "I thought that was just a mistake." I blushed immediately. *Of course God doesn't make mistakes.* "But he could be a bit more obvious that he exists," I said. "What happens to the people who have never heard of Jesus? Or the nice people who just never quite get round to it? Like Ms Sorenson."

"Who's Ms Sorenson?"

"Our Personal and Social Development teacher." I sighed before adding, "I kind of wish she was my mum." I paused. "Is my mum in Heaven?"

Summer gave a kind smile. "I don't know, Livi. But I know God loves her more than you'll ever know. I know he made her and

159

cried with her and laughed with her and will have pursued her every day of her life."

I swallowed hard. "But what if she's in Hell? Why did God let her die? I could have saved her if she'd lived." A tear trickled down my cheek and I hastily rubbed it away.

Summer leant over and squeezed my arm. "There are lots of questions I can't answer," she whispered. "But you need to know that God loves you and every single person in this world perfectly, passionately and relentlessly."

I nodded and wiped my eyes.

"And you don't need to do anything to try to earn his love," she added. "You were saved for free, by grace. All you did was believe! Don't try to earn it now."

I nodded again and let out a long sigh. "Okay," I whispered. "Thanks."

We sat in silence for a bit until Summer asked, "Is there anything else you want to talk about?"

I opened my mouth and closed it again. Eventually I said, "What about Joey?"

Summer tilted her head slightly. "What about him?"

"Did you know we're sort of a couple?"

She smiled. "I gathered that."

I shifted uncomfortably. "Well, is it alright?"

"What do you think?"

"I don't know. Sometimes I feel like it's wrong but I asked God whether I had to break up with Joey and he hasn't made me do anything."

"Why do you sometimes think it's wrong?"

"Just something Ruby said at the beginning." I blushed and corrected myself, "Actually it was something her *little brother* said. *'Anything that helps your relationship with Jesus is good and anything that hinders it is bad.'*"

"Good advice from Ruby's brother."

"He's four," I said dumbly.

Summer chuckled before looking at me very seriously. "Is your relationship with Joey bringing you closer to Jesus?"

I thought about it. "Not particularly."

"Is it driving you away?"

"No... Although, I suppose I sometimes think about Joey more than Jesus. Like..." I shrugged. "Sometimes I just want to miss church and see Joey instead. But we did once and I felt kind of guilty." I didn't add that I had almost stood her up to do it again.

Summer raised her eyebrows. "Do you like coming to church? Or do you just do it because you think you have to?"

"I like it!" I insisted. "But I also think I have to..."

"Whatever you do for God, do it out of love. Not because you think you have to. God values your friendship more than your obedience."

I blinked at her. "My friendship?"

"He loves you enough to let you choose what to do."

"Even whether or not to break up with Joey?"

"If he wanted slaves he wouldn't need our permission."

I was confused. "What?"

"He won't make you do anything."

"So... If I wanted to see Joey more than going to church..."

"He'd let you choose."

I sucked in my breath and sat back. I was stunned. Summer had offered me what I thought I'd wanted: the freedom to date Joey without anybody interfering and the reassurance that God wasn't going to come down and smite me. Yet, instead of feeling relieved, I felt utterly dismayed. "But... I don't understand," I muttered. "Is it right for me and Joey to date or not?"

Summer chuckled. "Why don't you ask God what he wants for you?"

"I did. I asked him for a sign."

"What kind of sign?"

I bit my lip. "I asked him to make one of my bracelets disappear if he didn't want me and Joey to be together." When Summer didn't reply, I added, "One time, I thought he'd done it... But then I found it under my bed."

Summer gave a thin smile. "Why don't you ask without setting the agenda? Just ask him what he wants you to do?"

"When? Now?"

"If you want."

"Can I pray in my head?"

"Of course."

I squeezed my eyes shut and prayed, *Okay, God. What do you want me to do about Joey? I don't know.* Immediately, a heaviness set in my heart and I felt a little sick. I opened my eyes and stared at Summer. "He didn't speak in any big way," I admitted. "But I just have this uneasy feeling. Like, I kind of think I *should* break up with Joey. But I don't know if I want to."

Summer nodded. "Did you want to talk about anything else?" She got up and started to clear our plates away. "Do you want another drink?"

"But what about Joey?" I demanded. "Should I break up with him or not?"

She looked at me. "What do you think?"

"It's too hard to work out! Just tell me what to do and I'll do it."

To my annoyance, Summer almost laughed. "I can't. That would be law. You're under grace."

"So I could keep going out with Joey if I wanted to?" I snapped. "You're not going to stop me? And God's not going to stop me either?" It sounded absurd. Surely Summer ought to be warning me about the dangers of disobeying God. I frowned as I asked hotly, "What if I got really serious with Joey and, you know, *did stuff* with him?"

Summer chewed her bottom lip. "Well... Our actions always have consequences. So I'd advise you to think very carefully about your choices. But God will still want you." She paused before asking, "How much do *you* want *God?*"

"I want him completely!"

"Sometimes that costs."

I rubbed my head.

"God can't give you his best unless you let him," Summer continued softy. "He won't force himself on you. And, sometimes, we have to give things up in order to get what he really wants to give us."

I blinked quickly and looked down. "But what if he makes me give up all my friends? What if he tells me I can't be a writer? What if I give up Joey and never have a boyfriend ever again?"

"You mean *what if God can't be trusted?*" She tapped the slithering serpent wrapped round the tree in the painting and whispered, "Oldest trick in the book."

I bit my knuckles as I considered her words. "But I like Joey," I protested. "And we're not doing anything *wrong*. Plus, Joey will be upset if I break up with him."

"Do you trust God with your whole life, even the really tricky bits?"

I sighed. "I want to trust him with all of it... But what if he makes me—"

"He won't make you do anything! He has good plans for you! Better plans that you could make for yourself. So many Christians don't really believe that. They love God and they trust him, but not completely. There's always something they keep out of his reach." I went to argue but Summer concluded, "Aim higher, Livi. You're destined for great things and I'd hate to see you play small. But God won't make you do anything. And neither will I. It's your choice."

I sat back in my seat, my head reeling. Although doing anything about it terrified me, the realisation sunk in that dating Joey really wasn't God's best plan for my life right now. But God wasn't angry with me. Nor was he going to make me do anything. It was completely my choice. I sniffed and rubbed my eyes, feeling utterly overwhelmed. "Maybe I just need more faith," I muttered.

Summer leant over and enveloped me in a massive hug. "You don't need more faith," she whispered. "You need more love."

~ 20 ~

Light a candle

I couldn't wait for Ms Sorenson's class. Our biographies were due and a certain somebody was finally about to get her comeuppance!

"Have you got Caroline's biography?" I asked Ruby gleefully on the way to school.

She gave a slow nod and patted her bag.

"Let me read it!" I exclaimed, holding out my hands.

Ruby squirmed and dug out her work.

Contrary to my suggestion, the front cover was not the photo of Caroline in a nappy. Instead, Ruby had drawn a picture of the Loch Ness Monster underneath the words, *'Caroline MacBrodie. Something real is hiding in the depths.'*

I raised an eyebrow. "That's a bit cryptic. But I'm sure it works..." I grinned at her and flicked to a random page.

She went pink as I read aloud, *"The divorce was not Caroline's fault. Neither was her mother's move to France or her father's choice to take up a series of Romanian mistresses. Although she didn't always feel it, Caroline was definitely as special as her two brothers, whose names I have forgotten..."* I looked up in confusion. "I don't get it. This is your great chance to make her pay."

Ruby shrugged. "I don't want to."

I was aghast. "Why not?"

"I was thinking about what Eddie's brother said the other night. Love is the one thing the devil can't use. And love always wins."

I opened my mouth and closed it again. "But still," I muttered, prodding her work. "We planned it... What about all our research? It was a complete waste of time!"

"No it wasn't," Ruby insisted. "Without it, I wouldn't have realised how sad Caroline must be."

I bit my lip. "She's not going to thank you for it."

Ruby gave a hopeful smile. "She might."

Despite mine and Annie's desperate pleas, Ruby refused to change her account of Caroline's life. She even kept it locked in her locker all day, afraid that we might get hold of it and make some alterations.

"I don't get it," Annie whined over lunch. "Caroline is really nasty. Why do you want to be nice to her?"

"Because Jesus told us to love our enemies," Ruby explained. "Caroline is our enemy so I want to love her."

Annie gave her a long look before saying, "Oh. Alright then... If that's what Jesus says..."

I rolled my eyes. It wasn't as simple as that.

To make matters worse, I tripped over on my way into Ms Sorenson's classroom and toppled sideways into Caroline's humungous chest.

She pushed me to the floor and sneered, "No thanks. I've got a boyfriend."

I turned and frowned at Ruby, my cheeks burning with anger.

Ruby gave me a sheepish smile and hurried to her seat.

Once everybody had sat down, Ms Sorenson rose from behind her desk and stood in the middle of the room. She waited for total silence before asking, "Do you all have your biographies?"

We nodded and waited for her to come and collect them.

Instead she said, "Great. Give it to your partner."

An anxious excitement filled the room as we looked at one another and exchanged our work.

Ms Sorenson cleared her throat. "Now then, you have before you your very own biography, as told by one of your peers. I want you to read it and spend some time thinking about your life up to this point. Then you've got till the end of term to write the rest of it."

"You mean the rest of our lives?" I asked in surprise. "Including how we die?"

Ms Sorenson nodded.

"But it hasn't happened yet," Annie said dumbly.

Our teacher smiled. "I know." She paused before adding, "You only have one life. This is your chance to think about where it's heading."

A collective murmur took hold of the class, followed by the sound of rustling paper as we turned curiously to the accounts of our lives to date.

I looked down at the biography Annie had written for me. She had plastered the front cover with feathers surrounding what looked like another mangled brain cut out from one of Mr Button's psychology magazines.

"What's with the brain?" I whispered, hoping Annie might say it was because I was the cleverest person she knew.

She beamed. "Because your surname is Starling. It's like, you know, 'Bird brain.'"

From the eager expression on her face it seemed this was supposed to be a compliment so, feeling a little nervous about the rest of the content, I forced a smile and turned to the first page.

'The first animal noise Livi Starling ever made was of a tiny baby mammal being born. I wasn't there, but I expect it sounded a bit like this: Wahhhhhhh!'

I chuckled to myself and flicked through. Other than describing Aunt Claudia as my *'favourite fun and friendly aunt,'* it was surprisingly accurate.

To my relief, Annie hadn't gone into much detail about my father, choosing instead to write, *'I could tell you a bit about Livi's dad. But it isn't his story, so I won't.'*

"Hey, this is really good," I whispered.

She looked up from the account of her own life.[42] "Ruby helped me," she whispered back.

I grinned before glancing across the room at Ruby. She was looking less than impressed with what Caroline had written about her.[43]

Beside her, Caroline was staring blankly at Ruby's work. She looked rather uncomfortable and the tips of her ears had gone bright pink.[44]

---

[42] She seemed to be enjoying my anecdote about all her hair being chopped off and made into a hedgehog.

[43] "She said I was born with webbed feet and the parts of a boy!" she complained later.

[44] She didn't say anything at the time although, later, with her friends, she claimed it was a *'poorly written piece of trash by an insignificant speck of a person.'* Ruby, to her credit, took this in her stride and simply whispered, "Jesus loves you, Caroline MacBrodie."

Ruby gave her a careful look before glancing across at me.

I shrugged and turned back to my own biography. I read through to the end where Annie had concluded with the words,

'And that was the story of our feisty heroine, Livi Starling. Right up to the moment where she reads about her life in her own biography. Spooky or what?'

I smiled to myself and pulled the lid off my pen. I couldn't wait to write about the rest of my life and immediately decided that I would start with the end. The only question was, could I stomach a gruesome death or should I opt for something a little more dreamy? I sketched out a large oval tombstone and tapped my pen against my teeth as I wondered what it should say...

'Here lies Livi Starling, who was swallowed by a lion in the prime of her life...' 'A memorial to Livi Starling, who vanished mysteriously whilst orbiting space...' 'You are standing on the bones of Livi Starling who died in the middle of writing a poem...'

I gave Annie a nudge. "Hey Annie, how do you want to die?"

She looked at me in dismay and indicated the blank piece of paper in front of her. "Die?" she muttered. "I don't even know how I want to *live.*"

I opened my mouth and closed it again. Then I folded up the sketch of my tombstone and pulled out a new piece of paper. I let out a long, slow sigh. *How did I want to live?* That was a much better question.

That evening, my dad rang with a bombshell.

"The wedding's off."

"What?" I stared at the phone in shock.

Dad gave an awkward cough and said, "Yeah... Erica consulted a psychic who said we didn't have the right chemistry."

"Right..."

I didn't know whether I was relieved or irritated. For the past few weeks their wedding had been looming on the horizon like an ominous iceberg and I'd fretted constantly over how it would feel to watch my father profess his undying affection to Erica and whether I'd be able to cope with any emotions that might surface. I'd wondered whether to go in boldly and introduce myself to all his friends as *'the daughter Charlie abandoned,'* or whether to just sit quietly at the back. I'd even considered not turning up at all just so that I could finally be the one to bail out on *him*. Now, even the chance to choose not to see him had been taken away from me. I couldn't help but feel rejected all over again.

"I thought I should tell you," Dad continued. "I figured you'd want to know."

"Well, obviously," I muttered. "There's no point in me coming if the wedding's not happening..." I waited to see if he might suggest meeting up anyway, for the sheer delight of seeing one another again.

But all he said was, "Right. Well, I'd better go. I've got six boxes of blue stones to return."

I hung up and let out a frustrated sigh. Then I wandered into the living room where Jill was watching a trashy soap opera. She looked bored and miserable. By her feet sat a pile of neglected work. I knew that she was depressed (as usual) because I'd heard her moaning to Aunt Claudia on the phone that afternoon.

She gave a glum smile. "Hi."

"The wedding's off," I told her.

Jill looked at me in surprise. "How come?"

"Something about a psychic."

She snorted. "Psychic? What an idiot."

"Indeed," I said. "But, actually, any path outside of Jesus is just as idiotic."

Jill glared at me. "Livi, don't preach, please."

"It's true!"

She shook her head and turned the volume up on the television.

"You need Jesus." I pointed to her pile of work. "Your whole life is a mess without him."

She ignored me.

I put my hands on my hips and went to stand in front of the TV. "If you don't turn to Jesus, you *will* go to Hell."

Jill gave an angry roar before flinging the remote control across the room. "I don't care!" she shrieked, her face red with fury. "Please shut up about it."

A lump caught in my throat as I searched for the right words to say. None came so, in the end, I ran up to my room and threw myself on my bed. Tears streamed down my cheeks as I hugged myself into a ball and tormented myself over and over with my inability to save Jill. I eventually composed myself and reached for my phone to call Summer. But, as soon as she answered, I burst into tears all over again.

"What's wrong, Livi?" she asked in concern.

I began to blubber as I told her about my conflict with Jill. "I can't save her! I just can't do it! She's been depressed since forever and I know God will help her but she won't listen to me. I told her that if she doesn't turn to Jesus she's going to go to Hell but she said she didn't care. I don't know what to do..."

Summer listened carefully before saying, "Sometimes we can bring someone the right message at the wrong time. Sometimes telling people how lost they are is a bit like walking up to them and telling them that they stink."

"But I'm right!" I exclaimed through sobs. "Aren't I?"

"Yes, Livi, you are. But it's not always about *being* right. You have to *do* right too."

I blew my nose heavily. "What?"

"*Sometimes,*" Summer insisted, "people just need to know God loves them."

"I've told her! I've told her so many times."

"I'm sure you have. But have you shown her?"

I opened my mouth and took a deep breath. Snot dripped down my face as I considered Summer's words.

"Most people already know that they stink," she continued. "They don't need you to shame them by pointing it out. You can't just yell at people until they believe."

My heart sunk as I realised that was pretty much what I had done to Jill over the past few weeks.

"Jesus loves your sister," Summer went on. "If you really want to help her, then you need to love her too."

I bit my lip in shame. Perhaps, in the early days, I had wanted to save Jill out of love. But now it was just pride; wanting to prove her wrong and shout, *'In your face!'* when she finally conceded that Jesus was real.

Summer paused before adding, "The Christian life isn't easy. But it *is* simple: Love God and let him change you; love others and let God change *them.*"

I dragged a hand across my face as her words danced through my mind. She made it sound so straightforward, as if the whole world could be mended with a good dose of love. But what on earth does that kind of love look like? And how do you love people who are so difficult to love? People like my dad or Caroline MacBrodie?

I immediately thought of Ruby and what it must have cost her to write such a nice biography for Caroline. Not only was Caroline dismissive of Ruby's gesture, but I had ridiculed her all the way home.

"I can't love," I whispered. "I'm not as nice as that."

Summer thought for a moment. "Ask Jesus and he'll help you."

Tears rolled down my cheeks. "But I've failed him so much! Why would he want to help me?"

"Because he loves you," she said. "And it doesn't depend on you. It depends on him."

"But—"

"God is good because of *his* faithfulness, not yours."

I let this sink in.

"It all comes down to love," Summer concluded. "Nothing beats it."

"Because love is the one thing the devil can't use," I muttered.

"Exactly! So when you find yourself facing a battle, don't curse the darkness. Light a candle."

I sighed. My head was growing heavy. "I'll try."

"You're doing well," she assured me. "Keep going."

"Thanks," I said weakly.

I hung up and leant against my bed. I wanted to run downstairs and tell Jill I was sorry. But deep shame rooted me to the spot and all I could do was bury my head in my hands and cry.

All of a sudden, my bedroom light went out and I sat bolt upright in panic. I heard Jill swearing downstairs as the television shut down. I glanced out of my window and saw that every house on the street was in darkness. A power cut must have hit our estate. In the eerie silence that followed, I was sure I could sense something lurking in the darkness, waiting to jump out at me. I was about to freak out and run downstairs but I had barely reached the landing before a sudden wave of peace washed over me.

Downstairs, Jill was muttering angrily as she ransacked the cupboards for a torch. "Stupid power cut... One thing after another..."

I took a deep breath and put a hand to my beating chest, tiptoeing back to my room as Summer's words echoed in my brain. *'Don't curse the darkness. Light a candle.'*

~ 21 ~

Who do you want to be?

Annie was supposed to have interviewed Old Budgie about the highlights of his long life to give us inspiration for the rest of our biographies. She met us in our form room the next morning with a huge beam on her face.

"Did you ask him?" I said eagerly.

"No," she exclaimed. "He died."

Ruby and I gasped. "Sorry," we muttered.

"It's alright," Annie assured us. "Right at the end, I told him about Jesus and he asked him into his life."

My mouth fell open.

"Wow," said Ruby. "That's amazing!"

I nodded. "How did you convince him?"

Annie cocked her head to one side. "I didn't really... I just asked him if he was ready to meet Jesus and he started crying and said he needed God to forgive him."

"What for?" we asked curiously.

Annie shrugged. "I don't know. He just said, *'Jesus, Jesus...'* and then he died."

I let out a long, slow breath. So Old Budgie had died and taken all his secrets with him. What had his dying thoughts been? Only God knew. I felt a pang of regret at never bothering to get to know him. I cleared my throat. "Are you still going to sing *'My Way'* at his funeral?"

Annie shook her head. "I think I'm going to sing *'Away in a Manger'* instead."

"Away in a Manger?"

"It was the only Jesus song he knew. Isn't it cool that God saved him just in time?"

"Yeah!" Ruby and I agreed.

"He'll be in Heaven right now," Annie continued dreamily. "I bet he's having a wonderful time."

Ruby smiled. "How old was he?"

"Ninety eight. And he'd never been to church in his life. Can you believe it?"

I sucked the insides of my cheeks as I marvelled at how patient God must have been throughout this man's long life. I could hardly bear to be in the same room as him, as decrepit and dying as he was, but God had been waiting with grace and tender mercy right to the very end.

Keen to make a start on the rest of my biography,[45] I ignored Fester's introduction to factors and spent the whole of Maths wondering what to do with my life.

I was having trouble writing the next part of my story. For one thing, I couldn't decide what to write about Joey. I chewed my pen as I wondered how long our relationship ought to last. Should I write that we grew up and got married? Or would I rather have something dramatic happen like him cheat on me or die in a fire? I rubbed my head and shuddered. With the power entirely in my hands, what did I want? Was Joey the person I wanted to share my life story with? The one I would grow old with? The one I imagined when I gazed at the moon on cloudless nights wondering if my future husband was out there, staring at the same moon, and dreaming of me too? Was that Joey? Would he love me right? Would we make history together? Was he the one God had chosen for me since the beginning of time? And, if not, then *how much* of my life did I want to share with him? He already had my first kiss. I spread out the pile of paper before me. How many more pages should I give him? I put my head in my hands.

Ruby glanced at me. "What are you thinking about?"

"Joey," I muttered.

She raised her eyebrows. "What about him?"

I sniffed. "Do you think I should break up with him?"

"I don't know. It's your choice."

I gave a growl and flicked my work. "That's what Summer said."

Ruby stayed quiet for a bit. Eventually she said, "If you think you should... Then maybe you should."

---

[45] There are less than three weeks left till the end of term and, since this will be my last ever assignment for Ms Sorenson, I'm desperate to make her proud.

I stared straight ahead. "Don't you ever wish you had a boyfriend?"

"Nope. Not yet."

I waited but Ruby didn't continue. "Why not?" I asked finally.

As I turned to her, Ruby gave a coy shrug and said, "My mum always says to me, *'You're a little carrot of a very high price. Don't give yourself away.'*"

I let out a splutter. "What?"

Ruby blushed. "Once a carrot gets bruised, it can't get un-bruised." I stifled a laugh but she ignored me and added, "One of the best things I can give my future husband is my purity."

The smirk fell off my face. "Oh."

"A kiss is never just a kiss."

"Hmmm." I turned back to my work, wishing I hadn't said anything in the first place.

Ruby didn't get the hint and ploughed on, "I want to get as close as possible to holiness rather than as close as possible to what I can get away with."

I felt my cheeks grow red. "Obviously."

"So that's why I'm waiting."

"Alright," I said quickly. "I get it."

Ruby paused. "I'm not judging you." She smiled and returned to her work.

I sniffed and gathered up my paper, determining not to think about it. I tried to fix my mind on the rest of my life instead. Immediately, I felt sick. The uncertainty was so depressing. I knew that I wanted to be a famous writer and perhaps own a horse or two but I hadn't planned much further than that. I started to draw a picture of a horse but found myself growing anxious over how long horses live and whether they incur expensive medical bills. At what point in my life story would the horse die? And what if I fell off it and lost both my legs? With endless blank sheets of paper in front of me, the future began to feel incredibly daunting and almost futile. I started thinking about Old Budgie and envied him being in Heaven and free from the troubles of this world.

I nudged Ruby. "What's Heaven like?"

She grinned. "It's like the best thing you can imagine, only better! Everyone is happy and your body is all glorified and there's no pain, or sadness, or fear, or anything bad. You get to hang out with Jesus forever and ever."

I sat back and gave a heavy sigh. If Heaven is so amazing then what could I possibly do on earth that would compare? What was the point in dreaming of having a nice house or a horse or a great career if, all the while, a better reality was waiting for me elsewhere? I began to feel a little annoyed. If Heaven is so much better than this life, then why doesn't God just take us straight there as soon as we believe? Why does he make us wait around?

"I'm glad you guys told me about Jesus," Annie said suddenly.

I gave a quick smile. "Me too."

"Do you realise that if you hadn't led me to Jesus, then I wouldn't have led Old Budgie?"

My heart leapt at her words. I felt a lump forming in my throat as I realised that, despite shying away from having anything to do with Old Budgie, somehow— by God's grace— I was still a part of his story. Right at this very moment, a man who had been redeemed and saved in the nick of time was dancing through the streets of Heaven and it was, *in part,* because of me.

I sucked in my breath. *So that's why I'm still here: to tell people about Jesus.* I bit my lip before correcting myself, *No! To LOVE them to Jesus, like Summer said.*

I made a firm resolution that I would spend my life loving as many people as possible and pulled out a fresh piece of paper to jot down some notes.

'At the age of ninety eight, Livi Starling won a Nobel prize for Love, having led hundreds of people to Jesus through the power of kindness...'

I smiled and drew a picture of myself with a massive heart.

My daydreaming was interrupted by the sound of Caroline and Kitty arguing at the side of the room.

"I'm totally as pretty as you," Kitty said haughtily.

"You wish!" Caroline retorted. "I'm a model, remember?"

Without thinking, I exchanged a mocking grimace with Ruby and Annie. Then I glanced back at my manifesto of love and immediately felt uneasy. Loving people was easy in theory, when they didn't have a face or a voice or any way to bother me. But I still wasn't any clearer on what it meant in practise.

I scribbled over my notes. Did I really want to love *all* people? Even the ones who would never, ever love me in return? I put my head in my hands as I muttered a hasty prayer. *God, if you really want me to love people, you're going to have to teach me how...*

~*~

Despite not fully expecting an answer to my prayer, and certainly not so soon, God decided to show me a little of what love looked like through a very unlikely candidate: Violet Rico.

I'd stopped to put my biography in my locker before lunch and had told Ruby and Annie I would meet them in the canteen. On my way, I took a short cut through the sixth form common room where I came across Violet who was surrounded by a bunch of girls in her year. They looked pretty angry and Violet was close to tears as one of them leant over and poked her. Although I couldn't hear what was being said, I was pretty sure that whatever had happened was probably Violet's fault. I kept my head down and attempted to dodge past without her spotting me. As it happened, she didn't spot me. But somebody else did: Jesus.

As soon as I left the common room, I felt him prompting me, *Go back and help Violet.* It wasn't a voice, as such, just a very strong feeling.

I shook my head. *That can't be God. He wouldn't ask me to do something so stupid.*

It came again, even stronger. *Go back and help Violet.*

By this point, I was halfway to the canteen. Ruby and Annie were expecting me. It would be rude to keep them waiting.

Go back and help Violet.

But God! She's dressed all in pink. She looks like a giant pimple.

His reply pierced like a sword. *She's mine.*

"I thought you liked me!" I said desperately. "Please don't make me look like an idiot!"

But the prompting wouldn't go away.

Even as I reached the canteen and went to open the door, I knew— I just *knew*— I needed to go back. So, muttering and groaning and calling God all sorts of names, I turned on my heels and marched all the way back to where Violet was being ripped to shreds. The girls were in the middle of taunting Violet for her shoes.[46]

---

[46] To be fair, they *were* rather strange: they looked like a pair of wellies which had been cut off at the ankles and spray-painted pink.

175

I lingered behind them and wondered what to do. Just as Violet finally cracked and burst into tears, I tapped the nearest girl on the shoulder and said in a loud voice, "Hey!"

The girl turned and glared at me. I braced myself for an almighty beating.

She looked me up and down before snarling, "What?"

"Leave Violet alone," I squeaked.

The girl looked at her friends and burst out laughing.

Behind them, Violet gaped at me through petrified eyes.

I had no idea what to do next so I raised my fists and said, "If you don't leave her alone... I might punch you, or something." A little nagging voice told me that probably wouldn't be very loving but I shoved it aside, my legs shaking like jelly as I tried to look tough.

As the girl snorted and came towards me, words from my unwritten biography danced through my mind. *'And Livi Starling died after picking a fight with Violet Rico's bullies.'*

I squeezed my eyes shut but, before I was annihilated, I heard a booming voice from the common room doorway, "Livi Starling!"

I looked up to see Mr Riley striding towards me.

"Hello Sir," I said, breathing a sigh of relief.

"What are you doing in the sixth form common room?"

I gave a nervous splutter. "Just saying hello to Violet."

Mr Riley shook his head and took hold of my shoulder before escorting me out of the building.

The mean girls stared after me, muttering to one another. Behind them, Violet shot me a thankful smile before slipping away.

Once outside, Mr Riley gave me a grand telling off and threatened to give me a detention. As he headed back into the sixth form common room, he turned and called loudly over his shoulder, "Don't let me catch you in here again. You can see Violet when school is over."

At that very moment, Caroline and her gang walked past and burst into raucous laughter. *"Freaky Von Freakshow loves Rainbow Drip!"* they sang.

I scowled and looked away, waiting until they were out of sight before letting myself cry. "God, why did you make me do that?" I said angrily. "Don't you love me?"

I love you completely, Livi.

I leant against the wall. "Then why did you make me do that? I feel so stupid."

Instead of answering my question, I felt God ask, *Who do you want to be?*

I blinked. *What?*

I know you, Livi.

I blinked again. *What?*

Just as I was tempted to conclude that God wasn't speaking to me after all and that this whole exchange was simply a product of my warped imagination, a heavy presence suddenly descended upon me. I was almost thrown off my feet by the overwhelming sensation of being known by God. I wanted to laugh and cry both at the same time and had to grip onto a nearby drainpipe to keep myself from falling over. Without warning, a vision of Violet danced before my eyes. She was dressed exactly as she'd been in the common room but, instead of looking like a giant pimple, she looked like a radiant flower. I gasped aloud at how captivating she was. Even more astounding was the intense compassion that I felt for her. I found myself almost breaking down in the middle of the playground as I made my way to the canteen. This was hugely embarrassing. I knew nobody would understand if I tried to explain that I was crying because Violet Rico looked so beautiful dressed all in pink.

God, what are you doing to me?

His answer made my stomach lurch. *I'm answering your prayer.*

"What?" I said aloud.

I'm showing you how I see Violet.

I was about to say that I hadn't prayed for that but was immediately reminded of my appeal for God to teach me how to love. I hadn't meant like *this*... I wanted to protest, '*Haven't you met Violet? She's so annoying!*' But how could I argue with the one who had made her?

I stumbled onto a nearby bench and wept as God continued to show me glimpses of his endless love for Violet. I began to see her as God saw her, beyond all the brokenness and awkwardness and offence and striving. I knew that this stunning flower was how he saw Violet and, oh, how he longed for her to see who she truly was.

As I marvelled at how very different this Violet was to the one I knew, a series of images flashed through my mind. I saw Violet as a small child lost in a supermarket and crying with fear at the thought that her family had left her behind. I saw her being ridiculed for being the last in her class to learn how to write her name. I saw her sobbing after a misguided teacher mistook her

177

desire to finish her work quickly for sloppiness. I saw her wracked with guilt after pushing Ruby off a swing and later cutting the hair off her own favourite doll in a vain attempt to make amends. I saw her looking utterly petrified as she stood by a hospital bed wondering whether her mother was going to die. I saw her holding her baby brother, Oscar, and believing that her parents loved him more than her because he was spoilt and a miracle baby. I saw her alone in her bedroom vowing to be strong after being taunted over and over by bullies who found her strange. With each new image that came into my mind, it was like being plunged deeper and deeper into Violet's heart. A battle raged within me as I felt the weight of her sadness, her fears and her insecurities warring against God's love and desire to see her whole and free.

"I don't know Violet like this..." I confessed, huge tears dripping down my cheeks.

She doesn't either, I felt God prompt softly. *But I do. I know her.* I gulped as God repeated in a whisper, *I know Violet. And I know you. I know everyone. Others may ask what you plan to do with your life, but I care about who you ARE.* There was a weighty pause, then God continued, *When you stand before me at the end of time, I won't ask how many people you saved or how successful your career was. But what will matter very much to me is the measure of your love.*

I nodded, feeling thankful and overwhelmed, barely noticing when Ruby and Annie came and sat beside me.

"Livi?" Ruby waved a hand in front of my face. "Are you alright?"

I wiped away a tear. "I just... I was just being Violet."

"You're not Violet," Annie said slowly. "You're *Livi,* remember?"

"Yes," I said. "Livi. That's who I want to be."

~ 22 ~

Let's be Jesus

Jill and I hadn't spoken properly since our regretful confrontation a few nights earlier. Part of me wondered whether to raise the issue and try to apologise. But, for fear of making her angry all over again, I decided to behave as though everything was normal. I sat sprawled out on the living room floor, my schoolwork splattered before me, as I attempted to make headway with my biography. Jill was sitting on the sofa, alternating between doing work of her own and flicking aimlessly through a magazine.

I shot her the odd glance before clearing my throat. "Jill?"

She looked up. "Yes?"

I pointed to my work. "Annie was going to ask her great uncle about his life so we'd know what kind of things are important and what to avoid. But he died. I know you're not really old, but I suppose you're old compared to me, so I'll ask you instead: What's your biggest regret?"

Jill looked affronted and turned away. "Don't ask."

"Why not?"

She ran a hand across her forehead and said nothing.

I got up from the floor and took a tentative step towards her. "Are you alright?"

She shook her head and stayed silent.

"Jill? You've been kind of sad for ages. What's wrong?"

She blinked quickly and avoided my gaze.

"What's wrong?" I repeated. "Tell me."

"Really?" She looked at me. "You really want to know what's wrong?"

"Er... Yeah," I said uncertainly.

She grabbed a tissue and blew her nose. Then she put a hand to her cheek and started to cry. I waited patiently and wondered what I was getting myself into.

Eventually, she said quietly, "I hate being alone."

"You're not alone," I said. "You've got me."

She shook her head. "I *am* alone..."

"No you're not! Maybe we don't spend as much time together as we used to, but you're not *alone.*"

"Livi—"

"I know I'm busy a lot and, okay, you don't have as many friends as I do. But you shouldn't compare yourself to me—"

"You don't get it," she whimpered. Before I could protest again, she said, "I want a man."

I stopped in my tracks. "Oh..." I said slowly. "You *are* alone."

I watched as Jill let out a sob and reached for another tissue.

My heart pounded as I sat beside her. *Please Jesus,* I prayed. *Help me love Jill like you love her. Help me stop trying to save her— that's your job. Help me just love her...*

In that instant, God began to answer my prayer and the feeling of calm melted over me as I gazed at my sister as though through fresh eyes. I saw that she was frustrated and lonely and really quite afraid. Deep down, it wasn't true that she didn't believe in God. She was simply angry with him for the way her life had turned out and, every time I mentioned Jesus, all I did was rub salt in her wounds. A lump caught in my throat as I glimpsed God's unceasing compassion for Jill's heartache despite her constant rejection of him. Before I could lose my nerve, I said very quickly, "Jill, please don't shout but... can I pray for you?"

She half shook her head before saying flippantly, "If you want."

My heart beat rapidly. "Now?"

Jill looked taken aback. "If you want," she repeated.

"Okay." I got to my feet and then sat back down again. I wasn't sure where to start. "Er..." I closed my eyes, hoping Jill would take that as a hint to close hers too. I didn't want her watching while I did this. "Dear God, thank you for Jill... Erm... Please will you give her a man..." I paused and opened my eyes.

Jill had her eyes shut and was looking serious.

I took a deep breath and finished, "And, please let him be someone who treats her nicely and who she really likes. Amen."

Jill opened her eyes. "Thanks, Livi," she muttered, turning back to her magazine.

I grinned, feeling relief and a little self-confidence wash over me. "Any time!"

~*~

It was a hot and humid night and I lay awake for hours, tossing and turning as I thought about how little I had sought to truly *know* Jill these past few months. I'd been proud and unforgiving in my ruthless attempts to convert her, never once realising that God was nowhere near as angry or impatient as me. I saw, clearer than ever, that all the clever words in the world are really not enough if I never learn to love people from the heart. I kicked my bed sheets to the floor as I wondered what I could do to show love to Jill— *real love*— for the sole purpose of being kind and without expecting anything in return. I debated sneaking downstairs and doing all her work for her but I quickly saw a flaw in that plan: *I don't know enough about chicken.* I chewed my bottom lip and tried to remember the last time Jill hadn't had to worry about work. I realised it had been years since she'd had a real break. "That's it!" I said, sitting up in my bed. "I'll give Jill a holiday."

I reached for my phone and rang Ruby.

Her phone rang seven times before she answered with a sleepy grunt. "Hello?"

"It's me! I've had an idea."

Ruby yawned before muttering, "What time is it?"

I glanced at my alarm clock. "Er... Half two... But this is really important."

Ruby sounded concerned as she asked, "What's up?"

I told her about my conversation with Jill and my desire to do something loving for her. "I thought I could take her on holiday. She's never been on a plane before. I was thinking somewhere like Spain."

Ruby thought for a moment. "That sounds nice. How are you going to afford it?"

I paused. I hadn't thought that far ahead. "I don't know."

"How about a jumble sale?" She yawned again.

"A jumble sale?"

"Yeah. We could bring unwanted items into school and sell them in the playground."

"That's a great idea! Let's do it tomorrow."

"Alright..." Ruby paused before adding in a whisper, "I have to go now. Violet's getting angry."

I said a hasty goodbye and hung up. Then I rang Annie.

I heard the confusion in her voice as she answered. "Livi?"

181

"Sorry to wake you. We're having a jumble sale."

She murmured sleepily, "When? Now?"

"Tomorrow at school. I need to raise money to take Jill on holiday. Have you got stuff round your house that you could sell?"

"Yeah," she said dreamily. "We've got lots of coats and cheese and feet..."

"Annie, wake up!" I yelled.

She gave a grunt. "What?"

"Bring things to sell tomorrow!"

"Alright." She paused before adding, "Livi?"

"What?"

"Are you really phoning me or am I dreaming?"

"I'm really phoning you. We're having a jumble sale tomorrow."

She muttered, "Bring some food for the jungle snail..." before falling asleep on the line.

Ruby met me the next morning with two backpacks crammed full of junk. "Ready to make loads of money?" she asked eagerly.

I patted my own bulging bin liner and grinned.

I had rung Annie first thing, in case none of my late night phone call had sunk in, but she assured me she had found *'loads of things to sell for Jill.'* She wasn't kidding. She turned up with a whole granny trolley of goodies, including half of her mother's make-up collection, a battered box of fireworks from her shed[47] and a bundle of old bow ties which had once belonged to Old Budgie. When I saw it all, I reassessed my original plan to take Jill to Spain.

"We might even make enough to send her somewhere exotic— like Hawaii!" I exclaimed as the three of us dragged our bags through school.

We hid everything in the Drama changing rooms until lunchtime where we forfeited our lunch in favour of setting up our stall. We found a spot between the canteen and the P.E block which we felt would pick up a lot of traffic whilst keeping us far enough away from the main building so as to remain undetected by any teachers.

Heads started to turn as we emptied our bags and began lining our wares up along the wall and, for the first few minutes, we had

---

[47] These were wrapped in several layers of cling film and contained the handwritten warning, *'Cover your eyes. Beware the sparks of doom!'*

quite a crowd. Unfortunately, they were less than keen once they saw what was actually on offer.

"It looks like you just brought in a load of unwanted junk from home," Georgina Harris complained, picking up a handful of *Colin's Tasty Chicken* promotional pens.

"What's this?" Darcy Bell added, turning Old Budgie's bedpan upside down.

I took the bedpan away. "You can have a free pen with every purchase," I offered.

They exchanged unimpressed glances before shaking their heads and wandering off.

A few feet away, a sixth former was haggling with Ruby over a little harmonica. "I've give you ten pence," he said.

"It's actually worth five pounds," Ruby replied. "I only got it last week."

The boy sniffed. "Twenty pence."

"Three pounds?"

"Fifty pence."

"One pound..?"

"Fifty pence, final offer."

I winced as Ruby sang, "Sold!"

As the crowd died down I rearranged our stall, grouping similar items together and pushing the more presentable things to the front. I came across Annie's little hedgehog made out of her own hair.

"Why is this here?" I picked it up. "And why is it £100?"

Annie beamed. "I figured it would be worth a lot because it's one of a kind."

I forced a smile. "It *is* one of a kind. But so is a lot of human waste and, unless you're famous, people don't tend to want to buy that kind of thing."

She blinked at me. "Oh! Maybe I should hold onto it in case I get famous one day."

I tossed it into her schoolbag with a giggle. "Yeah, maybe."

Suddenly, Caroline MacBrodie came slithering round the corner, encircled by Kitty, Molly and Melody. The four of them took one look at our stall and burst out laughing.

Caroline came right up close and started snooping though our things. I feared she was about to untidy it all but she just muttered, "Interesting," before giving us a cold look and slinking away.

Less than five minutes later Mr Riley, who had received an *'anonymous tip off that business was being conducted on school premises,'* came storming over in a rage. Wayne Purdy and Aaron Tang, who had been considering the box of fireworks and a bottle of Mrs Button's *Midnight Blue* hair dye, threw the items down and scarpered. Quick as a flash, I hid the fireworks under an old nightdress and turned to face our head teacher.

"What on earth do you think you're doing?" he roared, flecks of spit spraying out of his mouth as he stared at our stall. "This is an academic institution, not a marketplace!"

I blushed as I whispered, "We were just selling a few things to raise money for—"

Mr Riley cut across me with a growl and put his hand out. "How much have you made?"

I fumbled round in my pocket and pulled out our earnings. "Seventy eight pence, Sir." I carefully laid it in his hand.

He breathed out of his nose. "Pack your stall up," he said, handing me the money back. "And we'll say no more about it."

The three of us nodded and hastily threw the contents of our jumble sale back into our bags.

As Mr Riley strolled away I sighed and slid to the ground. "Now what do we do?"

Annie rooted through our junk. "We could give some of this stuff to Jill," she suggested, holding up the bottle of *Midnight Blue*.

I screwed up my nose. "She won't use that."

"Oh." Annie put it down in disappointment. "Jill would look really cool with blue hair."

I gave an exasperated cry. "It's not fair! I wanted to do something special for her and now I can't."

Annie looked a little thoughtful as she said, "I thought we needed money to give her a holiday. If you just want to make her feel special you can do that for free."

I chewed my lip as I considered her words. "I suppose…"

"I can't believe Mr Riley caught us," Ruby muttered.

Annie was wide-eyed. "Who do you think tipped him off?"

I rolled my eyes. "Caroline, of course."

Annie pouted and glanced from me to Ruby. "What should we do?"

"I don't know," said Ruby. "What do you think, Livi?"

I exhaled heavily. "I don't know." I was torn between the raging desire for revenge and the nagging pull of my conscience. I stuck out my bottom lip as I asked God, *Do we really have to love her?*

You don't have to do anything.

But you love her, don't you?

184

Infinitely.

I squeezed my eyes shut and put my head in my hands. I knew I had a choice to make. I could either aim to love people *completely* or I could admit that I wanted to pick and choose and only ever do it on my terms. I took a deep breath before saying quietly, "Let's give Caroline the money we made."

"What?" said Annie.

Even Ruby looked stunned.

"Let's give Caroline the money," I repeated. "And, no matter how nasty she is, let's keep being nice in return. Let's be Jesus to her."

Ruby gave a slow nod. "Alright..."

Annie beamed. "Shall we give her the hedgehog made from my hair too?"

I stifled a smile as I explained that Caroline might not receive that as a loving act. Then I picked up the paltry handful of cash that we had earned on our stall and gazed at the two of them. "How should we do this?"

They both shrugged and went bright red.

In the end, none of us had the courage to go up to Caroline in person so we stuck the money to her locker with a note which read, *'Buy yourself something nice. Love from The COOL Club.'* Then, after peeking from behind the drinks fountain until we saw Caroline go in and out of our form room, we returned to see whether she'd accepted our gift.

We were greeted by a less than courteous response on the white board. *'To The FOOL Club... Why don't you give your hard earned cash to a hopeless charity case? You'll find one by looking in the mirror.'* Our money was strewn across the floor.

I pursed my lips and rubbed her message off with my sleeve.

"Oh," Ruby said in disappointment. "I kind of hoped she'd be grateful..."

"What should we do?" Annie whispered.

"Keep being nice," I instructed them through gritted teeth.

"How?" asked Annie.

"I know how," said Ruby. She reached into her bag and laid the nappy advert on the table. "Let's get rid of this."

I gave a solemn sigh. It pained me to do something so merciful without Caroline even knowing about it but I knew it was the right thing to do. "Alright."

"We need to totally destroy it," Ruby continued. "We can't just scrunch it up otherwise somebody might find it."

"Should we burn it?" asked Annie. "Or eat it, like spies do?"

I sniffed. "We can probably just rip it up."

"And put half of the pieces in one bin and the other half in another," Annie suggested.

I frowned and turned to the picture.

We all stared at it, none of us quite willing to make the first tear. Suddenly the door swung open and in walked Caroline and her posse.

Annie grabbed the advert and tucked it under her arm.

She must have looked rather awkward because Kitty pointed at her and sneered, "The Shadow's hiding something."

Caroline came towards her. "What is it?"

Annie blushed and shook her head.

Caroline let out a nasty cackle and stuck her hand out. "Is it another weird note from The FOOL Club? Let me see."

Ruby shot me a worried glance.

I took a step towards Caroline. "You don't want to do that," I warned.

She glared at me. "Keep out of this, Freaky."

I sucked in my cheeks and willed myself not to get mad.

Annie let out a little whimper as Caroline reached out and grabbed her arm. Without warning, the advert slipped from Annie's grip and fluttered into the middle of the floor.

Ritchie Jones, who had just walked into the room, leant over and casually picked it up. His jaw fell open. Then, casting a sly grin at Caroline, he held it up for her friends.

There was a stunned pause while they took in what they were seeing. Finally, Molly let out a loud snort, Melody gasped and Kitty exclaimed, "Oh my!"

Caroline went as red as a beet and lunged at Ritchie.

He spluttered and danced out of her grasp, holding the advert tightly as he ran out of the room.

Annie sidled up to me and whispered, "Now what do we do?"

"I don't know," I replied. "That wasn't meant to happen."

Caroline turned, her face etched with fury.

I gave a sigh as I looked her in the eye. "I told you."

By the end of the afternoon, photocopies of Caroline's nappy photo graced every corridor in school. Caroline ran round in a frantic rage tearing them down but no sooner had she done so when new ones sprung up in their place. There was no way Ritchie Jones could be as speedy as that. I had a sneaky suspicion that he was getting help from Kitty, Molly and Melody, especially for the ones in the girls' toilets.

Ruby, Annie and I ended up in Mr Riley's office for questioning after he caught us taking posters down and assumed we were the culprits.

His moustache quivered as he shook one of the posters at us and roared, "Revenge for Caroline blowing the whistle on your little business venture, I presume?"

"No!" I said. "We were trying to love her!"

Mr Riley dropped the poster in confusion. "Pardon?"

"We didn't put them up, Sir," Ruby insisted. "We were taking them down."

Our head teacher eyed us suspiciously. "Taking them down?"

We nodded.

"Because Jesus says to love our enemies," Annie piped up. "And Caroline's our enemy because she's always so mean."

Mr Riley slowly opened his mouth. He looked a little dumbfounded.

"We were honestly trying to be nice," I whispered.

"We're Christians," Ruby added.

The three of us gave him beseeching stares as he considered us one by one. Finally, he shook his head and released us without a punishment.

We left school unwitting heroes as several of our classmates ran up to us and congratulated us for exposing Caroline so brilliantly.

"We didn't mean to," I muttered as Rupert Crisp approached me with one of the photocopies and asked if I would sign it.

Kitty and Molly walked by and I heard Kitty squeal, "Oh my goodness, can you believe how big Caro's bum looked in that nappy?"

They sniggered before looking up and catching me staring.

"Nice one, Livi," Kitty said with a grin.

"Yeah," Molly added. "Well played!"

I shook my head. "You're meant to be her friends!" I scolded.

They burst out laughing and sauntered off.

If I'm honest I still don't feel any love towards Caroline, but *trying* to love her was certainly worthwhile, not least because the look on her face when Annie offered to give her a hug made me feel mighty smug... But I'm working on that.

~ 23 ~

A very Violet party

A few days before her birthday-leaving party, Violet sent round a text to inform everyone that the theme of the party was going to be *'Things Violet will miss.'*

Keen to make a sincere effort to love her, I decided to dress up as her beloved dog, Dennis.

On the day of the party, I spent hours creating the best possible costume from an old grey cardigan (which I cut into stripes) and a pair of white pyjamas. I even made a pair of ears out of two socks attached to a headband and a tail from a stocking stuffed with newspaper.[48] Then I rummaged around in Jill's make-up bag and painted my face in extravagant lines, using up almost a whole bottle of mascara to capture the wetness of Dennis' nose. As I put my finishing touches to my feet (a pair of furry socks over my gym shoes), I hummed to myself and wondered whether there would be a prize for the best costume.

Jill refused to dress up. As we set off for the community hall where the party was being held, I gave her a disapproving shake of the head and warned her that she was going to feel very stupid when she turned up and was the only one not in costume. But, as it happened, the moment I walked through the door I realised it was *me* who was about to spend the evening feeling like a fool.

I cruised in, swinging my tail and giving my best *Disco-Dancing Dog* impression, only to be greeted by the confused gasps of a room full of people in regular attire.

"I thought it was meant to be fancy dress!" I hissed as Ruby waved and ran over.

"It was," she replied. "I wonder why nobody else has done it."

---

[48] I'd wanted to use tissues for a softer feel but Jill caught me and told me off for wasting them.

"You haven't even done it!"

"Yes I have! I've come as *me*. Violet will miss *me*."

I rolled my eyes and groaned.

Violet, decked out in what looked like a wetsuit with a tutu attached, came over to greet me. "Hello Livi! Thanks for coming. What are you wearing?"

I shifted uncomfortably and adjusted my tail. "I came as Dennis."

She looked at me in surprise. "Why?"

"Because that was the fancy dress theme, remember? Things you would miss."

Violet shook her head. "No... Things I'll miss is the theme for the games. For example, we're about to play *Leeds themed Charades.*"

"Then... what's the theme for fancy dress?" I spluttered, eyeing her wetsuit.

She gave a twirl. "It's not fancy dress."

I took a deep breath and reminded myself that God loved her very much. "Okay... Well, happy birthday."

She beamed and went to greet some more of her guests.

I turned to Ruby. "What should I do? I look ridiculous!"

She started giggling.

"Ruby!"

"Sorry!" She composed herself before asking, "Didn't you bring any other clothes?"

"Of course not! Why would I bring other clothes?"

She shrugged. "I sometimes bring spare clothes to parties in case I change my mind once I arrive."

I looked at her expectantly. "Do you have some then?"

She shook her head. "I didn't bother this time." She grinned and tugged on her outfit. "Do you like my dress?"

I growled and wiped the mascara off my nose. "Is it gone?" I asked desperately.

"No... You've sort of wiped it down your lip. It looks a bit like a moustache now."

I gave a whimper and ran to the toilets.

"You don't look too bad," Ruby assured me as I plunged my face under the tap and started scrubbing my nose. "If you take your tail off, you won't even look like you're in costume."

I turned to face her. "The tail's sewn on," I said irritably. "If I pull it off, it'll probably rip. Then I'll just be a girl who turned up in her pyjamas with a hole in the bottom."

Ruby pursed her lips and said nothing. She looked like she was trying not to laugh.

Try as I might, I couldn't fully remove the make-up from my face and was left with a dark smear across my nose and a couple of pointy lines over my eyebrows. I threw my ears away and did my best to tuck my tail out of sight but, even so, as soon as I emerged from the toilets I bumped into Belinda who looked me up and down and said, "Goodness, Livi! Look at you!"

Beside her, Oscar pointed at me and bellowed, "She's Dennis!"

As a few people turned to stare, I was torn between utter humiliation and a little bit of pride in what would obviously have been an award-winning costume had it been that kind of party.

I gave them a sheepish smile before running into a corner.

"Don't worry," Ruby whispered. "If anybody asks, just say you thought it was fancy dress."

That would have been wise advice had anybody bothered to ask. But it seemed that most people felt it would be inappropriate to direct any attention to what I was wearing. Instead, those who knew me gave me polite or patronising smiles. And those who didn't know me didn't speak to me and just gaped at me from a distance. For the rest of the evening I caught people looking at me as they whispered to one another, "Why is that girl dressed like a dog?"

Even Joey just stared at me long and hard before asking, "Is that a new suit?"

I shook my head and muttered, "I thought it was fancy dress."

I was hoping for some sympathy but, instead, he tipped his head back and roared with laughter. Then he grabbed his phone and started taking photos of me.

"Don't put them on FriendWeb," I warned, much to his amusement.

He giggled and said, "Oh! Good idea!"

I gave him a long look. All week, I'd been summoning up the courage to break up with him and had even brought his rocks with me as a parting gift. But, now that he was in front of me, the thought of saying anything that could upset him made me feel immensely sick.

Joey stopped taking photos and looked at me. "Are you alright?"

"I'm fine."

He grinned and cocked his head to one side. "You're not a pure breed, are you?"

My stomach lurched. "What?"

He pointed to my tail. "Nothing matches."

I snatched up the stocking. "Everything is pure cotton," I said indignantly. "Feel my tail." I held it out and then reconsidered. "Actually, don't. You might dent it."

Joey gave a bemused shrug.

Before I could say anything else, Violet got our attention from across the room. "Good evening everybody!" she roared into a megaphone. "And welcome to my party. If you brought a present you can put it on the table over there... We're going to start with a game."

Most of the guests were people from church and they graciously entered into the spirit of *Leeds themed Charades*. The others seemed to be relatives of Violet and Ruby who, from the looks on their faces, knew very little about Leeds and just watched from the side as the rest of us enacted various landmarks from around the city.

Violet grabbed her megaphone again and yelled, "Now then, if you'd like to take a seat, the show is about to begin!"

The guests mumbled to one another as Violet turned the lights off and switched on an overhead projector. What came next was almost forty minutes of bizarre artwork in the form of a slideshow accompanied by Violet's dreary commentary.

I tried to pay attention, reminding myself over and over that Violet was very special to God.

At one point, Joey put an arm around me and whispered, "This is so weird."

I forced a smile and wriggled out of his reach.

After the slideshow, Violet announced that it was time for another game. "It's called *Musical Family Members*," she explained. "It's a bit like *Musical Bumps* except you have to be holding onto somebody in my family when the music stops."

Oscar leapt up with a joyful squeal but Ruby and her parents looked a little alarmed. It seemed Violet hadn't consulted them before planning her games.

The music came on and the guests started to dance. I saw Jill bopping somewhat awkwardly at the side having been commanded over the megaphone to join in. I stayed as close to Ruby as I could and grabbed her arm as soon as the music stopped. Unfortunately, the game came to an abrupt end after several people fell on top of a screaming Oscar in their haste to stay in the game.

Violet grabbed her megaphone and said, "Oh dear. Whoops. Sorry about that."

She looked rather embarrassed as her brother went bright purple and screamed at the top of his lungs, "I hate this party!"

Belinda picked him up with a lot of cooing and took him off to the kitchen to pacify him with some jelly.

"Well, let's move on," Violet said hurriedly. "The next game is *Stuck in Leeds Ring Road*. It's a bit like *Stuck in the Mud* except you can only run in a circle..."

Once Violet had finished explaining the rules we started to run in a clockwise direction, pursued by Violet and three other catchers whom Violet had named after various teachers from school. I tried to keep up with everybody else but kept tripping over my tail and spent more time stuck than free. It wasn't long before I saw Jill give up under the guise of needing the toilet. One by one, people were dropping out of the game and Violet looked rather peeved.

"Come on!" she yelled through her megaphone. "Keep playing! Jill Starling, come back here!"

Jill turned back, a little red in the face, and a few of the guests got up and started running half-heartedly again.

From my frozen position in the middle of the room, I watched Violet and wondered whether she was having a nice time. There was quite a lot of concentration etched on her face and I couldn't help but feel sorry for her.

At one point, Jill jogged past and shot me a swift smile. I smiled back, feeling a combination of affection and sorrow at her depressed and lonely state. *God, I want Jill to know you. Deep in her heart, I want her to believe that you love her.*

I was caught off guard by Ruby scrambling through my legs to release me and toppled over with a yelp. She giggled and helped me up. "It's almost time for The Glory Seekers' performance!" she whispered.

I grinned. A new song was forming in my mind.

The game came to an end and I excused myself from the next one[49] and wandered over to the little stage at the front of the room where Ruby, Joey and Mark had gone to set up for their gig. The three of them looked up as I approached them.

"Hey," I said eagerly. "I've got a new song." I grabbed some paper from under their set list and started to write it down.

They looked at me in confusion.

---

[49] *I went to Leeds Petting Zoo.*

"We haven't got time to learn it," Joey protested.

"It's okay," I assured him. "It's the same tune as *'Don't go to Hell.'* It just has nicer words."

Ruby leant over and glanced at the song in my hands. "That's good," she said, taking the sheet from me.

"Thanks." I watched as they continued setting up.

The game of *I went to Leeds Petting Zoo* came to an end and Violet picked up her megaphone once more. "Are you ready, Ruby?"

Ruby blushed as the room turned to stare at her. Since I was standing so close to her they began to stare at me too and I saw several people nudge one another, perhaps expecting a skit of some sort.

I ran to the back of the room as Ruby told her sister shyly, "Yeah, we're ready."

Violet gave a nod and bellowed to her guests, "Right. This is the next bit of my party."

A few people exchanged bemused smiles as Joey tapped the microphone and said, "Hello everyone! We're The Glory Seekers and we're here to sing you a few songs." He grinned before declaring, "Our first song is called *'Dirty Deity.'*"

They launched into the song about Jesus' hygiene habits, much to the amusement of the guests. I saw Violet nodding in approval as she began preaching to some of her relatives. Not too far away, Jill had a rather scornful look on her face and I was hit once again with a pang of guilt at how careless I had been in my attempts to save her.

Joey's brow wrinkled in concentration as he slid his hand up and down his guitar and belted out the chorus, *"Jesus, my dirty deity... Became a grubby mess for me..."*

Beside him, Ruby and Mark clicked their fingers sombrely and added the odd, *"Oooh."*

The three of them sang a few songs before turning to the piece of paper I had given them.

"This is a new song," Joey announced into the microphone. "It's called, *'Don't go to Hell.'*"

"No it's not!" I piped up. "It's called, *'Come Home.'*"

Joey gave a confused nod. "Yeah, what she said." He started to strum on his guitar.

Ruby took the new words in her hands and grinned at me before breaking out in song.

'Can you hear him whisper to your bruised and battered heart:
"Meet me in the secret place
How I long for your embrace
You will be satisfied
Completely satisfied in me."
For the world and its desires will fade away
And in just a little while we'll see his face...'

I sidled up to Jill and whispered, "I wrote this one."

She looked impressed. "Well done."

"Thanks." I paused, wanting to ask what she thought of it. I had a vain hope that she would start crying and give her life to Jesus there and then. I was about to ask whether she wanted me to repeat any of the words but thought better of it. *Help me, God. How do I love her?*

God didn't give me any wise words to say so I kept quiet and, pretty soon, Jill wandered off to get a drink.

Summer came up beside me just as the song was finishing. "Did you write that one, Livi?"

"Yeah."

"I really like it."

"Thanks." I shrugged and fiddled with my tail.

Summer gave a funny smile as she looked at my outfit but she was too polite to say anything.

"I got the dress code a bit wrong," I muttered sheepishly.

"Oh right!" She chuckled. "Are you having fun?"

"Yeah, it's great. It's... very Violet."

She nodded. "How are things going with Joey?"

My stomach churned as I forced a smile. "Alright..."

She kept staring at me.

I sighed. "I'm not sure if... I mean, I don't *think* it's..." I paused and bit my lip. "I need to talk to him."

Summer smiled and squeezed my shoulder. "God will give you strength," she whispered.

I nodded dumbly and glanced at the stage. Joey had just begun one of his own compositions: *'Brother Noah trod on a Snail.'*

I exhaled slowly, forcing a smile as he caught my eye and bellowed, *"Oh what madness; what a lark! If you didn't want the poop to scoop you shouldn't have built the ark!"*

A few feet away, Jill had struck up a conversation with Eddie's brother, Stevie. "I'm one of Violet's neighbours," I heard her say, obviously feeling the need to explain why she was at such a strange party.

Stevie replied, "I'm from Violet's church. I'm Stevie."

I stole a quick glance at Jill, fearing that she might turn her nose up at the mention of church and walk off. But she just nodded and said, "I'm Jill."

They shook hands and Stevie asked, "What do you do?"

Jill fixed her *'I'm-so-glad-you-asked'* expression onto her face and said shortly, "I work in public relations."

"Oh really? Doing what?"

She blushed. "I work for *Colin's Tasty Chicken*."

Stevie raised his hands. "I love *Colin's Tasty Chicken!*"

Jill looked relieved. "It's not a great job," she confessed. "If my mother was still alive, she'd die all over again!"

I grimaced. Jill has never been particularly adept at flirting. Fortunately, Stevie didn't seem to mind and just laughed politely.

Ruby, Joey and Mark finished their performance and I joined the rest of the party in several rounds of applause. The three of them put their instruments down and posed for a photo with Violet who had run onto the stage. Joey cleared a space and stood on his head before springing to his feet with an eager grin.

He looked so happy and carefree. The idea of breaking up with him made me feel like I was incredibly heartless. I wondered whether I could get away with not saying anything. Perhaps I could let him go on thinking we were a couple and just hold his hand occasionally to appease him. I let out a moan as I realised that would never work. I would have to tell him at *some* point and, in the meantime, I didn't want to spend long hours together pretending to be a couple or being referred to by Janine as his *'special friend.'* Plus, he was bound to want to kiss me again soon. I suddenly wished that I had never gone out with him in the first place. It would have saved a whole lot of bother if we had just stuck to being friends. I wanted to tell Ruby that her way was right. I would definitely be waiting until I was ready for a serious relationship.

Can you help me, God? I prayed desperately. *Can you undo this mess? I'm sorry for giving Joey my first kiss.*

My stomach churned as Joey jumped off the stage and ran towards me. "Hey Livi!"

"Well done," I said, trying to smile.

"Thanks!" He grinned. "Let's get some sausage rolls."

He grabbed my arm but I pulled back. "Er... Joey?"

"What?"

I cleared my throat but, before I could say anything, Joey said, "Oh no!"

I blushed and said, "Yeah... I'm afraid so..."

"There's a storm coming."

"Not necessarily! I just..."

"This always happens when it thunders."

"What?"

"Have you got a tissue?" he continued as blood started to drip out of his nose.

I took a step back. "I'll get you one," I muttered, running over to my sister. "Jill, have you got a tissue? Joey's having a nosebleed." I pointed at Joey.

Jill looked at him in horror and pulled several packets of tissues out of her bag. "Give him these and don't touch him."

I trotted back to Joey. "Here you go."

He took a packet from me and tore it open, groaning as blood dribbled down his chin and splattered onto the floor.

I wondered whether I could leave him for a bit and come back once all the blood was gone but I wasn't sure whether this would be unkind. I lingered awkwardly, watching as he pressed tissue after tissue against his nostrils. It crossed my mind that, to an unwitting passerby, it could look as though I had just tried to murder Joey, perhaps as a desperate bid to dispose of him having never found the courage to end things properly.

"Hey, Livi," Joey said suddenly. "What are you doing tomorrow morning? Wanna hang out?"

"Actually, I want to go to church."

He shrugged. "Alright. Let's sit at the back."

I took a deep breath. "I've been thinking..."

He took a step back. "Uh oh!"

"I think we need to break up."

Joey frowned. "Did God say you had to break up with me?"

"No. He said I can have you if I want."

"Then why—?"

"I want him more."

Joey swapped one of his bloodstained tissues for a clean one and blinked at me. "You can have both of us!"

I shook my head and looked away. Trying to maintain any degree of seriousness was hard while he was staring at me with tissues rammed up his nostrils. "No I can't." I chewed the inside of my cheek before adding, "I'm not saying that I don't like you... and

I don't know what will happen in the future... But for now... it's not right."

He gave me a confused look. "I don't get it."

"I want to give God everything. Not because I have to. But because I want to."

"I still don't get it."

"I didn't think you would. That's why we're not right together." I fumbled around in the pockets of my costume and pulled out his rocks. "Here..."

Joey raised his eyebrows. "Don't you want them?"

I shook my head. "You should have them. I only collected them because you do. I'm not an expert like you."

"Oh!" Joey took the rocks and held them a little awkwardly. "Thanks." He bit his lip as he looked me up and down. "I should have said earlier; you made a great effort."

I smiled and picked up my tail, grateful that it was still intact. "I'll see you around."

~ **24** ~

Jill's Island

It was early on Saturday morning and I was on the Ricos' doorstep, frantically ringing their bell. I had been up for several hours putting the finishing touches to plans for a surprise party for Jill and it had just occurred to me that I hadn't thought to get a cake.

"How do I make a cake from scratch?" I asked as soon as Belinda answered the door.

She chuckled before saying mysteriously, "Well, Livi. If you want to create a cake from scratch, you first have to make the entire universe."

I kept staring at her until she offered to bake one for me and send it over with Ruby.

"Thanks," I said, breathing a sigh of relief. "And tell Ruby not to forget the eggs."

Belinda nodded. "I'll tell her." She paused before asking, "Livi, can I just check... You want me to invite Jill over at two?"

"Yes. And keep her here for at least half an hour."

"Right..." She looked a little apprehensive. "And what if she wants to leave?"

"You mustn't let her! Do whatever you need to do to keep her here."

"Alright..." She paused again. "Are the rest of us invited to the party or is it just Ruby?"

I took a deep breath. "It's just Ruby. It's sort of an exclusive thing. But maybe you could set these off when it gets dark." I handed her the battered box of fireworks from Annie's shed.

Belinda took them with glee. "I'd love to!"

I grinned and turned to go.

"Oh, Livi?"

I looked back. "Yes?"

"Jill really is blessed to have you. She's going to be so touched."

I swallowed hard. "I hope so."

In the end, Belinda chose to invite Jill over under the guise of needing some advice on her new underwear. I heard Jill muttering to herself as she hung up the phone and pulled on her shoes. "I'm just popping over to see Belinda," she called to me. "She's crying about pants."

I poked my head out from the living room. "Okay," I said innocently. "Take your time."

"Believe me, I won't be long."

I shrugged and opened the front door for her.

Five minutes later, Ruby arrived with a cake and a box of eggs hidden in her schoolbag. "The plan's working brilliantly!" she told me. "Jill's trying on a pair of my mum's tights."

I giggled and took the cake from her.

Moments later, Annie knocked on the door with a sack full of stuff that we had prepared earlier in the week. We took the hoard straight into the living room and began to set up.

"Did the photos arrive?" I asked Ruby.

"Oh yeah!" She dug around in her bag before pulling out a little envelope.

I recognised Aunt Claudia's uptight scrawl. *'Miss Livi Starling, care of Miss Ruby Rico.'*

I grinned and ripped the envelope open. A handful of old photos fell out and my heart leapt at the top one— a faded shot of Jill holding my hand on my first day of school. I had rung Aunt Claudia a few days earlier to ask if she could send me the photos. I'd said I wanted to show them to some of my friends which wasn't technically a lie since Ruby and Annie were looking at them now.[50]

"This one's hilarious!" said Ruby, holding up a shot of Jill smiling obliviously at the camera while I bawled as a sheep ate my hat.

I smiled and took it from her. "Go and do the eggs," I instructed. "I need to stick these up."

---

[50] My reason for using Ruby's address was less truthful as I'd claimed the postman was stealing our mail. Aunt Claudia must have taken this very seriously as Ruby told me later that she'd also received a frozen leg of lamb addressed to us.

Ruby and Annie nodded and headed for the kitchen where I had instructed them to put four saucepans on the stove filled with eight eggs and a selection of different singing egg timers.

I grabbed some tape from the cupboard and stuck the photos in a line along the hallway. Then I closed the living room door and popped my head into the kitchen. "How's it going?"

The two of them looked up from the stove.

"The water's starting to boil," said Ruby.

I grinned and was about to say something else when I heard Jill's key turning in the lock. "She's coming!" I hissed. "Hide."

Ruby tucked herself behind the dustbin and Annie lunged under the table. I ran out of the room, closing the door behind me, and fixed a nonchalant expression on my face as Jill came through the front door.

"That was horrendous," my sister groaned. "Belinda kept shoving her oversized pants in my face and asking me to feel them."

I gave a funny smile and said, "Oh dear."

"She wouldn't stop talking," Jill continued. "And then, as soon as I got up to leave, she fell to the floor and started screeching. I thought she'd had a heart attack. I was just about to ring for an ambulance when she jumped up and told me to put my phone away. Crazy woman!"

I coughed loudly so that Ruby wouldn't hear from the kitchen. "Ah, never mind," I said. "You're home now."

Jill started to reply and then caught sight of the old photos and gasped. "Oh Livi! Where did you get those?"

"I asked Aunt Claudia to post them."

Jill pointed to the one with the sheep eating my hat. "I remember that! You were so funny." She turned to face me. "Why have you put them up?"

I took a deep breath. "I was thinking about how much you've done for me over the years and I wanted to say I appreciate it."

Jill looked rather taken aback. "Thanks, Livi. That's sweet."

I was about to say something else when the choir of egg timers began to sing from the kitchen.

"What's that noise?" Jill asked in alarm.

I feigned confusion. "It's coming from the kitchen."

My sister raised her eyebrows and ventured down the hall. I ran ahead of her, trying not to grin as I pushed the door open. Jill jumped in fright as Ruby and Annie shot out from their hiding places.

"Surprise!" the three of us yelled.

Jill looked at me. "What's going on?"

"We're giving you a birthday party!" I exclaimed.

She gaped at me. "My birthday was three months ago!"

"I know. I wanted it to be a real surprise without any of the trauma of growing old. Plus, this way you don't have to worry about getting an offensive present from Aunt Claudia."

Jill gave a little splutter. "Right... Thanks."

"Sit down!" Annie said, dragging Jill towards one of the chairs.

Jill did as she was told and watched in astonishment as Ruby scooped out the eggs and laid them on a plate. "Oh, they look nice," she said quietly.

Ruby beamed. She had drawn a face on each egg.

"Eat them up," Annie said merrily, pushing the plate of eggs towards Jill. "And then we're taking you on holiday!"

Jill turned in shock.

I gave Annie a sharp nudge. "Not a proper holiday," I said quickly. "You'll see."

Jill nodded and started to eat her eggs. She got through three of them before saying awkwardly, "I'm getting a bit full. Perhaps I could save the rest for later?"

Ruby looked at me and shrugged.

"Yeah, that's fine," I said. "Put this on now." I held up a scarf and grinned at Jill.

She looked apprehensive as I came towards her. "What's that for?"

I giggled as I tied it round her face like a blindfold. "Hold my hand." Then I mouthed to Ruby and Annie, *"Go and get ready!"*

They nodded and ran into the living room.

"I'm taking you on a trip," I told Jill as I spun her round a few times to confuse her.

Jill gave a whimper. "Please don't take me outside with a scarf on my face."

"I won't! Don't worry."

She trembled and gripped my hand as I led her out of the kitchen, down the hall, up and down the stairs a few times and finally into the living room.

Ruby and Annie had exchanged their clothes for a couple of bird costumes which we had made that week out of a bag of feathers and several old pillow cases.

"I feel a bit dizzy, Livi," Jill muttered as I led her into the middle of the room. She went to remove her blindfold.

"Wait!" I yelled. "Not yet!" I hurriedly pulled on my own costume and flung my clothes behind the sofa. Then I nodded at Ruby who picked up her piccolo and started to play a tune. I gave Annie a poke and the two of us began to make raucous tropical bird noises.[51]

Jill almost covered her ears in fright. "What's going on?"

I threw in a few more screeches before yelling, "NOW you can remove your blindfold!"

Jill pulled the scarf from her face and looked around.

"Welcome to Jill's Island!" I exclaimed as Ruby went over to Jill and put a daisy chain round her neck.

Jill's mouth fell open as she spun round the room. We had spread out yellow towels all over the floor and covered them with flowers from the local park. Over the walls, we had stuck pictures of animals cut out from magazines and paper birds made by Ruby hung from string in every corner of the room. We had even covered the television with a piece of blue material which flowed out into the middle of the room like a little stream.

As Jill stared at us, I joined hands with Ruby and Annie and the three of us danced round Jill and chanted, *"Welcome to Jill's Island, make yourself at home! Here it's always sunny and you're never on your own!"* We broke apart and danced, flapping our elbows wildly with our hands tucked under our armpits.

Jill looked like she didn't know whether to laugh or cry. In the end, she did a bit of both. She stumbled back and plonked herself onto the sofa, shaking as she brought a hand up to her mouth.

I nodded at Ruby and Annie and the three of us hopped on one leg as we sang our song once more. We ended with a mighty roar and fell on our knees before Jill.

She wiped her eyes and applauded. "That was crazy!"

She started to get up but I pushed her back down and said, "We're not done yet."

"Oh!" Jill looked a little shell-shocked and watched in bemusement as the three of us exchanged our bird costumes for long coats.

That week in Drama the three of us had devised a short piece with the stimulus *'Interrogation.'* It wasn't particularly relevant to Jill's Island since it featured Ruby as a con artist hiding diamonds in ice sculptures but we performed it anyway. Then Annie recited

---

[51] I had spent a lot of time that week teaching Annie my *Paradise Parrot* impression and, aside from choking occasionally, she had got pretty good at it.

one of the war poems from Mrs Tilly's English class and Ruby gave Jill a wooden doorstop that she had made in Design and Technology. Next, I presented Jill with my gifts: a book entitled, '101 reasons why Livi loves you,' and a handful of vouchers offering 'Breakfast in bed' and 'Cleaning services.'

Jill opened the book and glanced at the first page.[52] She went pink and dabbed the corners of her eyes. "Thanks, Livi," she said quietly.

"Oh! I've got you a present too!" Annie exclaimed. She ran over to Jill and handed her one of her stuffed hedgehogs. On the plus side, it wasn't the one made of hair. However it *was* the one which read, 'Happy 40th birthday you old hog.'

Fortunately, Jill took it with a smile and set it down beside the book that I'd made.

"We've also got you a cake," Ruby added, running over to retrieve Belinda's homemade cake from where she'd stashed it underneath one of the towels. "Oh... whoops..." She held it up and grimaced. The cake had a giant footprint in the middle of it and what once was a smiley face now looked more like distorted sneer.

"Oh dear," said Annie. "I think that was me."

I bit my lip and turned to Jill but, to my relief, she burst out laughing. "That's brilliant!" she said through snorts. "I love it!"

I gave a relieved splutter and exchanged glances with Ruby and Annie. Then we pulled our bird costumes back on to sing 'Happy Birthday.'

Jill was laughing the whole time and, although I wouldn't have blamed her if she hadn't, proceeded to devour her squashed slice of cake with a massive grin.

After the cake, we played a game of *Pass the Parcel* in which each layer contained a forfeit and a *Colin's Tasty Chicken* pen.

When the music[53] stopped, Jill unwrapped the first layer and chuckled at the pen.

"What do you have to do?" Annie asked eagerly, pointing to the slip of yellow paper attached to the pen.

Jill grinned before unfolding the forfeit. *"Do an elephant impression."* She gave me a look of mock horror before protesting, "No! Don't make me do that!"

"You have to!" I exclaimed.

---

[52] I had drawn a picture of her holding me as a baby accompanied with the words, '1. You loved me first.'
[53] Ruby on the piccolo.

Ruby and Annie nodded. "Do it! Do it!" we chanted.

Jill covered her face as she squirmed and begged us not make her do the challenge.

We kept pleading with her until she took a deep breath and said, "Fine!" Then she crawled into the middle of the floor on all fours. She held one arm in front of her nose before bellowing in an almighty roar, "Harrrruuurrrr!"

The three of us shrieked with laughter as Jill went red and crumpled to the floor in stitches. She came back into the circle and gave me a friendly whack on the arm.

"That was great!" I told her.

She handed me the parcel and said, "Who's next?"

Ruby picked up her piccolo and started to play as we passed the parcel round. Once again, it stopped at Jill.

Jill looked at Ruby. "Not me again!"

Ruby just grinned and said, "Open it."

Jill tore open the layer of newspaper and snorted as another pen fell out. She pulled off the forfeit and read, *"Do a walrus impression... Livi!"*

"What?" I said. "There are lots of animals on Jill's Island."

"I don't even know what a walrus sounds like."

"Oh, I do!" said Annie. She stood up and made what can only be described as a strangled bleat. "Maaaah!"

We gawped at her.

Jill gave a splutter. "That's not a walrus... That's a goat."

Annie turned pink. "Oh yeah. I always get those mixed up."

The four of us fell about laughing and, once we'd started, we couldn't stop and ended up making an awful mess as we rolled all over the floor and across the rest of the cake.

Ruby and Annie stayed until dinner time. We had pooled our pocket money so that we could get Jill a takeaway but, in the end, she refused to let us pay and insisted on ordering the Banquet Bucket from *El Posho Nosho* which she usually deems far too expensive. When the party was over, she even offered to drive Annie home which has to be a first as Jill is normally far too busy to offer lifts to anybody. Ruby and I stayed behind to tidy up and made sure the house was completely back to normal before Jill came home.

"I'd better go now," Ruby said once we had cleared everything away. "I need to finish my biography."

My insides twisted at her words. We only had one more lesson left with Ms Sorenson and I didn't like thinking about our impending goodbye.

"Have you finished yours?" she asked as she pulled on her shoes.

"Not yet," I confessed. "I don't really know how to end it."

"Me neither. I'm thinking of writing that Jesus comes back before I get too old."

I grinned and walked her to the door.

Jill arrived just as Ruby was crossing the street. She ran across to give Ruby a big hug and thanked her for coming.

For the rest of the evening, Jill looked happier than I'd seen her for ages. She kept thanking me and welling up all over again.

"I'm glad you liked it," I said. "I wanted to take you on a proper holiday but I only made seventy eight pence and we gave it to Caroline MacBrodie because we were trying to love our enemies."

Jill nodded slowly and kept smiling.

"Because Jesus said to love our enemies—" I saw a flicker of irritation in Jill's eyes and stopped abruptly. "I mean... We don't have to talk about that."

"Thanks."

I took a deep breath. "Jill, I'm sorry for pushing things on you. And I'll try hard not to..." My stomach churned. "But I just want you to know that Jesus really loves you and, whenever you want to, all you need to do is open your heart to him and he'll be there."

She gave a thin smile. "I appreciate your efforts, Livi. And I'm glad you've found something that makes you happy. But it's not for me." She paused before adding, "I've done some horrible things. I don't deserve it."

Without thinking, I blurted out, "No, but Jesus deserves everyone he died for."

Jill looked up in surprise. Her cheeks went red and, although she didn't say anything, in the corner of her eyes was the faintest flicker of hope. She gave me a quick nod and looked away.

I almost started giggling, surprised at the words that had come out of my own mouth. I hadn't needed to plan or prepare; the Holy Spirit just gave me the right thing at the right time. My heart pounded as I wondered what I ought to do to capitalise on such a breakthrough. I opened and closed my mouth several times before realising that was all God wanted me to say in that moment. So I just leant over and gave Jill a hug. "Goodnight."

She held me tight and whispered, "Goodnight Livi."

I wandered up the stairs, thankful that God is God and rather relieved that I cannot figure him all out. I breezed into my room, a big smile on my face, and threw myself on my bed. As my head hit the pillow, I heard a faint clanging sound and looked down just in time to see one of my Jesus Jangles rolling off my bedside table. Immediately, I thought about Joey and how daft I had been to demand God give me a sign by making them disappear. Of course God's way was better than mine.

I leant over and picked up my unfinished biography. After thinking for a moment, I wrote, *'Following a couple of interesting life events, Livi realised that God can always be trusted, even though he doesn't always do what we want.'*

I lay back on my bed, pouting at the idea of Ms Sorenson's lessons coming to an end. Then I sat up and was about to pull my pyjamas on when I heard a loud bang from across the street. I peered out of my window just in time to see a flash of colour across the night sky. I gasped. I had forgotten about the fireworks! I scrambled off my bed and ran down the stairs shouting, "Jill! Look out of the window! Your day isn't finished yet!"

Jill was already standing at the window when I reached the living room. She turned to me and grinned.

"Surprise," I said in a whisper.

She put her arm out and I went to embrace her. As the sky lit up with a procession of rockets, I'm sure I saw a little tear streak down her cheek. My heart pounded as I realised with joy that I loved Jill more in that moment than I had ever loved her in my life. All term, I had thought that it was paramount that I save her before the summer, fearing that God would be watching with a disapproving frown if I didn't. I had been angry with him for not revealing himself more strongly, never once realising that he wants Jill saved even more than I do and is committed to pursuing her far beyond my measly deadline. I had been so blinkered by my own agenda that I hadn't stopped to ask God how *he* wanted to do things. Well, school finishes in three days which means the summer is officially here and Jill still isn't saved. But, now I see it was me, and not Jill, who God wanted to change all this time.

As the two of us stood in the window, watching the fireworks and shooting each other the odd smile, I thought about my life story and made a mental note to make a little alteration: *'...God can always be trusted, **especially** because he doesn't always do what we want.'*

~ 25 ~

Don't stop now

It was the day that I had dreaded for a very long time: our last ever lesson with Ms Sorenson.

I walked sadly to her classroom with Ruby and Annie, feeling as though we ought to be wearing black or something. I could hardly believe that the rest of our classmates were being so jolly. Everybody was getting excited for the summer holidays but, if I could have done, I'd have stayed at school forever having Personal and Social Development with Ms Sorenson.

I had spent a long time trying to figure out how to end my biography and it had finally come to me in the bath the evening before. I had leapt out with a jubilant cry and sprinted to my room, naked and dripping wet and grinning from ear to ear. After a few tales of myself as a very old lady going on wild adventures with my great great grandchildren and eventually dying after my *Reckless Rhino* impression fooled some hunters on safari, I wrote,

> *'In truth, Livi Starling died the day she gave her life to Jesus. And then, after a brief moment in time loving as many people as possible, she went home to be with him forever. So it didn't matter whether she died on safari, or as a hero, or quietly in her sleep, because what matters most isn't how you live or how you die but who you're living for.'*

I considered it now, outside Ms Sorenson's classroom, and wondered whether it was a little too fanatical. But, before I could change it, Ms Sorenson opened her door and told us to come in.

I took a deep breath and scurried in with the rest of the class. Once at my desk, I pulled my chair out ever so carefully, savouring the moment as fully as I could.

Across the room, Ruby waved and placed her bag on the empty seat beside her. Caroline had been away ever since the exposure of her nappy advert. If Kitty's rumours were to be believed, she had left to go to a boarding school on the other side of the country. Neither Kitty nor Molly nor Melody appeared particularly bothered about this and, from the stares that she'd received when she wore her new *Tizzi Berry* jacket, it seemed Kitty Warrington was officially the coolest girl in school once more.

When everybody had taken their seats, Ms Sorenson got our attention from the front of the room. "Well, 9.1, it's the end of term."

Most people cheered at her words but it took all my energy not to burst into tears.

"I've really enjoyed our lessons," our teacher continued. "And I hope you have too."

I nodded so hard that I nearly pulled a muscle.

Ms Sorenson went on to talk about how much we had grown in the time she had known us and how she was looking forward to reading our biographies. Then, after coming round to collect our work, she told us we could spend the lesson however we wanted. "But don't leave your seats," she added with a grin.

A few people gave cheeky groans but most of the class smiled and started to talk to their partner. It was a far cry from the lesson on the first day of term. It seemed that Ms Sorenson *had* known what she was doing after all. I'm sure I even saw Kitty Warrington and Rupert Crisp share a half-hearted joke.

Since Caroline was absent, Ms Sorenson let Ruby come and perch with me and Annie and the three of us spent most of the lesson planning a week-long sleepover for the start of the summer.

At the front of the room, Ms Sorenson sat at her desk, reading our biographies. I glanced frequently in her direction until I saw her pick mine up. My heart pounded as she opened the front cover and began to read.

Annie had just told a joke and she and Ruby were thumping the table in hysterics.

"Do you get it, Livi?" Annie asked. "I said: *What do you call a hedgehog with bananas in his ears?*"

Without taking my eyes off our teacher, I shrugged and muttered, "Don't know."

"*Anything you want; he can't hear you!*" she squealed.

I forced a smile. "Funny."

She and Ruby looked at me in confusion.

"Are you alright?" asked Ruby.

I kept my eyes fixed on Ms Sorenson. "She's reading my biography," I whispered.

The two of them turned to stare.

"Ooh," said Annie. "What do you reckon she thinks of your life?"

My stomach churned at her words. "I don't know."

I put my head in my hands, peeking through slits in my fingers as Ms Sorenson read to the end of my life story. I saw her smile once or twice but, to my disappointment, she didn't stop to look across or write anything down. Finally, she put it to one side and moved on to somebody else's. I let out a long sigh and slumped down in my chair.

Ruby caught my eye and smiled. "I think she liked it."

I bit my lip and looked away.

All too quickly, the cruel ring of the bell announced the end of the lesson and the room erupted with cheers and the thunderous scraping of chairs as my classmates got up to go.

"Well done on all your hard work this year!" Ms Sorenson called over the rumpus. "Come and collect your biographies on your way out."

The class chattered excitedly as they grabbed their things and went to pick up their work. After carelessly shoving their biographies into their bags, most people left the room without so much as a backwards glance. I packed up my belongings deliberately slowly, even taking the time to rearrange my pencil case unnecessarily, so that we would be the last to leave the room. I picked up my bag with a heavy heart and followed Ruby and Annie to Ms Sorenson's desk. The two of them picked up their biographies and tucked them into their bags but I held back, kind of wondering whether Ms Sorenson might like to keep mine.

She handed it to me. "This is really lovely, Livi."

I shrugged and muttered, "Thanks." Wondering how to further stall our farewell, I pointed to the poster we had put up for our 'God says' teaser campaign many weeks earlier. "Do you want me to take that down, Miss?"

She glanced at it before giving me a funny smile. "I'd like to keep it if that's alright? It's been quite a conversation starter in my classes."

"Of course!" I squeaked. I lingered awkwardly, wishing I could ask her for a hug but not entirely sure if that was allowed. "Er... Thanks for everything this year," I mumbled.

Ruby nodded. "Your lessons have been fun," she said shyly.

Ms Sorenson beamed. "Thank you, girls."

I took a deep breath and turned to go. Then I watched in astonishment as Annie started crying and threw herself onto Ms Sorenson for a hug.

Ms Sorenson laughed and put an arm round her.

Annie clung to her for a moment before stepping back. "Thanks, Miss," she said with a sniff.

Ms Sorenson just smiled.

"Can I hug you too?" I asked tentatively.

"Sure!" She held out her arms.

I went towards her, feeling stupid and clumsy as I buried my head in her shoulder and wrapped my arms around her. She gave me a quick squeeze and patted me on the back. I felt tears stinging my eyes as I pulled away. "I'll miss you," I whispered.

Ms Sorenson chuckled. "I'm not going anywhere, Livi. I'll see you in September."

"I know... But we won't have your lesson anymore and you're the best teacher ever..." I wanted to tell her how much she meant to me but a lump caught in my throat and my cheeks started to burn. I didn't want her lasting memory of me to be of some kind of snivelling stalker.

She smiled again. "Thank you, Livi. I've enjoyed getting to know you."

I had no idea what that meant and what she might have said if she could. *'I'll miss you too...'? 'You're my favourite student ever...'? 'I'd have been proud to be your mother...'?* There was no way of knowing because Ms Sorenson has always been a very no-nonsense teacher. So I just gulped as she walked us to her door and waved goodbye.

~*~

My dad called just as I was finishing my dinner. "Hey Livi. How's tricks?"

I winced at his all-too-familiar greeting. "Hi Dad."

"The wedding's back on."

My throat went dry. "Oh?"

"Erica's been reading up on inner energy and apparently ours is a near-perfect match!"

I sniffed. "Alright then." I paused, hoping for an apology for all the messing around.

But he just said, "Well, I thought I should tell you."

I murmured in reply and was about to hang up when he said, "Oh Livi?"

"Yes?" My heart leapt slightly.

"You can still hand out sandwiches, can't you?"

I squeezed my eyes shut. "Okay," I said in a whisper.

"Great! I'll see you then."

As soon as I hung up, I burst into tears. *I can't do this, God. I can't, I can't, I can't. It's too hard. I don't love him at all and I don't even want to.* I couldn't sense God saying anything and gave a shriek of anger at the idea that he had gone silent on me just when I needed him most.

Jill came out of the kitchen and looked at me in shock. "Livi? What's wrong?" She came and sat beside me, wrapping her arms tightly around me.

"The wedding's back on," I said though tears.

Jill frowned and held me closer. She called my dad a swear word under her breath and told me to forget all about him.

I nodded and wept and decided that she was probably right. What with the pain of saying goodbye to Ms Sorenson, I wasn't sure my heart could take much more.

I went up to bed believing that love was too grand a task after all. It hurt too much and cost too dearly and, if I couldn't hear God speaking as often as I wanted to, why should I push myself to such ridiculous extremes? But, that night, without even asking for it, I found myself in a dream in which God made his intentions for the rest of my life story perfectly clear.

I stood on a river bank, facing the many streams and the same wild river that I had dreamt of weeks earlier. This time I was standing beside the man in white, who I now realised must be Jesus.

As I considered each stream, wondering once again where would be the safest place to swim, Jesus pointed to the wildest part of the river. "Come to the deep," he invited me.

I gaped at him. "What if I drown?"

"What if you lose your life so that you can truly live?" He paused before adding, "Don't stop now."

I gulped. "But it's so *deep*... Don't you love me?"

His countenance changed as he said softly, "I love you completely, Livi. Do *you* love *me?*"

Without thinking, I took a tentative step forward and plunged in.

At that moment I awoke, spluttering for air as I wrestled with my sheets. Panting and gasping, I almost fell out of bed before I realised that I had been dreaming. I switched on my lamp and took several deep breaths.

"Jesus?" I cried aloud. "Are you there?"

He didn't reply and I was about to switch my lamp off and go back to sleep. But, as I glanced round my room, the sign beside my door caught my eye. *'What have you done for God this week?'*

A righteous anger rose up inside me and I sprang out of bed and tore it off my wall. Shame was displaced by a deep gratitude as I confessed to the Lord, *You don't want my labour; you want my love.* I burst into tears as I encountered, in the depths of my heart, God's enduring love for me and his gracious invitation to go deeper. I knew in that moment that even if I never did another thing for God, his love for me was complete and he would always, *always,* want me. The only question was how much did *I* want *him?* And would I still want him in the mystery of silence and in the pain of loss and through every season that I might face in this brief moment before he calls me home?

I threw the poster in the bin and, tears streaming down my cheeks, knelt before my bed as I began to pray.

"I want you completely, God, whatever the cost. And I want to love everyone that you love. You have to help me because I can't do it without you... Take *all* of me, Jesus. All that I am and all that I'm not. All of me for all of you..." I fell facedown as I finished with a sob, "Don't let me stop now. I'm just getting started..."

~*~

A love letter for you...

Dear Reader

*If Jesus was going to write you a love letter, I think it would go
something like this...*

'I know you.
I know you by name.
I know every hair on your head.
I know your deepest heart's desires.
I know all your weaknesses
and all the things you wish you could forget.
I know you better than you know yourself and
I know exactly what I made you for.

You are precious to me.
Long before you were born
I loved you and dreamed of all that you could be.

I want *you* to know *me* (not just know *about* me or settle for
somebody else's version of me).
I want you to encounter my love.
I want you to live *from* my approval, never *for* it.
I don't just desire your compliance.
I want to be your closest friend.

You have barely scratched the surface of all that I have for you.
Don't stop now. Don't play small.
I want to make history with you.

You may not know it but I'm in a good mood! I came to give
you life and life to the full. I am not put off by your mess.
You will never be too bad, too lost or too far away.
I will meet you exactly where you are.

Even in your darkest moments
I love you more than anyone could ever love you in a lifetime.
Even when you think you've messed up
I am fully committed to my plans for you.
Even if you never do a thing for me
My love for you is perfect and complete.
Even when you cannot feel me
I am closer than your own skin.

Don't stop now.

I've seen you fall and I long to catch you.
I've seen every tear you've ever cried and I long to heal you.
I've seen every page of your life story *(yes, even that)*
and I still want you.
I've seen every wrong that's ever been done to you
and I long to make everything beautiful.

Do not fear. It's not about you. It's all about me.
I've done it all. I've made a way.
I loved you first.

Jesus.'

— As imagined by Miss Ruby Rico, who wishes she could say it better but sometimes words aren't enough. Maybe you should ask him for yourself like this: **'Hey Jesus, what do you think of me?'**

Lightning Source UK Ltd.
Milton Keynes UK
UKOW03f2323070317
296055UK00002B/26/P